THE
SOWER

THE
SOWER

Book Two of the Chimera Chronicles

ROB JUNG

HAWK HILL
LITERARY
AN IMPRINT OF INGRAM

The Sower
Book Two of the Chimera Chronicles
Copyright © 2021 Rob Jung

Publisher: Hawk Hill Literary, LLC, an imprint of Ingram

This is a work of fiction. Names of characters, places and incidents are either the product of the author's imagination or are used fictitiously. Living persons or historical characters portrayed in this book are portrayed in fictional circumstances and settings.

Cover and Interior Layout Design by Inspire Books.
Inquiries should be addressed to:
Hawk Hill Literary, LLC
13274 Huntington Terrace
Saint Paul, MN 55124
Voice and Text: (612) 812-6060
ISBN: 978-1-7366108-0-0
E-book ISBN: 978-1-7366108-1-7
Library of Congress Control Number: 2021902451
Printed in the United States

WHAT THEY'RE SAYING ABOUT "THE SOWER"

"A relentless cat-and-mouse pursuit featuring a vicious murder, a conflicted detective, and one of the most cunning villains you'll come across."

—Brian Lutterman,
Author of the Pen Wilkinson series of corporate thrillers.

• • •

"It is an immensely enjoyable read for fans of sleuth novels with well-developed characters and twisty plot lines."

—Readers' Favorite Five-Star Review

• • •

"Between the tense encounters and the elaborate backstory, the varying pacing and mood, readers may be called to spend multiple sittings with this novel to appreciate its depth and nuance."

—Independent Book Review

• • •

"...what is she hiding that is so awful...? This book will likely resonate with modern art enthusiasts, mystery fans and members of the LGBTQ+ community"

—The U S Review of Books

• • •

"History meets mystery in the Chimera Chronicles trilogy and the second installment in the series, The Sower, promises to be another fast-paced, hardboiled thriller."

—Mindy Mejia,
Author of Leave No Trace and Strike Me Down.

ALSO BY ROB JUNG

The Reaper

"A tour de force story of one painting and a collection of characters whose greed, passion, and determination force them to come violently at odds over the span of decades." Judge, 28th Annual Writer's Digest Self-Publishing Book Awards.

• • •

"Wow, what a wonderful story. This book is well-written with an intriguing story-line and is incredibly engrossing. I had trouble putting it down. I love historical fiction and this is a great story." Dr. Patricia Eroh, reviewer.

Cloud Warriors

"Readers of thrillers that incorporate scientific discovery, deadly special interests, and confrontations between ethical and moral purposes will relish **Cloud Warriors** *…well written, replete with surprising twists and turns, and hard to put down; especially recommended for thriller readers who look for the kind of high-octane action, complex plots and powerful characterization mastered by such big names as Michael Crichton, H. Rider Haggard and Philip Kerr."* D. Donovan, senior reviewer, Midwest Book Reviews.

• • •

"A beautifully written, fast-moving novel with such an original, well researched plot that it has you hooked from page one and doesn't let you off until the final page has been turned…A hugely enjoyable book that I wouldn't hesitate to recommend to anyone." Veryan Williams-Wynn, author of *The Spirit Trap*.

DEDICATION

This book is dedicated to three women who helped me understand the joy and the trauma, the freedom and the loneliness, the pain and the triumph that accompanies gender transition. To Lauren Siegel and Geretta Rosemary Geretta, without whom the idea of *The Sower* would not have come into being, and especially to Ellie Krug, whose counsel and guidance made the character, Ronni Brilliant, possible, and whose own journey is so beautifully told in her memoir, *Getting to Ellen*.

AUTHOR'S NOTE

My novels arise from actual historical events. *The Sower* is a continuation of the saga of *The Reaper*, a painting by Spanish artist Joan Miro that disappeared from the Spanish pavilion at the end of the 1937 Paris Exposition. It is around that still-lost work of art that this story revolves. *The Sower* is entirely fictional, as are the characters, except in the case of living or historical characters who appear in fictional settings.

Rob Jung

>=<><=<

We are who we are
because we stand
on the shoulders
of a thousand yesterdays.

2009

JUNE 25

Lorraine heard the crunch of tires on the gravel driveway an instant before Barca let her know that they had visitors. She shushed the big golden retriever, then looked out her kitchen window as a white delivery truck came to a stop a few feet from the front stoop of the old farmhouse.

The passenger door with a "Bert's Appliance" sign on it, swung open, and a man holding a clip board in a gloved hand got out. The name Otto was embroidered over the pocket of his shirt.

She opened the door a few inches before he had a chance to knock. "Can I help you?" she asked.

"Are you Lorraine Blethen?"

"Yes. What can I do for you?"

Barca pushed his nose through the doorway, his tail banging against Lorraine's leg. "Barca. Get back," Lorraine admonished; then to the man: "Don't mind him. He wouldn't hurt a fly."

"We have appliances to deliver," he said. He had a slight accent. *German,* Lorraine thought.

"You must have the wrong place. I didn't order any appliances."

"Says they are a gift." He pointed to a box on the delivery ticket, and then handed Lorraine the clipboard through the partially opened door. "See."

"Well, I'll be," she exclaimed. She stood with her mouth open for a moment, astonished, until the deliveryman interrupted.

"Can we come in to see where the appliances go, and what we have to remove?" he asked.

"Of course. Of course." Lorraine opened the door. "Barca. Stay." she ordered.

The man hesitated.

"Um. Could I ask you to put your dog somewhere?" he said. "My partner is scared of dogs." He cocked his head, motioning toward the driver still seated in the truck.

"Oh. Of course," Lorraine replied, handing the clipboard back to the man and taking Barca's collar. She pulled the reluctant dog into a room just off the kitchen and closed the door.

The driver had a permanent half-smile, caused by a scar near his left eye which pulled the corner of his mouth upward. Short and muscular, Lorraine wondered how a man who looked so powerful could be afraid of dogs.

She turned and led the two deliverymen into the kitchen.

Without warning she was airborne, powerful arms lifting her like a rag doll and slamming her onto the kitchen table. In shock from the suddenness of the assault and the collision of her face with Formica, Lorraine tried to grasp what was happening. She felt herself being carried into the living room and flung on the sofa. Gloved hands wrenched her onto her back. Fear of sexual assault ripped her brain out of its malaise. A scream erupted from deep within her, but a pillow crushing down on her face muffled it before it reached her lips.

She struggled to breathe but the pillow was merciless, growing more oppressive by the second. She could hear barking; Barca, as helpless to protect her as she was to defend herself. Brutish hands pinned her body, throttling her feeble attempt to break free, but they didn't rip at her clothes. She wasn't going to be raped.

She was going to die

She felt her lungs coming apart as they fought for air that wasn't there. Reflections in her brain turned purple, then yellow, then orange. Pinwheels replaced the color, then turned into black holes. Her muscles grew taut as she strained against the unyielding hands, searching for any micron of oxygen.

Her body convulsed. Once. Twice. Words from long ago floated through her mind as her lungs exploded: *you'll be the death of me.*

Lorraine Blethen had lived in a turn-of-the-century farmhouse, a mile west of the quiet town of Zumbrota, for over forty years, the last thirty by herself after kicking out her philandering husband. She rented the tillable acreage to local farmers to support herself. She was shrewd in her business dealings, active in her community and church, frugal with her money and strict with her daughter, Mary, who fled from Zumbrota and her mother the day after she graduated from high school.

Lorraine's feisty personality, self-confidence, and willingness to share her abundant opinions made her a community gadfly, loved by some, hated by a few, given a wide berth by most.

A week after her passing, the Goodhue County coroner issued his report: Lorraine's death was, indeed, a homicide; the first in Goodhue County in over a decade.

The report caused a social earthquake, morphing the here-to-fore friendly community into a cesspool of innuendo and suspicion. Strangers were met with distrustful stares and cold shoulders. People made their children come into the house before dark and started locking their doors. Conversations over pancakes at Bridget's Café came with whispers and furtive glances.

As the investigation stretched into weeks, and then months, local police started receiving anonymous tips on who the murderer was, or might be, as neighbors saw an opportunity to settle old feuds.

The name most often heard when Zumbrotans whispered about "The Murder" was that of Lorraine's grandson, Hamilton.

"He's weird. Some kind of artist. Those artsy kinds are unstable, and they're always broke. Sonofabitch probably killed her for her money." "She didn't have any money." "She had that farm. That's worth a lot." "Hmmm."

"Can't trust him. He's Black, you know." "No, he's not. He's Middle Eastern, or East Indian. I met him once." "Black, brown, doesn't matter. Her daughter was so screwed up on drugs that she was probably doing a half dozen guys at the same time. Who knows what he is?"

"What about her daughter? Maybe she did it." "Hell, Mary ain't been around here for 30 years."

"Dorothy says it's somebody from an appliance company. Ya think Ralph mighta done it?" "Shit, Ralph couldn't organize a Sunday school picnic. Don't know how he finds his way home from the store at night." "Yeah, but…" "Yeah, but nothin'. That bastard grandson of hers probably hired someone. He did it, I tell ya." "Hmmmm."

Notwithstanding the rumors, suspicions, conspiracy theories and outright lies, and despite the best efforts of the Zumbrota Police, the Goodhue County Sheriff and the Minnesota Bureau of Criminal Apprehension, Lorraine Blethen's murder remained unsolved.

2014

SEPTEMBER 10, WEDNESDAY

For the umpteenth time, Ronni Brilliant read the five-year-old coroner's report as Delta Flight 1008 started its descent into Boston.

Conclusion No. 1: The scalp wound on Lorraine Blethen's right temple, if it had resulted from a fall, should have had a wide blood spatter pattern. The blood spatter pattern at the site was limited to the edge of the table where her head came in contact. In addition, the victim would have had a significant loss of blood. The blood pool under the victim's head had been small, the loss of blood minimal. The coroner had concluded that Lorraine Blethen was dead before her head came in contact with the coffee table.

Conclusion No. 2: Small blood spots, known as *petechia*, were found on the surface of her lungs and the inside of her lower eyelids, where capillaries had burst. This occurs when the victim is struggling to breathe. The skin around her lips had a bluish tint created by bruising, and there were teeth imprints on the inside of her upper lip, showing that intense pressure had been applied to the victim's face. Vacuuming her nose and oral pharynx disclosed tiny thread particles that were matched to a pillow on a couch in the living room where she had died. The bruises on her wrists and abdomen were consistent with being forcibly restrained. The coroner's second conclusion was that Lorraine was the victim of an intentional killing that had been staged to look like an accident.

Conclusion No. 3: The victim had never had a chance to defend herself. Examination under her fingernails produced no skin or other residue that could divulge the DNA of her killer.

Three-and-a-half years after the murder, Ronni's detective agency had been hired to do what local law enforcement had been unable to do, solve the murder of Lorraine Blethen. Their client was none other than Hamilton Blethen, Lorraine's grandson and the only "official" suspect in her murder. Hamilton, despite the efforts of local law enforcement authorities, had not been charged with the crime. The gathering of evidence had been severely hampered when Hamilton had been bludgeoned into a coma only a few days after his Grandmother's murder. The coma had lasted for nearly a year, and, even after he regained consciousness, Hamilton never fully recovered from the brain injury caused by the assault. Eventually, the law enforcement agencies gave up, and the case slid into the cold case files.

Twenty-one months after they'd been hired, the murder was still unsolved, and Ronni, as the lead investigator on the file, had been tasked by her partners to go to Boston and meet with their client face-to-face. She would provide an update and, reluctantly, recommend that they end the investigation.

As Ronni looked out the window of the Boeing 727, her dispirited state of mind was forgotten, blotted out by panic. They were about to crash into the ocean!

Magically, a concrete runway emerged out of Boston Harbor and collected the landing gear of the plane, as it had in thousands of previous flights, each one leaving first-time Boston travelers with palpitations and clenched bladders. Ronni, now among the millions of Logan Airport "survivors," exhaled. The momentary scare had snapped her out of the doldrums. *Nothing like thinking you're about to die to make you see things differently. Maybe something good will come out of this trip after all.*

In addition to meeting with Hamilton, being in Boston would provide Ronni an opportunity to follow a thread of information that might lead them to his estranged mother. Although unconnected to the murder investigation, Hamilton, who had been abandoned by his mother at age four, had asked the detectives to find her. She should, he reasoned, at least be notified that her mother had died.

Mary Blethen had been in her early twenties, in the middle of a decade of drug addiction, when she conceived and then abandoned Hamilton. He had not seen his mother in thirty-six years.

One of his few memories of his mother related to his high school graduation. He had received a card in the mail. It was inscribed with a single word, "Congratulations." It was signed "Magnolia." He didn't know anyone named Magnolia, but his grandmother had said it looked like his mother's handwriting. If it was, in fact, from Hamilton's mother, it was his one and only communication from her since he had watched her, in a yellow dress and with bright red hair, climb into a car that drove away down a gravel road, plumes of dust spurting from beneath the tires. At four years old, holding onto his grandma's finger with one hand, and a paper bag filled with everything he had in the world in the other, Hamilton had stood on the farmhouse stoop, his eyes wide in bewilderment.

The graduation card was a stinging reminder to Hamilton that he had been abandoned, unwanted. He threw it away in anger, but the name "Magnolia" had been forever etched in his memory.

The detective agency had tracked a handful of Magnolias during its investigation, but none had any connection to Hamilton or his deceased grandmother. The inability to locate Mary Blethen was another dead-end that the investigation had come up against.

In the last month a new possibility had arisen. Publicity surrounding a bid for the U.S. Senate seat in Massachusetts by a woman named Magnolia Kanaranzi had percolated all the way to St. Paul, Minnesota, and drew the attention of Ronni and her colleagues. There weren't many Magnolias, but this one met part of the profile they had developed for Hamilton's mother. She was a former drug addict.

Background research revealed that Kanaranzi had risen from the depths of heroin addiction to become the head of an East Coast media empire. The wealth and celebrity that came with that ascension had provided her a platform, and her public persona spread as a result of her outspoken advocacy of gender workplace equality and the rights of women and the LGBTQ community.

The trip to Boston provided a dual opportunity for Ronni. It would enable her to probe further into the miniscule possibility that Kanaranzi was actually Mary Blethen, but the second reason was personal. Ronni had come to admire Kanaranzi, both because of her rags-to-riches story, and, more importantly, because she was a champion of gender equality. As a "T" in that familiar string of letters, and a relative newcomer to the status of "W", Ronni wanted to meet Kanaranzi.

She caught a taxi from Logan to the *Boston Globe* for a prearranged meeting with Allison Long, a reporter and old college friend of Hamilton's. At his request, Long had agreed to introduce Ronni to the political and business beat writers at the *Globe* so she could question them about Kanaranzi's background. Long had also promised Ronni she'd try to arrange a meeting with the Senate candidate.

"Do you see Hamilton often?" Ronni asked. Even though she was five-foot-ten, with defined muscles amplified from weightlifting, her deep voice was always a surprise. It was the one remnant of being male that the years of operations, counseling and practice was unable to transform.

"I saw him right after he moved here a couple years ago, and once a few months ago at an art show, but that's all." Allison shouted, trying to be heard over the din of the *Globe* newsroom.

"How's he doing? I've only met him once in person, the day he hired me. The next day he moved to Boston. Is he still in a wheelchair?

"He'll be in a wheelchair the rest of his life," Allison responded, a trace of sadness in her voice.

"I talked to him when he arranged our meeting. He said you two have known each other since college. Was he in a wheelchair then?"

"No. Ham was a pretty good athlete. Played professional baseball for a while. And he was a really good artist. He's only been in a wheelchair the last four, five years."

"What happened?"

"I don't know all the details, but he was assaulted, I think about the time his grandmother was killed. Didn't you know that?" Allison asked.

Ronni responded with an animated head-shake, sending her razor cut black hair whipping back and forth. Her client had never mentioned the assault.

"To my knowledge, they never found the person who attacked him," Allison added. "I'm surprised he hasn't talked to you about it."

"Me too."

Eventually, their conversation turned to Magnolia Kanaranzi, and Ronni's desire to learn more about her.

"Why the interest in Kanaranzi?" Allison asked.

Ronni had anticipated the question. "Because of her stand on women's rights. She's one of the most outspoken advocates out there right now, and I'd like to know more about her. Did you have any luck setting up a meeting with her?"

"Sorry. I got in touch with her press secretary, but Kanaranzi's schedule is full until after the election. You know she just won the primary. She's probably going to be our next Senator."

Ronni, who had seen the *Globe's* blaring headline: **Kanaranzi Wins Primary**, nodded. "I'm disappointed, but I'm happy she won the primary," she said. "Hopefully she'll win the general election, too. We could use more people like her in Washington,"

Allison agreed. "Would you like a photo of Kanaranzi? It's not a very good consolation prize, but it's all I've got. I can get you one from her press packet."

"Sure."

"I'll leave it on my desk if we don't connect again before you're done. I've set up a meeting for you with a couple of our beat writers at Four-Thirty. They've followed Kanaranzi's rise since she became CEO of Kincaid Media. They might be able to provide you with the kind of information you're looking for."

"Did you tell them the purpose of the meeting?"

"I told them you wanted to know the candidate on a more personal level. The kind of stuff that doesn't show up in news stories."

Ronni thanked her and looked at her watch. She had two hours to kill before the meeting. She asked Allison if she could spend the time in the *Globe's* archives. Ronni had done an online search of Kanaranzi, but she might find something that hadn't found its way onto the internet.

The early newspaper articles, some of which she had already seen, were about Kanaranzi's sudden rise in Massachusetts' business circles. Several recounted her rags-to-riches story, describing her as self-made, intelligent, tough, a perfectionist, supporter of the arts, champion of women's rights, a philanthropist and member of numerous boards of directors. Even her apparent short-comings, impatience and a quick temper, enhanced her reputation as a strong, adroit and clever business person. There were some references to a quixotic personality, and to mood swings, but those were buried under the barrage of positive press Kanaranzi had received.

By all accounts, her life had begun in Sturgis, South Dakota, where she had met and been rescued from a life of drugs by the late Arthur Kincaid. She served as his trusted right-hand for nearly 30 years and, after his death, had gained control of Kincaid's substantial print media holdings. In less than a decade, she had consolidated her power and successfully expanded the business into television and social media.

Information about Kanaranzi's life before she met Kincaid at age eighteen, was nonexistent. Ordinarily, the absence of such information would not have caught Ronni's attention--*most people don't do anything newsworthy before they're eighteen*--except that there was no mention about her family or her childhood in either her announcement to run for the Senate, or in articles related to her campaign. This should have been ordinary fodder for such stories.

The only thing the articles mentioned from her past related to her early addiction to heroin. Kanaranzi had wisely gotten out in front of that potential issue, turning it to her advantage when she made addiction a focal point of her campaign, arguing her first-hand knowledge made her the perfect advocate for drug programs and modifications to the criminal justice system.

The newspaper stories felt a bit contrived, too perfect. As much as Ronni admired what Kanaranzi stood for, her investigative instincts made her skeptical. *I wonder if she has someone on the Globe payroll? Or maybe it's a code of honor among Boston media: you don't crap on me; I won't crap on you.*

Ronni had to remind herself she wasn't in Boston to get embroiled in a political race. She did, however, make a mental note to look into Kanaranzi's early years in Sturgis when she got back to Minnesota... even if she no longer had a case to investigate.

The two hours spent looking at old newspaper clippings turned up nothing that might link the Senate candidate with Hamilton Blethen. In fact, simple math suggested the opposite. Hamilton's mother abandoned him when he was four, thirty-six years ago. Kanaranzi was sixty-four according to newspaper clippings, meaning she would have had to abandoned him when she was twenty-four and would have given birth to him when she was twenty. But the newspapers said she met Arthur Kincaid in Sturgis when Magnolia was eighteen, so, unless she gave birth to Blethen after she met Kincaid....

A thought crossed Ronni's mind: *Could Hamilton Blethen be the rightful heir to Kincaid's fortune, the love child of Kincaid and Magnolia*

Kanaranzi? The intriguing thought stayed in the back of her mind as she met the two reporters.

After introductions, Ronni mentioned the possibility of a movie about Kanaranzi's life. She talked about the movie's production and casting, letting the reporters assume she was involved in the film, while being careful to avoid saying that she was. The mention of a movie was sufficient to get them both talking freely.

Her first question was whether Kanaranzi had children. They both said they weren't aware of any. To their knowledge, she'd never been married. After an hour of Q and A it was clear that neither of them knew anything about Kanaranzi's life before Kincaid, nor anything that could link Kanaranzi to Mary Blethen, or to her client.

On her way out, Ronni picked up the Kanaranzi photo from Allison's desk, an 8X10 black and white head shot. It made the candidate look like she was in her forties. Ronni wondered how long ago it had been taken.

With her mind still toying with the possibility of Hamilton Blethen as a love child, she caught a cab to a hotel on Copley Square: no smoking, state-of-the-art exercise room and room service. It was everything she would need for the night.

Sweat streamed down the exposed parts of Ronni's fine-tuned body as she pushed herself on a stationary bike, her idea of cooling down after a workout. Coming to a stop, she dismounted, stood for a moment listening to Billie Holiday singing the last bars of *Good Morning Heartache,* then removed her earphones and took a long drink from the water bottle in her backpack.

As she toweled off, the only other person in the hotel's exercise room said: "I got tired just watching you."

The woman, sitting idly on the seat of a lat pull-down machine, looked to be in her forties. She did not appear to have been working out, and her attire suggested she was not a regular inhabitant of exercise rooms.

Ronni nodded in her direction, acknowledging the remark.

"You must do it a lot," the woman continued.

"Daily."

"Are you an athlete?"

"Nope."

Ronni finished toweling off her face and neck, then wiped down her arms, taut skin over smooth, firm muscles. She had developed a workout routine that kept her arms and legs stretched, supple and strong, but avoided bulking up the biceps or calves like she had done when she was in the military, when she was still an "M". She bent down to put away the towel and the water bottle.

"My name's Virginia. Are you staying here?" The woman persisted.

Ronni nodded: "Just tonight."

"Me too. Any chance you're going to the lounge later? I feel so intimidated going into a bar by myself. If you're going later, maybe I could join you."

Ronni thought for a moment. "What time?"

The woman looked at the clock on the exercise room wall. It read seven thirty-five. "How about nine?"

"Okay. I'll see you there."

"I didn't catch your name."

"Ronni."

"Okay, Ronni. I'll see you at nine in the lounge."

Ronni picked up her duffel bag and left.

Magnolia Kanaranzi, owner of one of the great rags-to-riches stories in recent history, was now the odds-on favorite to become the next Senator from Massachusetts. However, the staccato clicking of her cobalt blue fingernails on the glass conference table proclaimed to those in the room that she was *not* happy.

"Early polls have you up by eight points over Metzger," Becky Lindstrom, a recent addition to the campaign staff, said, trying to brighten the mood. "You won the primary and you're up by eight. That's reason to celebrate."

Her circle of campaign advisors, seated haphazardly around the cluttered conference room of Kanaranzi campaign headquarters, held their collective breath. A few hesitantly nodded their heads in agreement. Others waited to see which Magnolia was in the room; the all-business, demanding and often angry Magnolia that they had come to fear, or the warm and caring Magnolia who occasionally appeared.

Jim Bean, the grizzled campaign manager, didn't wait to see.

"We haven't won anything yet," he growled. "Part of that is the bounce from the primary." He turned to his candidate, running a hand through his unruly hair. "Your lead is closer to three points."

"I don't view three points as a lead," Magnolia said. Her words cut the air like a razor. At five-foot-one and a mist of hairspray over a hundred pounds Magnolia wasn't physically intimidating, but when she was in her all-business mode people instinctively understood that you disagreed with her at your own peril.

"Metzger hasn't unleashed his attack dogs yet, and if he can't find any actual dirt, we all know he's capable of fabricating something," she said. "We need to hit him first."

"We can attack him on his record. Tie him to the President," Aaron Feldman, Kanaranzi's chief policy adviser, offered.

"Thanks for stating the obvious, Aaron." Her contact lens-enhanced navy-blue eyes flashed, saying as much as her words. Feldman, dressed in rumpled pants and a shirt that looked like he'd slept in it, shrunk under her gaze. She swiveled in her chair, turning her back to Feldman.

"He smoked marijuana in college," Lindstrom offered, still trying to be upbeat. "Flannery uncovered that in the last campaign."

"Yes, and Flannery lost by ten points. Do you think an attack based on marijuana smoking thirty years ago, coming from the campaign of a reformed drug addict, will be effective? If that's the best you can come up with, we might as well concede now."

Lindstrom's eyes found something on the floor that demanded her attention.

"We'll step up our opposition research," Bean rasped, his voice the timbre of a chainsaw. "I'll hire outside investigators, and we'll see what the national committee suggests."

"Get on it. All of you. Metzger's been a Senator for twelve years. Find out whose skirt he's had his hand under. He's got to have skeletons somewhere." Magnolia rose from her chair, her silver-white hair perfectly layered in a flawless razor cut, a sharp contrast to her explosive deep blue eyes. She seemed to tower over everyone despite her diminutive stature. Four-inch heels contributed to the illusion.

"This is the number one priority. I want *something* on Metzger by the end of the week."

As the staff filed out of the room, she leaned over and whispered in Bean's ear. "Find a replacement for Feldman. Don't fire him. Find him a project that will keep him busy, maybe develop a white paper on why a dual-state policy is best for Israel. That should keep him busy."

Bean rocked back in his chair, fixing Magnolia with a quizzical look. "A two-state solution? Feldman's not going to like that, and neither are your Jewish supporters."

"The one-state solution is on the wrong side of history, and the two-state solution can be good for Israel if you arrange the geography and the governmental structure the right way. Tell Feldman to be creative. We probably won't use what he comes up with, but I need a new policy advisor, a woman, who can focus the campaign on women's issues."

She beckoned her press secretary, Samantha Jones, to follow her. They walked out of campaign headquarters into the early evening twilight of Boylston Street. They looked like mismatched salt and pepper shakers, Jones, her skin the color of molasses, towering over her boss. Magnolia, the alpha dog, led the way to a waiting limousine.

"No news conferences this week, Sam, unless it's an emergency. Keep feeding the media our daily press releases with my itinerary, a policy blurb, and a quote or two from me. Until further notice, get the policy stuff from Bean, not Feldman. I want the policy statements to focus on gender, race and women's issues. You can make up the quotes, but run them by me before they go out."

A uniformed chauffeur, standing next to the open driver's side rear door of a diamond-white Cadillac, offered his white-gloved hand to Magnolia. The car and the glove were perfectly matched to her hair color, dazzling against the contrast of her cobalt blue custom-tailored suit and her Christian Louboutin pumps, both of which perfectly matched her eyes.

"Ma'am," Jones said.

Magnolia, already halfway into the limo, stopped and turned her head, her hand still holding the white glove. "What?"

"Someone has been asking about you, digging around in newspaper archives and talking to reporters."

"Metzger's wolves already at work?"

"My contact didn't think so," Jones replied. "It wasn't one of the usual political research hacks. He said it was someone from Minnesota doing research for a movie."

"Minnesota?" Kanaranzi's reaction was too quick, her voice too shrill.

Composing herself, she let go of the chauffeur's hand and finished sliding into the back seat. She settled into the lush leather, making Samantha wait. Finally, she looked up.

"Did you get his name?"

"It's a woman. Her name is Veronica Brilliant."

Kanaranzi nodded, and the chauffeur closed the door. As the limousine merged into Boylston Street traffic, she pushed the button that raised the glass partition between her and the driver, and dug in her purse for her "other" phone. She punched No. 1 on speed dial, then waited for the out-of-country call to connect.

"This is the office of Henri Hawke. Please leave a message."

"There's someone from Minnesota digging around in my past. How does that happen? You said you took care of everything. Call me immediately."

It was nearly 1 a.m. in Barcelona, but she knew Hawke would just be starting. She would get a call back within the hour, if he wasn't drunk or feeling obstinate.

With her mind running at full throttle, Ronni sat at the bar nursing her tonic and lime, waiting for Virginia.

The woman had not appeared to be coming on to her in the exercise room, and without sexual attraction as the impetus, the "can-I-tag-along-for-a-drink" request seemed odd. The verbal exchange had made her wary, and Ronni had stopped at the concierge desk on the way back to her room.

"I met a woman in the exercise room, and I need to leave her a message," she had told the young man sitting behind the desk. "Her name is Virginia. I didn't get her last name, but she said she was staying here."

The concierge tapped a couple of keys on his computer and scanned the screen.

"We don't have anyone checked in with the first name Virginia," he said.

Ronni cocked her head, a frown crossing her face.

"Do you have any rooms booked under a business name?" she asked. "Maybe she's registered under her employer's name."

"No. There're no rooms booked to businesses tonight."

Perhaps she had read the cues wrong, and the woman was propositioning her. In any event, it had confirmed Ronnie's suspicion that Virginia's presence in the exercise room had not been a chance encounter.

Feeling apprehensive, Ronni had dressed in black tights, a white shirt long enough to cover her butt, and her favorite Nike running shoes--clothes amenable to fight or flight—and went to the lounge at eight forty-five. A half hour later, she was tired of listening to piped-in music and watching the lime swirl in her glass. She checked her watch and then the lounge entrance. It was approaching a quarter past nine and Virginia had not made an appearance.

Maybe she'd been clocked by Virginia, who didn't want to be seen with her. It was always a risk, another reminder that she was not *woman enough*. Hoping she was wrong, Ronni decided to wait until nine thirty.

A man in a rumpled suit, open shirt collar and a bad haircut appeared out of nowhere.

"May I?" he asked, putting his hand on the bar stool next to Ronni. Without waiting for an answer, he pulled out the stool. As Ronni turned her head to look at him, she sensed someone behind her. She turned and was face-to-face with a short, massive human with a disfigured nose. Just seconds before, he hadn't been sitting on the stool. Now he was next to her, close enough for Ronni to smell garlic and body odor.

"You're not welcome here," the man in the suit said, just loud enough for her to hear.

She spun back to face him.

"We don't want queer people in Boston." His flat tone of voice and passive expression belied the threatening, ugly words. "Get on the next plane out of here and don't come back. If you do, the next time we see you will be in a dark place, and the consequences will be far less pleasant."

The brute on her other side slid off the stool, intentionally jostling Ronni. She bristled, jerked around to confront him, but he was already lumbering away. She spun to confront the man in the suit, but he too was waddling toward the exit. She suppressed her impulse to charge after them. Although a solid one hundred fifty-five pounds, Ronni was giving away more than a hundred pounds to the hulk. Even with her advanced martial arts training she was not sure she could take him. And if she did, she would most likely lose the argument with the police and be charged with assault. It didn't much matter if you were right or wrong if you were part of the LGBTQ alphabet.

She looked around the lounge to see if anyone had observed what had just happened, but the few patrons and the bartender were all busy with their own business. No one was looking at her, nor at the two men exiting the lounge. She scanned the room a second time. There were no furtive glances, no surreptitious looks, to suggest anyone had seen and then looked away.

Her hand trembled as she reached for her glass. Raising it, she caught the bartender's attention.

"Do you know the two men who were just sitting with me?" Ronni asked, trying to keep the glass steady and the quiver out of her voice.

"What two men?"

"There were two…," she hesitated, looked at the exit. They were gone.

"Can I get you something?" the bartender asked.

"A shot of Wild Turkey," she said, pointing at a bottle on the back bar.

Ronni had been threatened before when she'd been in the military police, but those threats almost always involved drunken Marines and a misplaced dose of machismo. She--he back then-- had usually been able to talk the would-be assailant out of following through on his unwise course of action. When that had failed, a quick bloody nose usually did the trick.

But this had been calculated. And threatening. And personal.

SEPTEMBER 11, THURSDAY

As the Lyft driver wove through the narrow streets of Boston looking for Hamilton Blethen's address, Ronni tried to tamp down the turmoil she still felt from the previous night. Ten years of passage from man to woman had taught her that every stranger you meet might go off on you, mocking or insulting, most of the time unintentionally. But this had been a premeditated threat to her personal safety unlike anything she had experienced since her transition. It had rattled her. She had even eyed the Lyft driver suspiciously until convincing herself that she was being paranoid.

She tried concentrating on the physical features of the two men. The man in the suit had been overweight and sloppy, but nothing else about him stood out. She doubted if she could pick him out of a lineup. But she would remember his voice: a flat monotone with a touch of New England nasal, a tone that might be mistaken as comforting except for the threat inherent in the words he spoke.

The hulk, on the other hand, was seared into her memory. His head was shaped like a bullet attached to his shoulders without benefit of a neck. His nose was bent against his cheek, having at one time lost a dispute with someone's fist. Beady eyes, too small for his massive head, had bored into her. And his scent...no...his stench; musk failing to cover up too many days without a shower. And garlic.

She could have reported the incident but knew it was unlikely that her complaint would be investigated. Based on past experience, a transgender private detective from Minnesota wouldn't get the time of day from Boston's finest, unless she had been beaten to a pulp. Or was dead.

Hamilton lived in an end unit of a row of rehabbed nineteenth century brownstones on Worcester Street, not far from the Boston Museum of Visual Arts. Ronni climbed the seven steps that led from the sidewalk to the ornate front door and rang the buzzer. She could hear chimes and the bark of a big dog. A woman with a shock of bright orange hair, piercing green eyes and a sea of freckles opened the door.

She had one leg awkwardly stuck out to the side, holding back an enthusiastic golden retriever. "Sit, Barca," she ordered, and the big dog immediately obeyed, although failing to corral his hyper-active tail.

"Hi. I'm Toni," the woman said with a sparkling smile. "You must be Veronica Brilliant."

Ronni stuck out her hand. "Please, call me Ronni. Nice to finally meet you in person."

The dog started to rise, and Toni fixed him with a stern look. The dog sat back down, this time sitting on his tail to keep it under control. His big brown eyes took on an apologetic, *my bad,* look.

"This is Barca," she said. "He's big and lovable, and he'll calm down in a minute, but I can put him in another room if you're uncomfortable with dogs."

"I'm fine with him as long as he's fine with me."

The two women and Barca rode an elevator to the top floor of the brownstone. Ronni, looking through the bars of the elevator door, was surprised by the austerity of the home. Hamilton had offered her detective agency a million dollars to find the person who killed his grandmother. In the twenty-one months they had been on the case they had burned through nearly a quarter of that. Each bill they sent had been met with a return check. No questions. No complaints. The only contacts between the detective agency and its client were regular telephone updates. Ronni had expected the home to reflect the opulence that would be associated with someone who could afford to pay a million dollars, but except for the elevator and the high, coved ceilings, there was no apparent reflection of wealth. The furniture was well-used, the hardwood floors well-worn and the art hanging on the walls of the third-floor room they entered was…well…primitive.

Except for flecks of silver in his black hair, Hamilton was just as Ronni remembered him: slightly hunched over in his wheelchair, deep brown eyes, perfect teeth, high cheekbones, strong chin covered in stubble. He was dressed in jeans and a loose-fitting ivory-colored sweatshirt that perfectly contrasted with his smooth, dark brown skin.

"Good to see you again," he said as Barca curled up beside him. "Have a seat. Can we get you anything? Coffee. Or juice?" He sat with his head cocked sideways on his tilted body, a quizzical look on his face.

"No. Thanks. I'm good," she replied.

Toni excused herself, saying, "If you need anything buzz me." Hamilton smiled at his wife, as Ronni reflexively nodded her head.

"So, what is important enough to bring you all the way to Boston?" he asked after Toni had left.

"We've been looking into Magnolia Kanaranzi," Ronni replied.

"The Senate candidate?"

"Yeah."

"When I first heard about her I did a little research. Found out, among other things, that she's a member of the Board of Trustees of the museum where Toni works. But from what I've read, I'm sure she's not my mother. We don't have anything in common--except for the physical resemblance." Hamilton chuckled at his own joke.

"We've come to the same conclusion," Ronni said, laughing. "About the 'not my mother', not about the resemblance. But there is one thread I want to follow before we completely close the door. I'd like to look into her early life, before she was eighteen. There's virtually no information about those years in the media or in any campaign literature."

Hamilton acknowledged her statement with a nod.

"How old were you when your mother left you?"

"Four."

"And how old was your mother?"

"Not sure. I think in her early twenties."

Ronni nodded. "That's consistent with everything I've learned." She talked about her meeting with Allison Long and the two newspaper reporters, and poked fun at herself as she told him of her momentary thought that he was the love-child of Kanaranzi and Arthur Kincaid.

Hamilton laughed. "Kincaid, a red-haired Irishman, and Kanaranzi, a white-skinned Italian. It would be some sort of miracle if they'd had a brown-skinned love child. Truth is, I never knew my father, and I doubt whether my mother did either. I'm the product of a seventies drug orgy."

His response created an uneasy pause in the conversation, giving Ronni an opening to ask the question that had been bothering her.

"Tell me about the assault that put you in a wheel chair?"

A long, cool quiet settled over the room. Hamilton's eyes lost their sparkle and slid slightly out of focus.

After minutes of painful silence, Ronni cleared her throat. "Mr. Blethen?"

Hamilton snapped out of his trance. "What?"

"Allison Long told me you were assaulted by someone, and that's how you ended up in a wheelchair. Could that be related to your grandmother's death?"

"I don't know anything," he snapped. "I don't remember anything, and I don't want to remember. I spent ten months in a coma and two years in a hospital," his voice escalating as he spoke. "I'd rather not relive that, and it doesn't have anything to do with my grandmother's murder!"

"I'm sorry I've upset you," Ronni apologized, trying to calm her angry client.

Toni rushed into the room, drawn by her husband's raised voice.

"What's going on?" she demanded, looking directly at Ronni. Hamilton shook his head and looked down, appearing embarrassed at his outburst.

"I'm afraid I've upset Mr. Blethen," Ronni said. "I asked him about being in a wheelchair."

"Why? Why would you ask that?"

"Well, truthfully, we have run out of leads on Lorraine's murder," Ronni said, blurting out the subject she had been trying to avoid. "I came to Boston to recommend that we abandon the investigation, stop spending your money. Then I was told about Mr. Blethen being assaulted shortly after his Grandma's murder. I thought there might be a connection between the assault and the murder."

Silence, like dense fog, again settled over the room.

Toni was the first to speak.

"Ham. Let's go in the other room," she said, signaling toward the doorway with a jerk of her head. "Give us a moment," she said to Ronni.

Ronni exhaled. *This trip is a disaster.* Certain that their engagement with this client was over, she checked her watch. How was she going to kill five hours until her flight left?

After ten minutes, she stood and wandered around the room, looking at the paintings. There were several that appeared to be without rhyme or reason. The brush strokes were crude, unconnected. In others she could identify the subject, a bowl of fruit, an old building. One was quite appealing, a woman with orange hair in dappled sunlight. She assumed it was a painting of Toni Blethen.

Another ten minutes passed--an eternity--until Toni returned.

"Ham is still upset. Not with you. He just can't deal with the memory, but we have agreed that you should pursue his assault and see if there is any connection with his grandmother's death."

Ronni nodded. "Has he ever seen a psychiatrist?" she asked.

"Yes, when he was in the military, and, again, a couple of years ago we tried but it sent him into such a state of depression that we stopped."

"How about hypnotism?"

The muscles in Toni's jaw visibly contracted, clearly annoyed at the continuing questions related to her husband's emotional and mental state.

"It's just that any investigation is going to be very difficult if we can't talk to Mr. Blethen about it," Ronni continued. "One of my partners has had good success with hypnotism."

"I'll raise the subject with Ham, but for now you'll have to do the best you can without talking to him. All communication from now on should go through me." She handed Ronni a business card. "All my contact information is on the card. I'd like a weekly progress report unless, of course, you find something important. Then let me know right away."

Ronni took the card. It read: "Boston Museum of Visual Arts, Antoinette Chapereaux-Blethen, Assistant Curator". Ronni now knew how she'd kill a few hours until her flight.

During the ten-minute ride to the museum Ronni breathed a sigh of relief. She'd provoked her client by confronting him about the assault, but she had at least kept the investigation alive to see if there was any connection between the assault and Lorraine Blethen's murder. And, although she'd found nothing to connect Magnolia Kanaranzi to her client, she would get a chance to look into Kanaranzi's childhood and teen years, while still getting paid.

Her thoughts drifted back to the previous evening. She rolled the events over in her mind: the encounter in the exercise room, the thug at her back who intentionally jostled her, the calculated threat by the man in the suit, the fact that "Virginia" wasn't registered at the hotel and didn't show up in the lounge. She had been the target of an elaborate setup. Her gender change seemed like a pretext. Her instincts told her there was another reason behind the threat, and the only reason she could think of was the investigation of Lorraine Blethen's murder.

Ronni browsed a Frida Kahlo exhibit, thinking that the artist must have been ridiculed about her unibrow and faint mustache, wondering if she was also an L or a T, and curious why some painters are famous and others are not. Personally, she didn't care much for Kahlo's paintings. She leaned more toward Claude Monet, Edgar Degas and other impressionists.

She moved on to the permanent collection and was reading the plaque next to a wall-sized mural, *The Reaper,* by Spanish artist Joan Miro, when her phone shattered the quiet of the museum. Embarrassed, Ronni fumbled for the phone and managed to answer it before the third ring. It was Allison Long.

"Let me call you back in a minute," Brilliant whispered.

Minutes later, outside the museum, Ronni returned the call. "Is there a movement in Boston that is openly, aggressively opposed to the LGBTQ community?" she asked.

"What? No. Not that I know of," Long sputtered. "Why?"

"Because I was threatened last night by a thug and a smooth-talking suit, and told to get out of Boston."

"What!!?"

"Two guys sandwiched me in the hotel lounge. One of them told me to get out of town on the next plane because they didn't want queer people in Boston. Said if I came back it would be very unpleasant."

"I've never heard of anything like this," Allison said, apologetically. "We've got our homophobes, but there's no concerted movement that I'm aware of. I didn't know things like that happen in Boston."

"Well, it happened last night," Ronni said. "And, in this case, the correct word is *transphobe.*"

She sat in the window seat in the second row of first class, ordered a tonic with lime, and gazed out the oval window at the people scurrying about on the tarmac, loading luggage, tending to the Airbus a321. It would be at least twenty minutes before they close the doors. *Maybe I'll get lucky,* Ronni thought as boarding passengers filed past her, hoping the seat next to her would remain unoccupied. She needed to think about what had happened since she'd landed in Boston little more than twenty-four hours ago. She didn't need a chatty neighbor to distract her.

They had been ready to pull the plug on the investigation of Lorraine Blethen's murder, but Ronni's presence in Boston had made someone uncomfortable. *It's certainly not impossible that someone, or some group, hates LGTBQ people enough to threaten them. It's happened before. But I was here less than half a day when it happened.* In Ronni's experience, transphobes were generally more reactionary than premeditated. *It's unlikely the presence of one transgender female would be sufficient to orchestrate such a detailed plan of intimidation, even if they'd had enough time to do it.*

She sipped her drink and again rolled the sequence of events over in her mind, concluding that it was unlikely that the threat had anything to do with her gender.

So, if that wasn't the motivation for the threat, who's responsible, and why? There were only a handful of people who knew she was in Boston: Allison Long and the two reporters at the Globe, Hamilton Blethen and his wife, Magnolia Kanaranzi's press secretary, and, perhaps, Kanaranzi, herself. And Ronni's partners. Maybe a few other people from Minnesota. *But I was specifically told to stay out of Boston, so it was unlikely that the source of the threat was from Minnesota.*

A passenger interrupted her thoughts with a smile and a nod as she passed the row where Ronni was seated. Ronni thought the woman looked familiar, and so did a man two passengers behind her. She couldn't place either of them, and went back to her own thoughts.

She discarded the idea of Long and the two reporters. She could conjure no possible way that Long was connected to Lorraine's murder, nor have any motive for threatening her. Unless, of course, she was transphobic. But their interaction had been cordial, even friendly, and Ronni had not sensed any animus emanating from Long. *Plus, she was helpful, setting up the meeting with the two reporters and giving me the information about why Hamilton's in a wheelchair. She's either a great actor or she's not involved.*

Ronni bet on the latter.

To the best of her knowledge, the two reporters she had interviewed were not even aware of Lorraine Blethen's murder. She had asked them no questions related to that; the interview being limited to Magnolia Kanaranzi's life story.

A thought flitted through Ronni's head: *could inquiring about her life story have been enough to precipitate a threat? What didn't she want someone to find out?* Her skepticism about the newspaper articles resurfaced. *Why were they so overtly positive? Were they covering up something? But did Kanaranzi even know I was in Boston? Her press secretary knew, but that didn't mean Kanaranzi did. The press secretary could have been trying to protect her boss. But protect her from what? From being identified as the mother of Hamilton Blethen? Hamilton had checked out Kanaranzi and come to the same conclusion we did: she isn't his mother. And even if she is, that doesn't seem like a big enough reason to have me threatened. Did she even know **when** I was coming to Boston? Unless Allison told her.*

Ronni tapped out a quick text to Allison, inquiring, then returned to her thoughts.

How could she have known that I was checking into her background? Unless Allison had mentioned it to the press secretary while she was trying to set up a meeting.

She tapped another text to Allison: *When you talked to Kanaranzi's press secretary did you tell her why I was going to be in Boston or mention anything about me looking into Kanaranzi's past?*

Ronni checked the time. She hoped Allison would respond before she had to switch her phone to airplane mode.

If she really is Hamilton's mother, what is she hiding that is so awful that someone thought a threat was necessary? Most likely it has nothing to do with being Hamilton's mother. More likely it's something from the thirty years when she was Kincaid's right hand. But it could be something in her first eighteen years that she's desperate to keep hidden? She's already come clean about her drug addiction. What could be worse? Maybe she killed her mother?

Ronni gave her head a hard shake, as if to eliminate the thought, then put both hands to her face and grimaced. *My, God. That's speculation on supposition on pure guesswork. I've gone from no proof that she's Hamilton's mother to her killing Lorraine. I've got to stop this.*

Her hands slid down her face, and she shook her head again, this time slowly. *But I'm definitely going to dig deeper into Kanaranzi's past.*

She swirled her drink, then tipped up the glass to take the last swallow.

That leaves Ham and Toni Blethen. They knew I was coming to Boston and maybe even where I was staying. And they really got upset when I raised the question of the assault. Why didn't he want to talk about it? Were the local police right all along? Maybe Hamilton was the killer. They just couldn't prove it. Did he stage the assault to deflect attention from himself? Maybe it went too far and left him an invalid? Did he hire us to investigate the murder to further divert attention? It's plausible, but the incident at the hotel took place before the meeting with Hamilton. He wouldn't have known, then, that I was aware of the assault, and even after he learned that I did, he let us continue the investigation. Plus, he could stop the investigation any time if we were getting too close. He's either got balls the size of a bull, or he really is innocent.

Ronni's thoughts were interrupted by a statuesque, Black woman ducking under the doorway as she entered the plane,

"Hey, girlfriend," she said in a deep, melodious voice. "We're going to be seat mates. Where y'all from? You like chocolate?"

The woman, at least six-four, with fingernails and eyelashes proportionately long, folded herself and her three shopping bags into the seat next to Ronni, never stopping to take a breath during her non-stop monologue. She rustled through one of the shopping bags, her long, sculpted fingers emerging with a bag of Hershey kisses. "You want one?" she asked. "My name's Geraldine. Geraldine Girard."

"Ronni–Brilliant." Ronni said, a bit overwhelmed by the bigger-than-life person now seated next to her. She took the offered chocolate, even though she didn't want it.

The flight attendant took Geraldine's bags and put them in an overhead bin. Geraldine declined the attendant's offer of something to drink

"My friends all tell me I should take up drinking just to get the free drinks in first class," Geraldine said, turning to Ronni. "But I don't fly first class to drink. It's because those itty-bitty coach seats won't fit my big ass. Besides, there are just some times when you need to pamper yourself."

Ronni nodded.

"How about you? You fly first class to pamper yourself?"

"Uh. No. I'm on business."

"What do you do that you're on business?"

"I'm a private investigator," Ronni said, her voice only a few notes higher than Geraldine's.

Geraldine pursed her lips and nodded. "The voice always gives it away, doesn't it? Both of us."

For two-and-one-half hours, until the plane touched down at Minneapolis-St. Paul airport, the two women shared their lives and journeys in the conversion from M to T to W. Geraldine, once a highly regarded college basketball player whose career ended when she came out, was now a playwright and theatrical producer. She and Ronni, ex-marine MP now PI, traded stories about the challenges they'd faced, the loneliness that still overwhelmed them from time-to-time, and the prejudice, both real and imagined. Ronni related the incident in the hotel the night before.

"Back when, you would have kicked their asses," Geraldine offered. "Being a woman is what I always wanted to be, knew I really was, but all that estrogen sure cuts down on your aggression."

"That and the surgeries," Ronni agreed. "Makes you feel more vulnerable. Back before the change, I would've challenged that ape. Might've kicked his ass. He might've kicked mine. But I wouldn't have hesitated."

"You look like you still could do the kicking," Geraldine offered.

"I was quite a bit bigger back then; more muscle mass."

"But you're lean and mean now. We've just got to keep reminding ourselves, girlfriend. We are women, but we are not weak. We still can kick some ass."

When they landed, before Geraldine went off to catch a connecting flight to Dallas, they hugged.

"Y'all stay in touch, now," Geraldine said. "Stay true to yourself, girlfriend."

For the first time in a long time, Ronni had let down her guard with the affable, ebullient woman who made her feel like they'd been friends all their lives.

As she waited for her luggage, she retrieved messages from her phone. Allison had responded. She had told Kanaranzi's press secretary when Ronni was going to be in Boston, but had not told her the reason Ronni would be there. "I only told her that you were a Kanaranzi fan and would like to meet her," Allison's message said. "I'm sure she gets a lot of requests. It's not likely she told Kanaranzi. Part of a press secretary's job is to be a gatekeeper."

SEPTEMBER 12, FRIDAY

"How do you want me to react when Bean tells me I've been demoted? Shocked? Pissed? Deflated?" Aaron Feldman sat, looking at Magnolia across the expansive living room of her Pier 4 penthouse.

"I think deflated," she replied. "Best to keep the impression that you're a meek soul with no backbone."

"Hmph," Feldman snorted through his nose. "What's your Bible say? The meek shall inherit the earth?" He chuckled.

"So, what have you found out about this person rummaging around in my past?" Magnolia asked, changing the subject.

"She's one of those queer people you're so fucking interested in giving rights to."

Magnolia stiffened. If Feldman wasn't the best political black ops operative in the country, she would have fired him--and not for the first time. "I know you don't agree with my politics, but please clean up your language. And wipe that smart-ass look off your face."

Feldman shifted his bulk on the couch and stared out the condo's glass wall overlooking Boston Harbor.

"Veronica Brilliant is a private investigator from Minnesota," he said in a voice with sharp edges, not looking at Magnolia. "She was a he until ten years ago, an M.P. in the Marines, discharged in 2002. Did a sex change a couple of years later. Set up her own P.I. firm seven years ago. Works mostly for insurance companies. Made a big splash a few years back when she recovered a piece of stolen art and saved some insurance company a bundle of money."

"Why is she investigating me?" Magnolia interrupted. "Who's her client?"

"Haven't gotten that far yet, but I will. Probably Metzger."

"Why would Metzger go to Minnesota to hire a P.I. to investigate me? There are plenty of them on the East Coast that would be happy to."

"Plausible deniability?" Feldman responded. "Anyway, we'll know by the end of the day. We'll just follow the money."

"I want this problem gone quickly."

"I've got it under control. She won't be a problem."

"She's former Marine and military police. That makes her a problem," Magnolia said. "Do you have a plan?"

"Better for you not to know, but I don't think the Marine MP thing will change anything. I have it on good authority that a sex change operation takes their backbone as well as their balls."

Magnolia bristled: "That's absolute bullshit. It's because of assholes like you that they need a champion like me!"

"But, I'm *your* asshole," Feldman smirked, unphased by the tongue-lashing.

"I don't want her hurt!"

"She won't be, physically, but she'll wish to hell she'd never stuck her nose where it doesn't belong."

The meeting with Feldman was the first of two unpleasant duties that Magnolia had to perform on this dreary Friday morning. Ordinarily, she would have taken her coffee on the balcony, enjoying a moment of respite from the campaign, relaxing in the serenity of being elevated above the hubbub of Boston harbor. Instead, a chilly drizzle kept her inside, pacing back and forth in the living room as her coffee sloshed in the cup, getting colder. She stopped only long enough to click the remote that turned off a voice-activated recording system that chronicled every conversation in the penthouse.

Maria, her current live-in housekeeper, came in from the kitchen with a fresh carafe. "Would you like more coffee?" she asked in Spanish.

"*Si. Gracias.*" Magnolia held out her cup.

It was almost time to change housekeepers, a transition that ordinarily occurred every three months. The agency that supplied her housekeepers always sent young women who spoke only French or Spanish, no English; who were legally in the United States; and who had been vetted for honesty, attitude and the quality of their work. Occasionally, one of the young women would show uncommon promise and Magnolia would, after they had left her employ as housekeeper, provide money for education and then have one of the companies in her media empire hire them.

Maria was not one of those. While competent and friendly, Magnolia suspected that she had violated the "no visitors" policy that applied to all her housekeepers. No visitors had been identified, but the suspicion lingered, so Maria would be sent on her way with a small bonus and a recommendation.

At the moment, however, Magnolia didn't have time to break in a new housekeeper. Replacing Maria would have to wait until after the election.

Magnolia took the fresh cup of coffee into her office, closed the door and settled into one of the two Philip Arctander clam chairs that sat opposite her desk, tucking her legs beneath her. She spread the linen fabric of her royal blue caftan over her legs, then fished a phone out of the caftan's over-sized pocket and listened again to a phone message from the night before.

Henri Hawke had been drunk when he returned her call, a condition that was not uncommon whenever she tried to reach him during evening hours in Barcelona. Remarkably, the next day he never seemed to have any ill effects from his previous evening's imbibing. As usual, she had elected to wait to talk to him. She punched No. 1 on the phone, launching a call to the only number for which the phone was used.

"To what do I owe the pleasure." Hawke's syrupy French-accented English greeted her.

"This is not a social call!"

"It never is."

"Are you alone?"

"No, but I will be in a moment."

Magnolia heard him shoo someone away, in flawless Catalan, telling them it was a business call he had to take in private.

"I am now alone," he said, switching back to English.

"There is a private investigator from Minnesota digging around in my past. You told me you fixed that."

"Madame, I have taken care of it by making you invisible. All traces of your past have been erased--no court records, no school records, no employment records, no relatives. And I have created in its place a new you: pure, pristine and innocent. Like Phoenix rising from the ashes. I cannot, however, erase everyone who might want to know more about you now that you have chosen to become a public figure. Congratulations on your primary victory, by the way."

She wanted to be angry at Hawke, but he was right. He had warned her about running for political office, about the exposure it would inevitably bring. Because of their past association, it posed a huge risk for her and for him as her fixer. But the lure of power had drawn her, like a moth to a flame.

"Do you want me to handle it?"

"No. At least not now," she replied. "I do have something I need you to take care of when the election is over though."

"Another case of collateral damage?" Hawke said, using a catch-phrase Magnolia had coined five years earlier when she had first come to him needing someone in her circle to disappear.

"Yes."

"Just remember, no public figures. The lights are too bright."

"This one is anything but public. You might even consider him a competitor."

"In that case, it will be a pleasure. Let me know when I may be of service."

"You're sure about the invisibility," Magnolia asked, returning to their earlier topic of conversation.

"Absolutely," he answered, "and it's time you get a new phone. Don't forget to remove the SIM card."

Magnolia hung up. She hated dealing with Hawke. He was smug and overconfident. He was also the only person in her circle she could not control.

Someday, she thought, *he will become collateral damage.*

Ronni sat with her elbows on the conference room table, her hands steepled over her nose, her chin resting on her thumbs. She had told her partners, Carrie Waters and Holly Bouquet, about her meeting with Hamilton and Toni Blethen, including the assault on Hamilton five years ago. Neither of her partners had been aware of the assault, and all three women found that omission to be, at best, curious, and at worst, damning.

"This just doesn't add up," Ronni said. "If he killed her, why would he agree to continue the investigation?"

"Same reason that he started it in the first place," Holly offered. "To divert attention."

"I thought of that," Ronni said, "but there really is no attention focused on him now. The prosecutors gave up on him before we were hired, and if he stops paying us, we stop the investigation. It just doesn't make sense."

"Maybe that's the whole thing," Holly continued, her left hand brushing a lock of blonde hair away from her blue eyes. "He doesn't make sense. Maybe he's one of those psychologically messed up people that needs to keep revisiting his crime. Like an arsonist who goes back to watch the fire or a murderer who attends his victim's funeral. Maybe keeping the investigation alive is his way of doing that."

The brows of both Ronni and Carrie furrowed, as they often did when Holly explained a theory or offered an opinion. Holly was the acknowledged intellectual leader of the group. Stunningly attractive, and with multiple degrees in the field of criminal justice, her insights and intuition had led to the resolution of more than one case. Her combination of charm and beauty frequently enabled her to access information that was beyond the reach of her partners.

"I wonder if he's ever had a psychiatric evaluation," Carrie, the youngest of the three, interjected.

"He's had psychiatric treatment, but he quit because it made him depressed," Ronni answered. "That's what his wife…Toni… told me."

"Maybe it wasn't depression," Carrie observed. "Maybe it was getting too close to the truth. Maybe it's the same reason he went ballistic when you brought up the assault. The same reason you got threatened."

"There's no chance of getting him to see a psychiatrist again," Ronni said.

"I'd sure like to hypnotize him," Carrie continued. "Even take a shot at trying to communicate with his grandmother."

It was Carrie's psychic abilities that first drew the attention of Holly and Ronni, and resulted in her becoming part of the detective agency. She was also the reason the agency was named "The Monet Detective Agency". Carrie had neither the education nor the work experience to become a licensed private investigator, and, without a P.I. license, she couldn't legally be a partner, nor could her name be part of the agency's name. But she could be a consultant. And Carrie, with her rare gift of spiritual communication, was listed on the agency's website as a consultant on psychological and ethereal investigation.

The three women, who considered themselves equal partners notwithstanding the legalities, selected the agency's name because "Brilliant, Bouquet and Waters" made them think of Claude Monet's painting, *Water Lilies,* and Monet was Ronni's favorite artist. So, they had become the Monet Detective Agency and had purchased a large, framed copy of *Water Lilies* which now hung on the wall of their conference room.

"Neither of those are going to happen," Ronni said. "At least not now. All communication has to go through Toni, and she's very protective."

"So, how do you want to proceed?" Holly asked, getting up from her chair.

"I think we need to look into the assault, with or without his cooperation," Ronni replied. "Even if he wasn't involved in the murder, the assault may tell us something about what's driving him. At least we'll know more than we know now."

Hollie and Carrie agreed.

"You have the best rapport with the local police." Ronni said, directing her comment toward Holly's back as the blonde P.I. used the wall to do stretching exercises. "Why don't you track down Hamilton's assault, and then talk to the investigating officers. Maybe you can sweet-talk them into looking at their files since it's a cold case."

"Guessing the assault happened sometime in July, 2009? Maybe late June?" Holly queried over her shoulder.

"Sounds about right. Probably didn't get press coverage, though. Call Toni Blethen to get the exact date if you have to. I've worn out my welcome with her. Maybe she'll give you authorization to look at medical and police records."

"What do you want me to do?" Carrie asked, shifting uncomfortably in her chair. "I can free up some time tomorrow."

"See if that neighbor woman who found Lorraine's body is still alive and in possession of her faculties. If she is, see if she'll agree to let you hypnotize her. "

"She wasn't cooperative before."

"This is different. Before you were asking her to participate in a séance so you could try to communicate with Lorraine. That freaked her out. This time, we're just trying to see if, under hypnosis, she recalls something that is beyond her conscious recollection. Like the name on that appliance truck."

"I'm going to make a quick trip to Sturgis, South Dakota, as soon as I get a couple of things wrapped up here," Ronni continued. "Maybe there's something in school or in public records there that will shed some light on Kanaranzi's early years. Maybe I can track down an old classmate or two."

The meeting broke up with Ronni returning several phone calls and jotting dates on her calendar of meetings and events that had been scheduled while she was in Boston. She checked with their receptionist to be certain nothing else required her attention, then left to pack for the trip to Sturgis.

Home was a retrofit condo in what was once one of the grand homes in the Cathedral Hill area of St. Paul. Ronni lived by herself in a one-bedroom unit with a detached, dilapidated garage. It wasn't much, the once-stately building now on the seedy side from lack of maintenance, but it was all hers. And she loved the friendly, gentrified neighborhood with its restaurants, bars, coffee shops, book stores, hipster night spots and tolerance. She always felt safe.

Ronni walked up the flight of stairs to her third-floor unit. The door to her condo was ajar. *Did I forget to close it?* She remembered activating the alarm and locking the deadbolt when she left. *Or did I?* She stopped outside the door and listened. She wished she had her gun, strapped under the driver's seat of her car, but made the conscious decision not to take the time to go and get it. Gathering up her courage, she pushed open the door and yelled, "Who's in here?" Only the sound of splashing water answered.

Cautiously, she looked in the bathroom. Water was pouring over the sides of the sink, the faucets running at full blast. Half submerged in the overflowing sink was a framed photo of her sister, the one that Ronni always kept on the dresser in her bedroom.

"What the…?" She shut off the faucets and lifted the picture out of the water. Water sluiced off the corner of the frame. The photo was ruined.

Oscillating between anger and anxiety, Ronni checked the rest of her apartment. Nothing else seemed out of place.

"Brilliant's P.I. firm has several clients but only one located in Boston," Feldman said. "It was a bitch to find it, but I finally did. It's called the Lorraine Blethen Legal Fund. It's located in Cambridge and has an account at Cambridge Trust on Huron Avenue. Does any of that mean anything to you?"

The fine hairs on the back of Magnolia's neck stood on end, and the corner of her left eye fluttered. She paused, fighting to suppress the rage that welled up within her.

"No-o-o," she said, drawing it out as she slowly shook her head, winning the battle with her inner fury and maintaining her outward calm. "Find out who's behind it. Maybe it's a stealth political action committee of some kind."

Feldman left and Magnolia poured herself a dollop of single malt scotch, neat. It was a taste she had cultivated in recent years. So far, in the exalted social and political circles in which she traveled, it had been enough to illustrate she was one of the "boys." But she could foresee the time when she would be compelled to indulge in expensive cigars, a recent trend among powerful women.

Dressed in a pink hooded robe of Sherpa fleece, Magnolia sat on her deck, sipping the Speyside Scotch and watching nighttime boat traffic, the robe's collar snug, high around her neck, her feet curled under her against the chill.

She knew who was behind the Lorraine Blethen Legal Fund. But how had Hamilton made the connection? Unless, of course, Hawke's claim of invisibility had a flaw.

She looked at her watch. It was one a.m. in Barcelona. She set her drink on the table next to her chair and picked up her new phone. She stabbed the number one with her fingernail. As expected, she got voicemail.

"Hawke. We have a new problem. Call me immediately."

SEPTEMBER 13, SATURDAY

Hamilton leaned forward; the brush handle clamped tightly between his clenched teeth. Slowly he manipulated the bristles, applying streaks of blue-green paint to the canvas, creating depth and contrast to the seascape. He'd been working on the painting for more than a month. It would take at least another to complete it.

He had reluctantly agreed to try painting again as part of an occupational therapy program. His first attempts resulted in spilled paint, frustration and a lot of curse words. His first "painting" was little more than smears and streaks. But with angry persistence, guidance from the therapists at Spaulding Rehab, and never-ending encouragement from Toni, he learned to control his temper and develop his technique. His painting had improved a thousand-fold, but he was still a long way from attempting the one thing that he had been so good at in the past, copying the works of famous painters.

Before the "accident," Hamilton was a sought-after art copier. Private citizens and businesses hired him, and his copies of Vermeer, Gainsborough, Steen and Caravaggio paintings hung in homes, offices and businesses across the country. His peerless copies created the exact mystique that his clients coveted. Was it an original? How much did it cost? Where did you get it? That's what his clients wanted their friends and customers to wonder. And envy.

Even to the expert eye, Hamilton's pre-accident paintings were nearly indistinguishable from the originals. Seldom did anyone look close enough to see the disclaimer, "copy by H. Blethen", painted in small letters in a discreet place, usually hidden beneath the frame. If asked, Hamilton would admit he was the painter, but he was seldom asked, and he had learned early that discretion was as important to an art copier as were his brushes and canvas.

Even though he was among the best at his craft, he was never able to instill the same mastery in his own work. Copying others' work had been his bread and butter.

As he painted the seascape with tiny strokes, deftly creating light from the setting sun as it filtered through the crest of a wave, he knew he would never recapture the delicate touch required of his previous specialty. He had reconciled himself to that reality, and, since they no longer had to rely on his paintings to put food on the table and keep a roof over their heads, he was more or less satisfied with showing steady improvement in his craft.

Today, however, it was a struggle. He dipped the bristles into the paint and returned to the canvas time-after-time, but thoughts of his meeting with Veronica Brilliant kept disrupting his concentration. Finally, he placed the brush in a solvent-filled glass, released it from the grip of his teeth, and wheeled out of his studio.

He wished he hadn't lost his composure. Perhaps it *was* time to call a halt to the investigation of his grandmother's death. The detective said they had run out of leads, and he really didn't any longer care whether they found his mother. Save the money. Avoid having to confront his ugly, painful past. Dodge his own demise.

Toni had argued in favor of allowing the detectives to reopen an investigation into the assault that had occurred more than five years ago and left him nearly a quadriplegic. He knew what she was doing. She was hoping that solving the question of who assaulted him would give him closure, free him from the evil that continually surfaced in recurring nightmares. At the very least, she hoped he would finally confront that devastating night that had irrevocably altered their lives.

Hamilton also wanted the nightmares to stop, but reliving that night was a price too big to pay. The wraith with the baseball bat, that came out of the dark in his nightmares, felt like death. As it approached through the mist of his subconscious, the fear rose in his throat. Just as the bat was about to smash his skull, and as the assailant's mask was about to fall away, he would wake up screaming, sweating, shaking. It would take hours for him to calm down.

As irrational as it might be, Hamilton was convinced that if he learned the true identity of the phantom behind the mask, he would die.

He was not ready to leave Toni, nor to end this life in which he had just begun to feel comfortable.

"Hamilton Blethen has hired a private investigator to search for his grandmother's killer, and the P.I. is now investigating me!" Magnolia screamed into the phone.

Mon dieu. How could that happen? Hawke's mind raced as he tried to digest her tirade. He had arranged, through one of the best hackers in Europe, to expunge all electronic records of Mary Blethen prior to her ascension from the 1976 Sturgis Motorcycle Rally as Magnolia Kanaranzi. County records, school records, court records, jail records, all wiped clean.

Concerned that records in Zumbrota, Minnesota, where Mary Blethen was born and grew up, would not have been digitized as far back as her birth in 1953, he dispatched one of his most trusted operatives to investigate. Finding, as expected, that the county, city and school records from that era were kept on microfiche and not in computerized form, the operative simply asked to view the county birth records, deftly slipped the microfiche in her pocket and walked out of the courthouse, creating a one-month gap in the Goodhue County birth records.

A request for information about the Zumbrota High School Class of 1971 had been rebuffed by a no-nonsense matron who considered the school's historical archives her personal fiefdom. The human hurdle was easily overcome, however, thanks to an unsecure school building. The records of the Class of '71 disappeared, the professional burglary was never discovered, and the warden-in-charge didn't realize there was a gap in her historical records until years later, by which time she had long forgotten the operative and her request.

To create Magnolia's backstory, the hacker had planted a false birth certificate in the Meade County, South Dakota records. To anyone who searched, she was born Mary Stumpf in the Sturgis regional hospital in 1958, to Agnes Stumpf, now deceased. No father was listed. Five years had been trimmed off her age to create a false narrative in which anyone looking into her past would stumble. And, it had made Magnolia happy.

School records from Sturgis Brown High School had been digitized, so it was an easy task to inject the grades, attendance and graduation of Mary Stumpf who now, for the purposes of history, was not only born in Sturgis, but also graduated from high school there in 1975 at the age of seventeen.

Finally, the hacker burrowed into the Clark County, Nevada, archives. Magnolia had officially changed her name from Mary Blethen to Magnolia Kanaranzi while she was a pit boss in a Las Vegas casino. It was child's play to change the county records to show that it was Mary Stumpf who changed her name to Magnolia Kanaranzi on her eighteenth birthday. As far as Las Vegas was concerned, Mary Blethen never existed. It had all been scrubbed clean.

It had been a very expensive undertaking, but the results were impeccable. That Hamilton Blethen was now having Magnolia investigated left Hawke puzzled

"Well?" Magnolia asked, her scalding tone breaking the silence.

"Well, what?"

"Well, first, where did you screw up? How could Hamilton Blethen have connected the dots if they had all been erased, as you claim? Second, how are you going to fix it?"

"I didn't 'screw up', as you so quaintly put it, and the simplest solution would be to terminate him."

Magnolia thought for a moment about the prospect of killing her son. "Too risky," she said. "It might end the investigation into Lorraine Blethen's death, but there would be an investigation into his death, and because of that damn painting, and your mistakes, it could lead back to me."

"It will look like an accident," Hawke consoled, ignoring her accusations about his mistakes.

Unseen by Hawke, Magnolia shook her head on the other end of the call, a spark of motherly instinct welling up from somewhere inside. "We need something to make it impossible for him to continue the investigation."

"Money." Hawke crooned without hesitation. "Cut off his source of money, and you end the investigation. Private investigators don't work free, as you know so well."

The lilt in Hawke's voice irritated Magnolia.

"We'll use the painting against him," Hawke went on. "We'll contact the Boston Museum of Visual Arts and question the authenticity of *The Reaper*; tell them we have first-hand knowledge that *The Reaper* was destroyed in a fire in 1937. That will send the Museum into a tizzy. They'll hire a bunch of experts to investigate, question the painting's provenance. They may force him to buy it back, or, prosecute him for selling the Museum a forgery. He will have to spend huge amounts of money to defend himself. If he has to choose between defending himself or continuing to investigate Granny's death, he'll choose the former."

"I like it," Magnolia responded, a touch of excitement in her voice. "An art copier, hired to paint a copy of a long-lost painting, has his services terminated when his customer dies. A few years later, in dire financial trouble, he suddenly sells that very same painting to the museum for thirteen million dollars, claiming that he inherited the painting. It will be virtually impossible for him to defend himself. We just need one expert to say it's a forgery."

"With all the dilettantes in the art world that will not be difficult," Hawke assured her. "I can arrange for that expert, and you, as a board member of the museum, may be able to subtly influence which expert they hire."

"Since it was my million dollars that was the last piece of the thirteen million they paid him, they damn well better take my advice on who to hire."

"Delicately, my dear," Hawke whispered. "You must be subtle when you exert your influence. You do not wish to draw attention to your role in this matter."

"Someone other than myself will have to contact the museum," he continued after having given his advice time to take hold. "Hamilton would recognize my name."

"I'll arrange for someone to do it," she said. "I want him and his investigator off my back A.S.A.P.!"

Ronni reported the break-in to the police and called her insurance agent to report the damage. As always, the damage didn't exceed her deductible. At least he recommended a service company to clean up the mess.

She also called her sister.

"Maddy. It's Ron."

"Hey! Nice to hear your voice."

"Yeah. Sorry I haven't called more often, but something's come up that's got me a little concerned."

"And you called me?"

"Yeah. It has to do with you. Someone broke into my apartment yesterday. I keep a picture of you in my bedroom…"

"Really?"

"…and the burglars moved the picture from the bedroom to the bathroom. Have you seen or heard anything out of the ordinary lately?"

"No."

"Well, let me know if anything comes up. Strange phone calls. Someone following you. Anything."

"What's this all about?"

"I'm not sure. It may be nothing. Maybe just a B and E. Maybe he thought you were cute and was going to take your picture with him."

"That's creepy."

"Sorry."

"Did they take anything?"

"Not that I've been able to determine. Just moved your picture and left the water running in my bathroom. I might have interrupted him. I've got some water damage. Hope the people downstairs don't."

"I'm sorry, Ron. Anything I can do to help?"

"No. I've got it under control. Just wanted you to know. We need to have lunch soon."

"Sure. I'll check my calendar and get back to you."

Ronni knew she wouldn't. It was better when they communicated from a distance so that Maddy could hold onto the charade that Ronni was still her big brother, Ron.

SEPTEMBER 14, SUNDAY

"Miss Kanaranzi. Miss Kanaranzi."

Magnolia jerked as she heard her name. "What? Where am I?"

"We're almost at the Springfield Armory. Are you all right?" It was Samantha Jones speaking from the opposite seat of the stretch Chevy Suburban that was transporting Magnolia, Samantha and an advance man, Brian Flaherty, between campaign stops.

"Uh. Sure. Uh. Remind me about this stop," Magnolia responded, trying to fight her way out of sleep exhaustion and gather her thoughts.

"It's a rally. You're speaking to a group of outdoors organizations. You're going to tell them that you aren't going to be taking away their guns or Second Amendment rights, but that you are in favor of banning military-style automatic weapons."

"Oh, right. Right."

"We picked the Armory because of its historical significance as a former gun manufacturing facility," Samantha reminded her.

It was the third and final campaign stop of the day for the Kanaranzi caravan. Trailing the Suburban were two cars filled with campaign staff and volunteers, that had worked the crowds before and after the candidate's speeches, collecting names and contact information. The staff members had been invigorated by the reception at each of the first two stops, but rather than being energized, Magnolia had grown more tired as the day wore on.

The Suburban pulled up to the Armory's main entrance where a handful of people with picket signs milled about.

"What's this about?" Magnolia inquired, craning her neck to look out the window.

"PETA. Animal rights people," Flaherty said. "They show up wherever there's a large gathering of outdoor groups or hunting advocates."

The driver opened the passenger door and offered his hand to Magnolia. The protesters stopped and watched. One booed. Another yelled, "Give'm hell Magnolia!"

Flaherty and Samantha followed her out of the vehicle, and were joined by the other campaign workers who cordoned off the protestors. With Flaherty leading the way, Magnolia and her entourage entered the two-hundred-year-old facility that had been converted to a museum and convention hall. A small crowd was scattered around the thousand-seat auditorium.

"About one fifty," Flaherty guessed at the crowd size. It felt like considerably less.

Magnolia exhaled angrily through her nose at the spectacle of the mostly-empty cavernous hall.

"Son of a bitch," Flaherty exclaimed, feeling her noisy expiration required some response. He peeled off to find the local organizers, and in so doing he missed the tiny spasm that momentarily inflicted Magnolia's left eye.

"Who organized this?" she snarled, turning and directing her wrath at Samantha.

"The local Democratic committee."

"Who was our liaison?"

"Flaherty."

For a half hour Magnolia stuffed her rage, shaking hands with local elected officials and party minions. As Magnolia spoke from the proscenium to the small gathering, now clustered in the front of the auditorium, Samantha worried about her candidate. The sleep-induced, disoriented incident in the limousine was the second in a week. Neither time did Magnolia appear to be asleep, but her mind was clearly not on the campaign or the event at hand and, although her eyes were open, she did not appear to be aware of her surroundings or the people she was with. Luckily, she had recovered quickly on both occasions.

And then there were the surges of anger. It was understandable that she'd be upset by the size of the crowd, or by being booed by a protester, but Magnolia's recurrent rages were wholly out of proportion.

Could it all be from sleep deprivation, Samantha wondered? She'd check with her doctor about getting something to help the candidate sleep. She knew that neither Magnolia or Jim Bean would slack off on Magnolia's schedule, but the doctor might prescribe something that would allow her to reach REM sleep quickly and wake up fully refreshed. Samantha would also ask him if it was possible for someone to sleep with their eyes open.

Her speech concluded to polite applause, Magnolia was busy shaking hands and chatting with a few of the audience members who approached her. Samantha allowed it to go on for ten minutes before telling Magnolia it was time to go.

"Where's Flaherty?" Magnolia asked as they left the building.

"Talking to the local committee officers."

"He should've done that before this event. Not after."

The two women climbed into the back of the limousine. Magnolia pressed the intercom button and signaled the driver to leave.

"What about Flaherty?"

"Leave him."

"But…."

"Leave him. He's fired."

Oh, shit. I'm going to have to fix that tomorrow, Samantha thought. She was afraid to tell Magnolia that she couldn't fire Flaherty. He was a volunteer.

SEPTEMBER 15, MONDAY

Ronni pushed the speedometer over eighty, heading southwest on Highway 60 as the sun began to peek through the rear window of her Dodge Dakota. She had left St. Paul while it was still dark. Sturgis was still six hours away. Her thoughts kept going back to the running faucet and her sister's photo.

The last few days hadn't been the best of Ronni's life. She'd pissed off a client, been threatened by two thugs, had her home broken into, and her sister's photo had been ruined in an overflowing sink. It was as if a black cloud was following her. She adjusted her rearview mirror to keep the sun out of her eyes and revisited the questions that kept nagging at her.

The warning to stay out of Boston has to be tied to the Lorraine Blethen case. There's no other logical explanation. I don't believe it was a random act of a couple of transphobes. But why? Ronni had gone to Boston ready to pull the plug. They had hit a wall in their investigation and, at least to her knowledge, hadn't turned up any evidence that would make anyone feel threatened. But someone had. What was she missing?

Could it be Hamilton? He didn't know we were ready to quit. Was my going to Boston enough to spook him? Was Carrie right? Is he an adrenalin junkie who needs to be on the edge of a cataclysm to feel alive? Was his blow-up staged? Did he stage this whole thing? Even his own assault?

Ronni wasn't ready to buy that theory. She had been there and seen it. She felt Hamilton's meltdown was real. *And he could have just ended the investigation. Instead, he separated himself from it, and his wife became the gate keeper. That doesn't sound like someone who needs to be close to the flame. But if not him, who?*

She had no good answer.

And then there's the break-in. Coincidence? Half a continent separated St. Paul from Boston, and Ronni wouldn't have thought the two events were linked, but her sister's picture in the sink troubled her. Maddy was not involved in Ronni's work in any respect. *Why would the asshole who broke in put Maddy's picture in the sink? Unless he was some kind of pervert. Or was it meant to intimidate me?*

Ronni looked down at the speedometer. Nearly ninety, accurately reflecting both the speed of the Dakota and her racing mind. She eased off. The road sign read: "Worthington 7". The Dakota slowed, but her thoughts didn't.

What about the woman on the airplane? Geraldine. Was she for real?

Ronni had liked Geraldine, but in light of everything else that had happened in the last week, nothing could be taken at face value. The tall, Black trans woman with the exuberant personality had been a great travel companion, but, in hindsight, her willingness to divulge her innermost secrets to a complete stranger was suspicious. Trans people ordinarily kept their gender change well-guarded, except to very close confidantes. *Had she been planted next to me? What did I tell her?*

As Ronni tried to recall her two-hour-long conversation with Geraldine, the one phrase that kept coming back to her was Geraldine's admonition: "We've just got to keep reminding ourselves, girlfriend. We are women, but we are not weak. We still can kick ass."

That's the struggle, isn't it, Ronni thought. *We want to be both. Feminine. Pretty. Caring. But we also want to kick ass. We want a man to want us, but we're scared to be vulnerable.* Ronni's go-to reaction was to withdraw when approached by a male in a social setting. The more aggressive the man, the more withdrawn she became until he crossed a line. Then she reverted to kick-ass mode. After ten years of transitioning to W, and as much as she wanted a relationship, she still hadn't figured it out.

She eased the truck to a stop, then spun the wheel as she turned on to I-90. The grain elevators of Worthington passed on her left as she accelerated toward Sturgis. "Luverne 31" the road sign said. She flipped open the leather case lying on the seat next to her and fished out a CD, *The Best of Etta James*, and listened to Etta's version of *At Last*. Ronni relaxed.

Analysis was not her strong suit. That was Holly's forte. Ronni was better with confrontation, action. She was muscle. Holly was brains. And then there was Carrie, who added an element to the Monet Agency that defied description but had proven invaluable. Maybe Carrie would hit on something in the netherworld. Otherwise, there seemed little chance that they would solve Lorraine Blethen's murder, and failure was not something Ronni suffered graciously.

She had been a winner all her life: as an athlete and an MP when she was still a he, and as a private detective after her conversion. Defeats were rare, and they chewed on her like a flesh-eating virus. Both her commanding officers and her P.I. partners had attempted to pry Ronni's hands from cases that seemed lost or unsolvable, but she seldom agreed to let go.

Tenacity was a virtue, a psychologist had once counseled her, but tenacity had to be coupled with reason. It was not a virtue if it was compelled by the need to prove her invincibility. It was perfectly acceptable to walk away if the circumstances dictated that was the best course of action. To walk away in that situation was not a defeat or a failure.

This advice was given when Ronni was undergoing counseling while in the midst of the multiple operations that reshaped and recast her body, one of those vulnerable times when she doubted her decision and her self-esteem was in the toilet. A period when she spent most of her time in pain.

It had been good advice, but she knew that wasn't why she couldn't let go.

It was a December night in the port city of Aden. The *U.S.S. Cole* had been attacked by al Qaeda two months earlier, and Ron Brilliant was among the United States forces deployed to support the counter-intelligence personnel that had been dispatched to investigate the bombing. The Cole had long since been returned to the United States but the investigation continued. On this particular December night, an American, Joel Cosgrove, had failed to return from a meeting between U.S. and Yemeni officials.

Ron had gotten to know Cosgrove well enough to learn that he was gay and struggling with his sexuality. Ron had come close to revealing his own sexual struggles to Cosgrove, but fear of reprisal from his own unit kept him quiet. Nevertheless, he empathized with Cosgrove's situation and genuinely liked the man.

When Cosgrove failed to return to base, Ron was part of a patrol sent to look for him. The six heavily armed soldiers split into groups of three and combed the streets of Aden. At midnight, after three hours of scouring every alley and doorway within a mile of the base, the corporal in charge of Ron's group called off the search, opining that Cosgrove was probably shacked up for the night with some whore.

Ron bristled at the comment, but said nothing.

The next morning Cosgrove was found, his throat slit, less than half a block from where the patrol had ended its search. Ron vowed he would never again quit.

Even if Hamilton and Toni hadn't agreed to continuing the investigation, Ronni knew that the memory of Cosgrove and the Boston incident would have compelled her to make this trip to Sturgis and to continue the Lorraine Blethen murderer investigation. Finding the killer was still longer than a long shot, but someone was worried. Ronnie had to find out what had caused them to worry.

In the meantime, however, finding out more about Magnolia Kanaranzi, and whether she could be Hamilton's mother, was the immediate goal.

Okay. Get your head together. Ronni thought. *What am I looking for? Birth records first. Then marriage records. Death records, too, just to be sure.* Luckily Sturgis was the county seat and all records were public and in one place. *Then a visit to the school. That might require a little persuasion, but I should at least be able to find out when Magnolia went to school there. Maybe get an address where she had lived. Then contact any relatives she might learn about from the county or school records. Evening might be the best for that.* She decided she would have to stay overnight.

A road sign flashed past on her right. At eighty miles per hour, it took a moment for the sign to register in Ronni's brain. She slammed on the brakes and the truck fishtailed, leaving rubber stripes on the interstate. She regained control and coasted to the gravel shoulder. *Whhhhh,* she exhaled. *Good thing no one was behind me.*

Ronni carefully backed the Dakota down the shoulder toward the sign, now a hundred yards behind her. Twice she stopped to let oncoming traffic pass. The sign finally glided past the right side of her truck and she stopped. It was an ordinary road sign, informing the reader that at the next intersection, if you turned right, you went to Magnolia. If you turned left, you went to the town of Kanaranzi.

BINGO!

Ronni dialed her phone.

"Holly? You won't believe this! Magnolia Kanaranzi is a road sign."

Toni's fork pushed the green beans around her plate, forming geometric patterns on the light-colored stoneware.

"Something bothering you, Hon?" Hamilton asked. "You haven't eaten a thing."

Toni sat for a moment, looking at her plate.

"This is going to upset you," she said, looking up.

"So, tell me." Hamilton cocked his head as if to deflect the blow.

"I got called into Meredith's office this afternoon."

"And?"

"The museum knows that we sold them *The Reaper.*"

"How did they find out?"

"It gets worse. They received a call raising questions about *The Reaper's* provenance."

Hamilton struggled to sit up straight. "What kind of questions?" Irritation crept into his voice.

"They questioned its authenticity."

"What!" Hamilton shouted, as the lid came off his temper. "Who?"

"She wouldn't tell me."

"Somebody is claiming it's a forgery and we don't know who? How the hell are we……. did she fire you?"

"No. I told her we sold it through a blind trust so that it wouldn't affect their consideration of my employment. I'm guessing whoever made the complaint knew we were the sellers."

"Did she believe you?"

"I don't know. She said the museum would do a full investigation, and wanted to know if you'd cooperate."

"That damn painting has caused us nothing but grief. Lawsuits with your family. Tax issues. Now this."

Five years earlier, he had agreed to paint *The Reaper,* but the man who had commissioned him to paint it died and the project was canceled.

With the cancellation, a million-dollar commission had also evaporated. The amount of the commission; the sketchy reputation of Arthur Kincaid, the man who was willing to pay the million dollars; and his demand for absolute secrecy--backed by a veiled threat-- screamed forgery. Hamilton had struggled with his conscience but eventually convinced himself, despite the feeling in his gut to the contrary, that he had no real proof that Kincaid would pass off his painting as the original. He decided to paint it. Greed had triumphed over ethics, only to have fate intervene.

He was now being accused of forging the painting he had almost forged. The irony of the situation in which he now found himself was not lost on Hamilton. *Karma,* he thought. *The gods of art are getting even.*

Toni remained silent, knowing anything she said would only add fuel to her husband's simmering rage. She knew Hamilton was right. The painting, inherited from a senile distant relative of Toni's, had resulted in a lawsuit by one of Toni's uncles, claiming that the old woman was incompetent when she signed her will. Ham and Toni ultimately prevailed, but it cost them nearly a quarter million dollars in legal fees and drove a wedge between Toni and much of her family.

Toni bent over and wrapped her arms around her husband. "Don't worry. We'll get through this, like we have everything else."

"It's got to be your uncle, getting even for losing the lawsuit? Who else would know that we were the sellers?"

Toni nodded. She didn't want to believe that her own family would do it, but she couldn't think of any other explanation. "I'll try to find out from Meredith when I go back to work tomorrow," she said.

They had sold *The Reaper* for thirteen million dollars. The legal fees they had paid to establish their legal right to the painting threatened to bankrupt them, but the sale of the painting to Toni's employer had saved them. Those legal fees, the money Ham had set aside for the investigation of his Grandmother's murder, and the purchase of their home in Cambridge were the only money they had spent from the proceeds of *The Reaper* sale. Eleven million dollars remained in reserve, another three-quarter million in escrow for Lorraine's investigation. It was Toni's salary as assistant curator of the museum, Hamilton's disability payments, and interest from their small personal investments that provided their lifestyle. Luckily, the Veterans Administration picked up the tab for Hamilton's rehab and medical needs.

"Let's talk about this in the morning. After we've had a night to digest it," Toni suggested.

Hamilton spun his chair away from the table and rolled out the dining room door, causing the reclining Barca to lurch out of the way. The big dog looked up at Toni with sorrowful, what-did-I-do-wrong eyes. She sunk to the floor and put her arms around the golden retriever as tears escaped down her cheeks.

"Nothing," she whispered into the dog's fur. "You didn't do anything wrong."

Jim Bean sat behind his desk at election headquarters, listening to Samantha voice her concerns about the well-being of their candidate.

"So, you think she should take some time off?" he growled. "Or see a shrink. Are you kidding me? We've got less than eight weeks to the election, we're in a dead heat with Metzger and he's just released an attack ad. She doesn't have time to take time off, and we sure as hell aren't going to give Metzger ammunition by sending her off to a shrink. She can sleep after the election. Besides, she'd kick my ass out of here if I even suggested she take time off."

Samantha stood, taking the berating in stride. She hadn't thought her plea would do any good, but she had to try.

"I understand," she said. "I just hope we don't push her over the edge while we're trying to win the election. You should've been there. She went from half-awake to angry to cruel in a split second. She was like a different person,"

"She's tough, and this is what she signed up for. She can handle it."

Samantha backed out of Bean's office and went to her desk, checking the day's schedule: four events, starting with a luncheon and ending with another rally, this time in Lowell. Lowell was Metzger's back yard but, hopefully, this rally would be better attended than the one last night in Springfield.

Harking back to the Springfield rally reminded her that she had to return Flaherty's call. He was angry. He had every right to be. Samantha needed to get him reimbursed for the cost of the cab fare from Springfield and talk him down, maybe get him to come back into the campaign. At least she needed to make sure that he didn't let his anger spill over to Metzger.

The attack ad Metzger had released was all about how Magnolia mistreated her employees. It featured a couple of disgruntled former employees that had been terminated, unjustly according to them, from one of Magnolia's companies.

A similar ad about mistreated campaign volunteers would be devastating.

At the end of the day, Ronni called Holly to report that she had found nothing in the county records referring to a person named Magnolia Kanaranzi, nor did the Sturgis school district have any record of someone by that name.

"As we expected," Holly said.

After discovery of the highway sign on Interstate 90, they had agreed that Ronni should continue her trip to Sturgis to research local records even though neither of them thought she would find anything.

"I've been looking at the picture of the road sign you texted me," Holly continued. "She may have risen from the ashes in Sturgis, but it appears she got her name four hundred miles east of there from this sign. It certainly increases the odds that Magnolia Kanaranzi is Hamilton's mother. Do you think we should tell him?"

"Not yet," Ronni said. "It increases the odds a little, but she could have come from anywhere. I don't want to give him any false hope."

"My guess is that she was traveling to Sturgis for the motorcycle rally, saw the sign, liked the name and took on the identity," Holly speculated. "I'd say the first place we look is Zumbrota. We know Mary Blethen left Zumbrota right after high school, running away, so to speak. Just maybe, she was running to Sturgis to become Magnolia Kanaranzi."

"The timeline doesn't work," Ronnie countered. "She's too young to be Hamilton's mother."

"I still think it's worth looking in Zumbrota, and, besides, Carrie's going there tomorrow to talk to Dorothy Proost…"

"The neighbor?"

"…Yeah. Carrie can check county and school records for both Mary Blethen and Magnolia Kanaranzi while she's there."

"Has Proost agreed to be hypnotized?" Ronni asked.

"Not yet. She's in a nursing home. Carrie wants to visit her in person to assess her mental faculties before suggesting hypnosis."

"What time is Carrie's appointment?"

"I think it's at one, right after lunch."

"I'll leave here early tomorrow. Tell Carrie I'll meet her in Zumbrota. I'll call her when I get close and we can pick a place to meet. I can do research while Carrie is talking to Proost."

"You don't need to do that," Holly said. "Carrie can handle it."

"I know she can, but after Boston I feel like I have a personal stake in this investigation. If it turns out that Magnolia Kanaranzi is Hamilton's mother, I'd like to lock that down and be the one to tell him."

"It *would* be a nice consolation prize to reunite our client with his mother," Holly said, "Even if we don't ultimately solve his grandmother's murder."

SEPTEMBER 16, TUESDAY

"Ham will cooperate with the museum's investigation," Toni said as she stood in the doorway to Meredith Glenn's office. "What would you like him…us…to do?"

"We've turned the investigation over to our lawyers. They'll let us know."

Toni hesitated. "Am I in any kind of trouble?"

"No. No. But I'm sure they'll want information from you too. Probably a statement of some kind."

"We'd really like to know who raised this issue," Toni continued. "We might be able to resolve this in a hurry if we knew who it is."

"I'm not at liberty to tell you that. I'm sure the lawyers will let you know at the appropriate time."

Frown lines appeared at the corner of Toni's eyes, showing her frustration. "We think it's a relative. We had to fight a lawsuit started by one of my uncles, challenging Ham's right to inherit the painting. We're thinking that it's probably him trying to get revenge. If we're right, we can probably settle this by paying him something."

"I don't know, but I'll pass that information on to the lawyers."

"Should we get our own lawyer?"

"That, probably, would be a good idea."

"Okay if I take the rest of the day off to look?" Toni asked.

"Also, a good idea," Meredith responded. Her demeanor was friendly, but a thick tension now existed between the two women who had worked together so closely over the past two years.

Despite Meredith's assurances Toni knew that if the allegations became public, her time as assistant curator would be over. Museums of the stature of the Boston Museum of Visual Art do not like controversy and, even if she was exonerated of any wrong-doing, Toni would be a pariah in the professional art world, tied forever to a suspected art forger. Her career would effectively be finished just as it was getting started.

On her way out of the museum, Toni saw two members of the museum's custodial staff working around *The Reaper*. She changed course to confront them, and asked: "What's going on?"

"We've been told to take it down and put it in storage," one of the workmen said, pointing at *The Reaper.*

"Senator Metzger has accused you of vindictive and arbitrary actions related to the firing of two of your employees. Do you have a response to his claim that you mistreated your employees and had a personal vendetta against them?" The question, posed by a Washington-based reporter, didn't come as a surprise.

Until that moment, the press conference had gone smoothly. Magnolia had championed her plan for pre and post-natal education. Samantha had planted questions with friendly journalists and, as expected, Magnolia had hit the softball questions out of the park with her answers. But, all of that would be forgotten in the next news cycle if she fumbled her response to *the* question.

Magnolia took a deep breath and slowly let it out, shaking her head slowly from side to side with a I-can't-believe-you-asked-me-that-question look on her face.

"I assume you're referring to the recent attack ad posted by Metzger's campaign," she said.

"First of all, this is a personal attack that has nothing to do with my qualifications to serve as your next Senator. Second, they were not *my* employees. They were two of hundreds of employees of Kincaid Media. I did not hire either of them. I did not know them socially. I did not personally terminate them. I imagine that there isn't any company with a thousand employees that doesn't have at least one or two that are unhappy.

"Having said that, I was aware of both of these people professionally. As CEO of Kincaid, it is my duty and obligation to run and operate the company in the best interest of its shareholders, just as I'll run my Senate office in the best interest of the citizens of Massachusetts. These two employees had repeatedly shown they were no longer capable of fulfilling their duties. Their performance had become a detriment to the company. That is the reason they were terminated. I had, and have, no vendetta against either of them. I suspect they are just repeating words that Metzger's attack dogs put in their mouths. If my opponent continues to make personal, unsupported attacks on me as the focus of his campaign, instead of focusing on the real issues that face the people of Massachusetts, he should look first in his own cloak room and keep his hands where they belong."

The last comment caught everyone by surprise, and brought a volley of shouted questions and raised hands from the attending media.

Samantha quickly stepped to the podium.

"No more questions," she said. "Thank you all for coming." And, with that, guided Magnolia out of the room.

"What the hell was that about?" growled Bean after they were out of media earshot.

Magnolia turned on her campaign director.

"Shut up and listen," she hissed. "You haven't found shit about Metzger. I know he's dirty. Anyone with his level of testosterone and position of power has groped more than one page in his day. All I've done is sow the seed. Just wait. Someone will come out of the woodwork in the next week or two. Then we'll have him by the balls."

"You don't know that! This could blow up in your face."

"How? Metzger will howl his denial and indignation, and in a week, this will be old news. *Or,* his denial will become the big news of the campaign if someone comes forward. And they will. I guarantee it."

Bean threw up his hands. "I hope you're right."

"We always knew it was going to be a dirty fight," Magnolia said, "and I intend to win it by a knockout."

Samantha and Bean watched Magnolia walk away down the corridor, her four-inch spikes clicking on the Terrazzo floor.

"Stilettoes," Bean muttered. "How fitting."

Ronni pulled into the diagonal parking space in front of Bridget's Café, next to Carrie's dilapidated Subaru.

"When are you going to get a new car?" she asked her partner as she slid a wooden chair up to the opposite side of the table where Carrie was sitting.

Carrie, a piece of half-eaten strawberry pie in front of her, wiped a bit of whipped cream from the corner of her mouth. "Suzie and I go way back," she said. "She gets me where I have to go. She got me here from California. She always starts. So, she's a little worn around the edges, but that's no reason to kick her to the curb. Oops. Sorry about the pun."

Ronni smiled at both the pun and Carrie's attachment to the car named Suzie.

"You want something?" Carrie asked with a grin. "Best pie in Zumbrota."

"No. Did you get a chance to talk with Dorothy Proost?"

A waitress who had been eyeing Ronni from behind the counter, sauntered over. "Can I get you something?"

"Just coffee. Black."

She wrote it down on her pad, all the while looking over her glasses, inspecting Ronni.

"Guess they don't get many trans patrons," Ronni said after the waitress left, thinking she'd been clocked.

"I think it's the leather pants and the piercings. Probably not the ordinary dress code in Zumbrota," Carrie said. "She probably thinks you're a biker." She took another bite of her pie as the waitress returned with Ronni's coffee.

"I did talk to one of the caregivers at the local nursing home where Dorothy is living," Carrie continued, after washing down the pie with a slurp of coffee. "She told me to come back at three, after Dorothy has had her afternoon nap. She said Dorothy is having a few short-term memory issues, but nothing serious."

"Did Holly tell you what I found out in Sturgis?"

"Yeah. Weird. What do you make of it?"

"I want to stop at the local newspaper and check their archives for anything about Mary Blethen, or Magnolia Kanaranzi," Ronni said. "Do you have time to run by the school before you meet with Dorothy to see if they have any records on either of them? I think they might respond better to you than me."

Carrie looked at the clock on the restaurant's wall. "No problem. That three o'clock is not hard and fast. I just need to wait until after her afternoon nap to see her. Want to come with me?"

"I'd love to, but I might freak her out."

Ronni walked the block to the newspaper office and found that the *News/Record* had not moved into the digital age. Her search would have to be done the old-fashioned way: one old, dusty newspaper at a time.

She focused her search on the decade of the 1970s. *That should cover her high school years and then some,* she thought. She skimmed the newspapers, working backwards in time, looking at headlines and photos, stopping only to read articles about school activities or the occasional story about some young person's achievements. She had gone through all of 1979 and half of 1978 when Carrie called.

"The school has no record of Mary Blethen after eighth grade, and no records of any kind about Magnolia Kanaranzi."

"The Kanaranzi thing doesn't surprise me. Blethen must have left Zumbrota before high school," Ronni said.

"Or maybe she was home schooled, or went to a private school," Carrie said.

If she was home schooled, it's unlikely she'll show up in the newspaper, Ronni thought. All the articles about school-age kids were about sports or other extra-curricular activities connected to the high school.

"I'll check the area for private schools later," Carrie continued. "Right now, I'm heading to the nursing home. I'll call you when I'm done."

"There's a restaurant on Highway 52 on the way out of town. Let's meet there," Ronni suggested. "I'm going to stay here and look through newspapers until they close." She checked her watch. The newspaper office closed at five, and she needed to narrow her search.

"What year was Mary Blethen in eighth grade?" she asked. Ronni could hear Carrie shuffling paper.

"The 1966-67 school year."

"Are you sure?"

"That's what the person at the school told me."

"Okay. Thanks."

According to what she had learned in Boston, Magnolia Kanaranzi emerged from Sturgis, South Dakota, in 1975 right out of high school. If Mary Blethen was in eighth grade in 1967, she would have graduated from high school in 1971. *Damn!*

Ronni wrestled the loose-leaf binder that contained all fifty-two newspapers from 1971 off the shelf and laid it on the table where she had been working. She located the edition for the week of May 31. No mention of high school graduation. She flipped back to the week of May 24. There it was: photos and the story about the graduating class of 1971 and the list of all the graduates. She'd had a hunch that in a small town like Zumbrota they would list the entire graduating class. The edition that featured high school graduation week was probably the biggest seller of the year.

There was no Magnolia Kanaranzi among the graduates, as expected, but there, under the "B" s, was Mary Blethen.

Strange. Carrie said that the school had no record of Mary Blethen in high school.

Ronni looked at the picture of the graduating class, squinting to locate Mary Blethen among the 70-plus graduates. The picture was too small and grainy to get a good look at any specific graduate.

"Excuse me," she said, after hunting down the lone person working in the office. "Would you still have the high school graduation photos from 1971?"

The woman shook her head. "You might find something at the library," she offered. "It's open until eight tonight."

Ronni thanked her and went back to the newspaper archives. She quickly skimmed the remaining newspapers for 1971 and all of 1972. She found no mention of Mary Blethen. She thanked the woman again, and left.

At the library, the woman working behind the counter directed her to a section devoted to local high school memorabilia.

"I don't think we have graduating class photos," she said, "but you might try looking in the yearbooks."

There was no yearbook for the Class of '71, but there was one for the Class of "69, and there, in the thumbnail photos of the sophomore class of that year was Mary Blethen, dark rings under her eyes and a sullen look. Ronni recognized that look. She was willing to bet that Mary Blethen, at age fifteen or sixteen, was already on drugs.

Ronni snapped a picture of Mary Blethen's photo with her cell phone, then took the yearbook to the receptionist's desk and asked if she knew any of the students from the sophomore class.

"I've only moved here three years ago, but Helen…she's a volunteer…has lived here her whole life," the receptionist said. "She'll be here tomorrow."

Carrie and Ronni met at the Covered Bridge Café on the north edge of Zumbrota.

"She remembered the name on the door of the truck," Carrie said, recounting her session with Dorothy Proost. "Bert's Appliance. And she remembered that the vehicle was a delivery truck with a square box, that it was white and that there were two people in it. She was outside hanging up clothes when she saw the truck pull out of Lorraine's driveway. She walked over to Lorraine's to see if she had gotten a new stove. Other than that, the hypnosis didn't turn up anything new."

"Did you ask her if she saw a license plate?"

"She said she didn't, and she didn't remember anything on the side of the truck other than the name of the appliance company. I googled Bert's Appliance and found several, but the closest one is in Indiana. Nothing remotely close to here."

"Let's think about it overnight and meet with Holly tomorrow," Ronni said.

Their conversation was interrupted by a waitress. They hastily ordered burgers. Carrie added a beer to her order. Ronni settled for water, knowing that getting pulled over with the smell of alcohol on her breath was the only excuse local police would need to lock her up, and it wouldn't matter what her blood-alcohol reading was.

"Mary Blethen graduated from Zumbrota High School in 1971." Ronni resumed the conversation. "I found a picture of her in a yearbook when she was a sophomore."

Ronni scrolled to the photo on her phone and showed it to Carrie.

"There's a woman at the local library who might know some of the people from the class of '71," Ronni continued. "She works tomorrow, so I'll be coming back to Zumbrota."

"Does she look like Magnolia Kanaranzi?" Carrie asked, referring to the photo on Ronni's phone.

"I don't know. I'll compare it to the campaign photo I have of Kanaranzi when I get back to the office, but I doubt that there is any connection. Mary Blethen graduated in 1971. According to what I learned in Boston, Kanaranzi appeared in Sturgis in 1975, right out of high school."

"Well, we know Magnolia Kanaranzi's not her real name, or at least not the one she was born with," Carrie said. "If her name's not real, maybe the dates aren't real either."

SEPTEMBER 17, WEDNESDAY

Monet's *Water Lilies* floated on the conference room wall as the three private detectives sorted through the fragmented facts of Lorraine Blethen's murder.

"So, if you were going to arrange a hit on an old lady in a small town, knowing what Carrie just learned from Dorothy Proost, how would you go about it?" Holly asked.

Ronni rattled off a simple faux plan: "Hire a hit man. Rent a generic truck. Have a couple of those magnetic signs made to put on the doors to make it look like a thousand other delivery trucks. Scout the place for a couple days to determine her schedule. Pick a time when you know she's alone. Then do the deed and drive away."

"Why the signs on the doors?" Carrie asked.

"To give them cover in case they're stopped," Ronnie replied. "If they were really good, they would have a couple of old appliances in the back of the truck."

"And to send anyone who investigates down a dead end," Holly added.

"Why two hit men?" Carrie continued her questioning. "She's an old lady. One could certainly have taken care of her, and two doubles the risk of someone talking about it."

"That's a puzzle, Ronnie said. "Maybe because of the dog? I can't think of any other reason, unless the hit was ordered by someone who already had them on their payroll and the second man was just backup."

"That suggests organized crime," Holly said. "What motive could they have for offing an old woman in rural Minnesota?"

"Drug deal? Sex trafficking?" Ronni responded. "An old woman in need of money, living by herself on a farm midway between Rochester and the Twin Cities, would be a perfect conduit for the Mafia or one of the cartels. Maybe a deal went bad and they snuffed her. We know the hit was done by professionals."

"I'll go back through our file to see if there is anything in the police reports that might lend itself to that theory," Holly said. "I'm sure they did a search of the house at the time of the murder."

"I'll bet they didn't search it for drugs," Carrie said.

Ronni nodded. "I'm guessing that if there were any drugs, or if this was a holding place for sex trafficking, the killers wiped the place clean. When I go back to Zumbrota this afternoon, I'll stop at the police department and ask if there were any complaints or reports of unusual activity at Lorraine's place."

"I think the organized crime theory is unlikely," Holly said, "but we should follow it, at least for a little while, if for no other reason than to eliminate it."

"I agree," Carrie chimed in. "I can spend some time tomorrow at the BCA seeing what information they have about drugs and sex trafficking in southern Minnesota, but what about the theory that Hamilton did it? Except for the mob idea, he's the only one with motive."

The three women sat for a moment, pondering the Hamilton-did-it theory. Carrie stared at the mottled carpet on the conference room floor, scratching the back of her neck with her index finger, trying to conjure another suspect. Holly gazed out the window, deep in similar thought.

"If we knew the motive, we'd know the killer," Ronni said, breaking the silence. "We can follow both paths. For the sake of argument, let's presume our client *is* the killer. He lived in St. Paul, so he probably would have rented the truck and had the door magnets made in the Twin Cities. Carrie, in addition to checking out the BCA, can you do some digging on where you could rent a white delivery truck and have door signs made back in 2009?"

"I can do it," Carrie nodded.

"I'll do a background search on Lorraine. Look for her connection to the mob," Holly snickered.

"While you're at it," Ronni said, ignoring Holly's sarcasm, "check Zumbrota area hotels the week before Lorraine was killed. Include Rochester. See if any of them had two men staying in the same room there the days before Lorraine's murder. It's a long shot, but that's all we have. Hopefully, they'll still have records back that far. Meanwhile, I'll go to Zumbrota and see if I can find Hamilton's mother."

Minutes later Ronni stood in the parking garage staring at a flat tire. *Shit!* She dug in her purse for her phone to call roadside assistance, then stopped. *Ten years ago, I would have changed this myself. What the hell? Thank God I didn't wear a dress today.* She put the phone back in her purse, popped the trunk and looked for the spare tire. It was one of the skinny, temporary kind. She wrestled it out of the trunk. The jack was bolted to the trunk floor underneath the spare. Luckily, the wing nut wasn't rusted. Fifteen minutes later Ronni was dirty and disgusted, the flat tire was in the trunk and the Dodge Dakota was sitting at an ungainly tilt because of the undersized spare. She would have to get cleaned up and get the regular tire fixed before she went to Zumbrota.

"That tire's been slashed," the young technician at Discount Tire on University Avenue told her. "You'll have to buy a new tire. In fact, you'll need to buy two because your other front tire is worn to the point that putting a new tire on one side and leaving the worn tire on the other will make your truck difficult to drive, unsafe."

Ronni wasn't sure she believed him, but she didn't have time to argue nor go somewhere else.

Feeling violated by both the person who slashed her tire and the up-selling technician, she struggled to keep from lashing out. "How much?" she asked through clenched teeth.

She settled on a pair of mid-range radials: two-hundred-seventy-eight dollars plus tax, a dent in her checking account she hadn't counted on. This was becoming one of those days that made her want to crawl into bed and pull the covers over her head.

By noon the tires were installed and Ronni was back at her condo getting cleaned up. The tire change had done a number on her black slacks and white blouse. She felt dirty even after taking off her clothes. She showered for the second time. By the time she'd washed the dishes after a lunch of tomato soup and half a chicken sandwich, it was two-thirty. She headed for Zumbrota.

As she approached the last exit to Cannon Falls, heading south on U.S. 52, her phone rang. Ronni fumbled in her purse but didn't get to the phone in time. She recognized her sister's number, and punched redial.

"Hi, Maddy. It's Ron. What's up?"

"You...you said to call if anything happened." Her voice was trembling, like she was about to cry.

"What happened?" Ronni shouted into the phone.

"Somebody forced me off the road."

"Are you okay?" The alarm in Ronni's voice turned to concern.

"I'm at the hospital. Bumps and bruises. They're going to keep me overnight."

"What happened?" Ronni repeated.

"I was turning onto Cedar Avenue from the crosstown and a truck pulled up beside me on the exit ramp and forced me off the road. I went through a fence and the front of my car was in a pond before I stopped."

"You sure you're okay?" Ronni exhaled, realizing she had been holding her breath.

"I think so. Hurting a little, and stressed out, but I'm okay."

"Did you see the person who did it?"

"No. I just saw the side of a truck, and then it hit my fender. It was like the truck just leaned into me and kept forcing me sideways. I couldn't get away from it. Another car saw it and stopped to help me."

"Did you get the name of the person who helped you?"

"No, but I'm sure the police did. Someone must have called the police."

"What did the truck look like?"

"It was just a big white truck. One of those delivery trucks with a square back."

Ronni slammed on the brakes and skidded onto the left shoulder, considered the condition of the median, then put her truck in four-wheel-drive, turned left and charged into the tall grass. The footing was solid and she was in the northbound lanes in a flash, accelerating back toward Minneapolis.

"What hospital are you at?" she asked, her voice now angry.

"What was all the noise?" Maddy asked.

"Just did a U-turn. What hospital are you at?" she barked.

"Fairview Southdale."

"I'll be there in a half an hour. Tell them you don't want any visitors. Not until I get there."

"Why? What's going on, Ron!"

"We'll talk about it when I get there."

Ronni punched the end call button with her thumb. Maddy's picture in an overflowing sink took center stage in her mind as the Dakota's speedometer approached one hundred.

He pressed hard with all eight fingers on his skull, trying to alleviate the pain of the headache, or at least create a different pain to momentarily divert his attention. He hooked his thumbs under his cheekbones for leverage and pressed harder, but the pain in his head, the vise around the base of his skull and the nausea would not go away.

Hamilton's headaches had become more frequent, and more severe. He had been afraid to tell Toni. Afraid that it would lead to more surgery. Afraid that surgery would lead to…. He could never finish the thought.

"I'm getting a migraine," he told the physical therapist. "I think I'm going to be sick."

An hour later, after puking his insides out and taking two hundred milligrams of Topomax, Blethen sat slouched in his wheelchair, trying to concentrate on a conversation with his psychologist.

"That was a bad one," she said.

"Mmph," he grunted.

"Have they become more frequent?" she asked. Hamilton nodded, hoping the movement wouldn't reignite the nausea.

"Has something changed that would trigger the migraines? Are you feeling more stress than usual?"

A shroud passed over his face. *More stress? Nothing important. Only that I'm being called a fraud, a forger. We're going to lose everything. Toni is going to lose her job and her reputation. No. Nothing stressful at all!*

"No," he said.

As predicted, Metzger howled his indignation at the insinuations Magnolia had made at the conclusion of her press conference.

"I have never, ever forced myself on a woman," he wailed. "I have always treated women with the utmost respect. If I have ever done anything that has made a woman uncomfortable, I assure you it was unintentional."

"Methinks he protesteth too much," Bean said, paraphrasing Shakespeare as he watched Metzger's news conference.

"If I have ever done anything to make a woman feel uncomfortable, I apologize," Metzger continued, "But I have nothing to apologize for. It is my opponent who should do the apologizing for making this kind of scurrilous accusation. She's trying to drag this campaign into the gutter because she knows she can't beat me on the issues. I ask you, the voters of Massachusetts, is this the kind of person you want to represent you in Washington? I have represented you for twelve years...blah...blah...blah."

Bean switched off the television and turned to the other campaign staffers in the room.

"He's going to beat that drum until we hear it in our sleep," he said. "I don't want *any* of you to give it credence by responding to it. I don't care who's asking the question or begging for an answer. Your response is 'no comment'. This needs to go away, and responding will only keep it alive. Impress that on all the volunteers. No matter the question, the answer is 'no comment'."

The staff filed out of the room, except for Samantha who held back to talk to Bean.

"Do you want me to brief Magnolia?" she asked.

"I'll take care of it," the campaign manager replied.

"Be a little gentle. She's really feeling stressed."

"She created her own stress with this," Bean growled.

"That's not what I mean. You know the dust-up with Flaherty in Springfield? I was prepping Magnolia for a meet-and-greet yesterday and she asked if Flaherty had done the advance. Like she had no recollection of Springfield. I'm telling you; she needs some time off."

Bean tilted his head and massaged his scalp with his right hand. "Maybe you're right," he said. "This would be a good time for her to lay low with this groping allegation hot. It will be out of the news cycle in forty-eight hours." He nodded his head. "Good time to take a breather."

"She's got a fundraiser tonight. I'll cancel her campaign events for the next two days."

"Cancel them, but she has to be back in the saddle on the twentieth," Bean said as Samantha started to leave. "This young actress, Emma Watson, is speaking before the United Nations on gender equality. Starting a UN initiative called *HeForShe*. Get Magnolia plane reservations for the morning of the twentieth. Plan to go with her. I'm working an angle to get her on the stage with Watson and have a couple of minutes with her for a photo op. Watson's speech is scheduled for two p.m."

Samantha was fairly skipping as she left the conference room. Campaigns were twenty-four-seven hard work. There wasn't much you could classify as fun until you won, but the chance to meet Emma Watson made this trip to New York an exception.

Toni dropped her purse and coat on a chair and carried the grocery bag into the kitchen.

"Ham?" she called. He didn't answer and Barca was nowhere to be seen. *Must be upstairs painting,* she thought. She punched the intercom button to the third floor. "Ham?" she repeated.

Puzzled by his lack of response, she took the elevator to the third floor and was enthusiastically greeted by Barca and his constantly-in-motion tail.

"Good boy," she said, ruffling the fur on his head. "Where's Ham?"

She followed Barca through the great room and into Ham's studio. He was slumped in his wheelchair. Toni raced across the room and grabbed his left shoulder, shaking her husband. "HAM!"

His head lolled to the side, and he blinked several times as if trying to focus. His eyes were dilated. "Whazzit" was all he uttered before his head slumped to his chest.

Toni spun around, looking for the drugs. Sitting on his desk was a bottle of Topomax. She raced into the bathroom, but found nothing that could have caused his condition. She dashed back into the studio. Ham's condition hadn't changed. She grabbed the vial of Topomax and took the elevator downstairs to get her phone. She found the Regional Center for Poison Control on her internet app and dialed the number.

"I think my husband may have overdosed on Topomax," she said as soon as the phone was answered.

"I'll send an ambulance," the person on the other end said.

The estrangement of her only sibling was one of the few things that Ronni truly regretted, a regret that was driven deeper into her heart as she walked into Maddy's hospital room. There was no greeting from her sister. No look of relief. Instead, Maddy turned her head and looked away.

Although they managed to communicate long distance, where she could still pretend that Ronni was Ron, face to face Maddy turned cold. The person she now saw had stolen her big brother, her hero: football star, United States Marine, military policeman, macho man.

"How you doing?" Ronni asked. Her attempt at a hug was awkward, and met with a tepid response.

"What's going on, Ron?" Maddy's use of the old male nickname stung, even all these years later. Even to her sister, she would never be enough of a woman to be accepted. Ronni tried not to let her hurt show.

"I'm not sure. It might just be a case of a drunk driver. I don't want to jump to any conclusions," she said.

"That's bullshit! You didn't race over here to tell me it was a coincidence that I got run off the road by a drunk. And you told me to make sure no strangers came in my room. And your call about calling you if anything strange happened. What's that all about? What is going on!"

Ronni paused, surprised by the fury in Maddy's voice. "There's this case I'm working on."

Maddy glared back, a look of loathing on her face. "So?"

"I can't tell you about it," Ronni said, "but I've been threatened recently. When I didn't back off, I think they thought they could get to me through you."

" Well that's…just…great," Maddy huffed.

"We're going to solve the case," Ronni lied, "but until we do, maybe you should go on a vacation someplace. I'll pay for it."

"I have a job, Ron. I have kids. I have a life." Maddy's voice began to rise again.

"I know. I'm sorry, but…"

"You have no idea! You've screwed up your life. Now you're screwing up mine…"

"But, I…."

"Get out! Get out! I can take care of myself. Leave me out of your life!"

SEPTEMBER 18, THURSDAY

"You look like hell."

"Up all night." Ronni, her voice flat, depleted, answered Holly's question. "I never made it to Zumbrota. Someone ran my sister off the road."

"Is she all right?"

"Yes. No. I don't know. She kicked me out of her hospital room."

"I'm sorry. Why?"

"Because of the Blethen case."

"What? What's that got to do with your sister?"

Ronni's shoulders sagged.

"I wasn't going to tell you, but I was threatened in Boston. It was a transphobic threat, but I think that was just a cover. Now I'm sure it had to do with the Blethen case. After I got back, my condo was broken into. They left the water running with my sister's picture submerged in an overflowing sink. Yesterday my tires were slashed, and then, on the way to Zumbrota, I get a call from my sister saying she'd been run off the road, almost ended up in that deep pond at Cedar and the Crosstown."

"You told your sister?"

"I didn't tell her all of that, just that I'd been threatened, and they might be trying to get to me through her."

"She threw you out of her hospital room because of that?"

Ronni shrugged, then nodded and slumped into her office chair, tears running down her cheeks.

Holly shook her head in sympathy for her friend and colleague. "Tell me about the threat in Boston. "

A deflated Ronni told her about the two thugs and how she'd been set up.

Holly's instinct was to walk around the desk and hug her friend, but she checked herself. Ronni wasn't into hugs, and this might not be the best time to make her feel more vulnerable. Instead, she broke the news.

"Well, you won't have to go back to Boston, and you can take the rest of the day off."

Ronni looked up at her partner.

"We've been officially terminated from the Blethen case. I called Toni Blethen this morning to give her our weekly report, and she told me to stop investigating. We're off the case."

"Why? What happened?" Ronni didn't know whether to be relieved or angry.

"She said it was too stressful on Hamilton. We're supposed to summarize what we've learned and send it to her with our final bill and the balance of the retainer after we've subtracted our fees."

Ronni was shocked. "Did you tell her about the road sign?"

"I didn't get the chance. I'll include it in our final report."

"Have you told Carrie?"

"Not yet. She hasn't come in yet. I think she's out looking at records of truck rentals."

"That reminds me," Ronni said. "The vehicle that forced my sister off the road was a white delivery truck. Maybe whoever is behind this didn't have to rent a truck."

"We're off the case, Ronni."

"That's just wrong!" Ronni made up her mind. She was angry. "We touched a nerve with someone in Boston. We should be allowed the time to figure out who and why."

"Let's meet tomorrow morning at nine to go over everything we know. I'll compile it into a report," Holly said, dismissing her partner's plea and backing out of Ronni's office

"I'm going home." Ronni said, her anger at being tossed off the case morphing into deflation and sadness. "Try to get some sleep. I'll see you tomorrow."

"If there's a silver lining in any of this," Holly offered, "you can tell your sister the investigation is over and she won't be the target of any more threats. And you won't be threatened again, either"

"I'll leave her a voicemail. I tried to call her last night. She hung up."

Sound sleep eluded Ronni, even with two Unisom tablets in her system. Maddy's angry voice shouted at her from a photo floating in a car filled with water. Road signs with the words "Kanaranzi" and "Blethen" on them flashed by. Screams, as white trucks rushed at her, stopped as she woke up just before the trucks hit her.

Ronni stopped the revolving nightmare by getting out of bed. She left a message on Maddy's cell phone. She was no longer on the case. Maddy had nothing to worry about. She turned on a twenty-four-hour news channel and made herself lunch.

As she sat in her underwear, sipping a bowl of hot tomato soup, the news network's coverage was interrupted by a promo for an upcoming event at the United Nations. Actress Emma Watson, of *Harry Potter* fame, was to address the general assembly on the issue of gender inequality. Ronni made a mental note to watch the speech. *I wonder if Kanaranzi will be there?*

With that thought, and nothing to do the rest of the afternoon, she decided to make the hour-long drive to Zumbrota. *Maybe we can at least put something in that report that will help Hamilton find his mother.*

She decided against wearing leather pants. She put on jeans and a long-sleeved turtleneck that covered the tattoo on her neck. She checked herself in the mirror, and decided she looked conservative enough to satisfy Zumbrota standards.

Helen was a portly woman with gray wisps of hair that escaped from under a red kerchief. Her jolly face jiggled each time she emitted a nervous laugh, which happened with almost every sentence.

She studied Ronni's private investigator card carefully, then laughed, jiggled and agreed to tell everything she knew about Mary Blethen, Lorraine Blethen and whatever else about Zumbrota that Ronni might be interested in.

After an hour with Helen at the Zumbrota library, Ronni learned that Helen didn't have a very high opinion of Lorraine ("always had her nose in everybody's business") but didn't think she was ever in trouble with the law. She didn't know much about Mary except "she was one of *those girls;* always flirting with trouble." She did provide the names of two of Mary's classmates that still lived in Zumbrota.

Ronni's next stop was going to be at the police department but, instead she decided to look up Mary Blethen's classmates. She would check with the police later, even though she felt confident that she would find nothing there. If Lorraine had brushes with the law, Ronni was certain that Helen would have known about it.

Ronni found one of the classmates, Anna Bridgeman, at home.

"We're trying to locate her" Ronni explained to the thin, timid woman peering back at her through a slightly opened front door of a weather-beaten two-story house. "There is a family matter in which she has an interest."

The statement had its intended effect. Anna opened the door.

She and Mary were never good friends. Mary ran around with a bunch of kids that were always in trouble. When they were together in class, Mary seemed smart.

"Can you describe her for me, physically," Ronni asked.

"She was little. Smallest in our class, I think," Anna replied. "Not much more than five feet."

"What about hair, eyes?"

"Black hair. Don't know if it was natural or out of a bottle. Not sure about her eyes. Blue, I think."

"Any distinguishing marks?"

"I may have a picture with her in it. She and I were in a play together once. Somewhere I have a picture of the whole cast. She'd be in it."

Anna went to look for the picture, leaving Ronni to ponder life in a rural Minnesota town as she looked around the living room cluttered with collectibles, throw rugs and well-used furniture. A CRT television, *circa* 1990, sat on a cheap table. There was not a book, magazine or newspaper in the room. *Sometimes it would be nice to live in a bubble,* she thought. *No stares, no threats, no worries.* Ronni was checking to see if she'd gotten a return call from her sister when Anna shuffled back into the room, weighed down by several photo albums.

"The cast picture should be in one of these," she said, setting them on the table and motioning to Ronni to have a seat next to her. She began paging through albums with Ronni looking over her shoulder.

"Oh, here's one I'd forgotten," Anna said, turning the album she was looking at toward Ronni. "This is Mary." She pointed at a dark-haired girl dressed in jeans and a loose-fitting top. "This is at our high school picnic."

"Mind if I take a picture?"

"No. Go ahead."

Ronni took out her phone and shot three photos of the girl in the picture. She did the same when Anna found the cast picture.

"You said she ran around with a bad crowd," Ronni said after they had finished looking at the albums. "Are any of them still living around here?"

"None that I know of. I've never seen any of them around town, or at church, or at a class reunion, either."

"How about names? Could you give me the names of those in that group? Particularly the boys."

Anna looked puzzled. "Why the boys?"

"Easier to trace. Not likely they've changed their names."

With a short list of names in her possession, Ronni thanked Anna and headed for the Zumbrota police department.

"We're too small to have that kind of specialty," said the young police officer behind the front desk, responding to Ronni's inquiry about whether the investigator in charge of drug or sex trafficking was available. "You'll have to talk to the chief, and he's out of town until Monday."

"Please tell your chief that I'll call him next week." She handed the officer a business card and left.

Toni eased the van to a stop in the hospital pickup area. She pushed a button, the passenger-side door slid open, and the wheelchair lift unfolded. Hamilton maneuvered his wheelchair on to the hoist.

"What were you thinking?" Toni asked after Hamilton's chair was locked in place.

"I had a migraine."

"But you took six hundred milligrams. That could've killed you."

"Maybe it would have been better."

"Don't say things like that!"

"Sorry. I didn't mean it. The pressure just got to me."

She pulled the van away from the curb.

"I relieved some of that pressure this morning," she said as she turned onto Worcester Street, breaking the silence that had permeated the van on the ride home. "I know you wanted to end the investigation into your grandmother's death, so I did it this morning. I let the private investigators go. They're going to send a final report and the balance of the retainer."

Hamilton's exhale was audible. "You're the best," he said, turning in his chair to look at his wife.

"This---what shall we call it---episode? This episode made it clear to me that we didn't need any more stress, or expense." Toni shook her head, orange curls quivering. "We can always go back to it later if we want to, after *The Reaper* thing is taken care of."

"Anything new on that?"

"Nothing. I took today off. I'll ask tomorrow when I go back."

"Thanks."

"For what?"

"For being you. For loving me. For sticking with me." The look in his eyes would have done Barca proud.

"I'll always love you, Ham, but you've got to promise me one thing; no more overdoses." Her green eyes flashed.

"I promise."

Magnolia curled up on a teal-blue chaise, her back to the glass wall that overlooked Boston Harbor, and wrapped her black silk jacquard robe around her legs.

Feldman, rumpled and overweight, slopped over the edges of the too-small chair, facing her.

"She's on the run," he said. "So much shit raining down on her head she doesn't have time to investigate you, or anything else. In a week she'll be ready for the loony bin."

"You said she wouldn't be harmed." Magnolia recoiled, her face registering alarm as the tone of her voice conveyed genuine concern.

"I said I wouldn't physically hurt her, but this ain't no kids game. You said you wanted this investigation to stop. I've stopped it, and she doesn't have a bruise on her body." Little beads of sweat popped out of Feldman's forehead. He had expected Magnolia to be pleased with the results of his operation. "Don't worry. She won't bother you again. Right now, she's probably curled up in a corner whimpering like a little bitch."

Without a word, Magnolia uncoiled from the chaise and glided across the expansive, white-carpeted living room. Feldman stared at her legs, alternately freeing themselves from the folds of her robe as she walked

She pushed open the swinging door to the kitchen. "Maria, bring us some coffee and pastries," she said in terse Spanish.

She ambled back, aware that Feldman was fixated on her legs. Avoiding the chaise, she grabbed an open-back dining room chair, spun it around, and straddled it, facing Feldman.

"I have another project for you," she said. The dismay in her voice had been replaced by a stony timbre.

Feldman's Adam's apple bobbed as he gulped. "Yeah?" It came out hoarse, cracked.

They waited as Maria entered with a carafe, two cups and several pastries on a silver tray.

"Put it there," Magnolia directed, pointing at a coffee table next to Feldman. "Do you take cream or sugar?" she asked him.

"Yeah. Both," he croaked. Maria went back into the kitchen and returned with a cow-shaped pitcher and sugar bowl.

"Help yourself," Magnolia said. "And bring me a cup, black, with one of those Danish. The apple one."

Feldman blinked, thinking for a moment the order was directed at Maria, but Maria had gone back into the kitchen. With a scowl, he heaved himself out of the chair, put the apple Danish on the crystal plate, poured coffee from the carafe and shuffled across the room. Sweat trickled down his cheek and bumped across the rolls of his neck

"You forgot the napkin," she said, taking the plate and cup from him with a churlish smile. She saw something flash in his eyes, but he turned and, rocking from side to side, waddled back to the coffee table.

"You really should lose weight."

Magnolia took the napkin from his hand and laid it over a bare knee. Feldman stared for a split second, then returned to his chair. He poured himself a cup of coffee, regular. He didn't add sugar. He didn't take a Danish from the tray. Magnolia reveled in the power she held over him.

"Women need to come forward in the next week or two, claiming Metzger groped them or had sex with them since he's been a senator. Could be a hooker or two, but it would be better if they were a page or a former staff member. Best scenarios would be if he forced himself on them. Can you handle that?"

"Easy," he said, sitting up straighter now that the conversation was in familiar territory.

"I'm sure there are women out there whom Metzger has harassed," Magnolia continued. "Find them and get them to come forward. If they're pros and you have to pay them, tell them it's for the publishing rights to their story. Either way, we need someone to step up and accuse Metzger of harassment."

"I need resources."

"I'll put another ten thousand in the account. I want a progress report from you by Tuesday. I don't want anything to go public before then."

Feldman put down his half-full coffee cup. "Ten thousand's not enough if I have to…"

"Okay. twenty," she said, interrupting.

"I'm on it," he said.

Feldman lumbered toward the door, picking up his mobile phone from the table by the entry where he had been required to leave it. Magnolia watched him leave, then checked her watch: 10:14 a.m., 4:14 p.m. in Barcelona. Hawke should still be sober. She retrieved the single number burner phone from a drawer in her bedroom and punched "1".

"Mademoiselle, it is always a pleasure to hear your voice." Hawke's voice was slithery. He *had* been drinking.

"A little early in the day, isn't it, Henri?"

"My judgment improves as the night proceeds," he responded, unfazed by her rebuke. "How goes the campaign?"

"Close, but we're about to land a knockout punch that Metzger won't recover from."

"Impressive. But I know you didn't call to discuss campaign strategy."

"Actually, I did. Remember I mentioned that there was something I wanted you to take care of after the campaign is over? I want to expedite it."

Hawke listened as Magnolia told him about Aaron Feldman.

"My. My. What a nasty fellow he is," Hawke dead-panned.

"Save the sarcasm. He's smart, crafty and has connections."

"Hmm."

"Here's how I want it to go down," she said. "Feldman is currently locating women who have been sexually harassed by my opponent. A week before the election, I want it leaked to Metzger's campaign that Feldman is the one who found the women. Two days later I want Feldman to have a suspicious accident. If the news media doesn't do it for us, we'll suggest Metzger did it out of revenge. Of course, he'll deny it, but the insinuation will remain in the news cycle through the election."

"Very clever. You get rid of this Feldman, who could be a problem for you in the future, and get an election boost in the process. Very clever,"

You're next, Magnolia thought. *When the election is over.* But before the call ended Hawke changed the subject, at least temporarily altering her secondary plan.

"I have found the expert to challenge the authenticity of *The Reaper*," he said. "His name is Tomas Fabregas, currently at the *Sophia* in Madrid. His credentials are impeccable, and he's an expert on avant-garde art."

"Will he give us the answer we want?"

"Mon dieu. Would I ask the question without knowing the answer? The right answer has been bought and paid for," Hawke teased. "I'll send you information about him. I trust you can pass it along to the proper people at the Boston museum. They should be more than happy to hire such a renowned expert for their investigation, and he won't be unreasonably expensive because he is so excited for the opportunity to examine one of history's iconic avant-garde paintings."

SEPTEMBER 19, FRIDAY

Ronni was putting on her bi-weekly estrogen patch when the front door buzzer went off. She hobbled to the intercom panel, pulling up her jeans. "Yes?"

"Package for Veronica Brilliant."

"Leave it by the door. I'll be right down to get it."

She slid her feet into her fluffy bunny slippers and padded down the staircase to ground level. The scuffed wood floor and yellowed, peeling wallpaper that reached all the way to the eighteen-foot ceiling of the theater-sized foyer gave the place a dilapidated feel, like an old mansion past its prime which, indeed, it was. The massive, oak front door opened to a large veranda that dominated the front of what was once among the most elegant of homes in St. Paul. Leaning against the outside wall was a courier-sized envelope. Ronni flipped it over to see who had sent it. There was no return address.

Back upstairs in her condo, she kicked off her slippers and poured the last cup of coffee from the morning pot. She sat down at the living room table and ripped open the envelope. Inside was a single page of newsprint with a short, typed note stapled to it: "Everything you touch DIES."

Ronni recoiled, dropping the note as if it was a snake.

Shaking, she reached down to retrieve it. The newspaper page was from the *Dallas Morning News* three days earlier. A small grainy picture peered out at her. The picture and accompanying story were outlined in yellow marker.

"Fourth Trans Woman Murdered" the headline said. The story identified the victim as Geraldine Girard, an activist in the LBGTQ community, and the fourth transgender woman of color to be murdered in the Dallas area in the past three months.

Ronni's hands flew to her mouth as the name registered. She looked again at the grainy picture. It was the woman from the plane. She remembered the hug and Geraldine's last words: "Be true to yourself, girlfriend." Tears blurred Ronni's vision. *Oh my God! She's dead because of me!* Ronni's thoughts flashed to her sister. *I could have killed Maddy, too.*

A scream of anguish erupted from deep within her as she collapsed on the kitchen table. Tears fraternized with spilled coffee as she convulsed in torment.

Magnolia stood at the windowed wall of her penthouse, looking across the gray-brown water at The Institute of Contemporary Art. She had given her housekeeper the day off. Magnolia wished to be alone on this day of reprieve from the campaign.

She checked with her secretary at Kincaid Media and was pleased that nothing needed her attention, so she ran a bath in the Jacuzzi and luxuriated for the next forty-five minutes to the sounds of Count Basie, leisurely shaving herself in the process. When done, she carefully placed the razor on the edge of the tub, then stood and dripped her way across the bathroom floor to the shower.

She switched the shower to a steam setting and stood motionless as the temperature climbed and her pores sweated themselves clean, then reversed the setting and rinsed off under a cool shower. Stepping out of the shower, her body covered in goose bumps from the chilled water, she dried herself off, rubbing briskly to return circulation to her skin.

Thoroughly cleansed and invigorated, she looked at herself in the mirrored bathroom wall. She was pleased with what she saw: a body still trim and lithe; breasts that were still, with a little help from a surgeon, firm with no signs of sagging; a flat tummy. She slipped into loose-fitting gaucho pants and a fleece top.

Now, her second cup of coffee in hand, she contemplated how to use the remainder of the free day she had been given by Jim Bean.

Her phone rang, jarring the peace and contentment. Magnolia slowly turned to face the annoying instrument. A tic in the corner of her left eye seemed to alter its usual vibrant color, turning it a dull blue. She hesitated, then answered after the third ring.

"Sorry to bother you on your day off," Samantha said from the other end of the call, "but we need to go over logistics for tomorrow. I'll have a car pick you up at 7:30. I'll meet you at LaGuardia. We have a 10:00 a.m. flight to New York. You need to be at the U.N. by 1:30.

Bean has arranged a meeting with Emma Watson after she addresses the U.N. general assembly."

"Who's Emma Watson?"

"English actress. Young. Was in the *Harry Potter* movies. She's an advocate for gender equality. She's the keynote speaker in the kickoff of a U.N. campaign called *HeForShe*. I'll brief you on it on the flight to New York."

"There are only forty-five days to the election. We're spending a whole day on this?" Magnolia's voice elevated.

"Bean thinks it's worth it," Samantha responded. "National exposure. All the major networks will be there. Provides a great opportunity for people to see you as a national advocate for gender equality. This is right in your wheelhouse."

"What time do we get back?"

"Flight gets in at 6:05 p.m. There's a fundraising dinner at 7:00. We may be a tad late for that, but that's okay. Give them a little more time to drink and loosen their purse strings. You should be home by ten," Samantha said. "I'll bring makeup. We may need to touch you up a bit before your photo op with Watson."

"This is not my first rodeo," Magnolia snapped. "I was on national television long before I hired you."

"Oh. Sorry. I didn't…"

"You stick to scheduling and logistics. I don't need your advice on how to appear before the media."

"Yes, ma'am."

Magnolia ended the call without saying goodbye.

Maria's wave caught the attention of the woman who had just entered the coffee shop. Isabella, of Mexican heritage like Maria, waved back and made her way between the closely packed tables.

"Can I get you something?" she asked.

"*No. Gracias,*" Maria answered, lifting her half-filled mug to demonstrate. Isabella veered toward the coffee counter.

Maria had met Isabella while waiting to check out at a nearby super mercado, Maria's go-to place when she needed something to complete dinner preparations. Isabella had initiated the conversation, saying she was new to the area and asking for information about local pharmacies, dry cleaners and restaurants. They agreed to meet for lunch the next time Maria had a day off.

The lunch had lasted two hours and, for Maria, it was wonderful to be able to talk to someone from "back home". They bid each other good-bye with promises to meet again soon. *How fortunate I am to have made a new friend,* Maria thought.

They met over coffee a week later and exchanged their life stories, including Maria's desire to bring her younger brother to Boston. Isabella offered to help, saying that she worked in government and might be able to pull some strings. Yesterday Isabella had called, saying she had some good news. She suggested meeting at the coffee shop so she could deliver it in person.

Maria watched as Isabella ordered her coffee. She was older than Maria and wore the carriage and dress of a professional woman comfortably. Tall and slender, she was the counterpoint to Maria's short, round body, but for Maria there was no envy. She was too happy to have Isabella as a friend to be jealous. Isabella joined her at the table.

"I've got good news," she said, getting right to the point of the meeting. "I think I can help you get your brother here from Mexico."

Maria's face lit up. It had been her dream since coming to the United States as a teenager to have her younger brother, Jesus, join her; to get him away from the gangs, the drugs, the violence. She prayed often for Jesus, hoping it was not too late for him.

"I have a little money…"

"Don't worry about money," Isabella interrupted her. "I told you, I work for someone in the government, so I don't need your money, but I do need some information so that I can fill out the proper forms."

For the next half-hour the two women sat at the small table, Isabella quizzing Maria about her brother and taking notes.

"I think I have everything I need," Isabella finally said. "I'll get the forms filled out and have them ready for you tomorrow."

"We could meet back here," Maria offered.

"Could we meet where you work?" Isabella asked. "As a personal favor. I'm a very big fan of your boss. If I could vote, I'd vote for her. I'd love to see where she lives, maybe meet her."

Maria hesitated. *There was the no-visitors rule, but Magnolia would be out of town. And Isabella was going to bring Jesus to the U.S.*

"You can come to where she lives…where I work…but you won't be able to meet her. She's out of town tomorrow," Maria said. "Can you come by at noon? I'll fix us lunch." Maria gave her the address.

"Perfect. I'll see you tomorrow at noon. I'll have the papers for you to sign. Your brother will be here before you know it."

They sat over a second cup of coffee, compliments of Isabella, and talked of life in Mexico when they were children, of the struggle to survive in the United States, of the upcoming election and Magnolia's chances of becoming the next senator from Massachusetts.

Maria felt pangs of guilt as she left the coffee shop, but Isabella had become such a good friend, and Jesus would soon be here because of her. Her excitement trumped any qualms she had about breaking the no-visitors rule. She started planning lunch.

Ronni was still shaking internally as she walked into the offices of the Monet Detective Agency three hours later.

"What's wrong?" Carrie asked as Ronni joined her colleagues at the conference room table. "Is it your sister?"

"This." Ronni pushed the envelope across the table toward her partners.

Carrie opened it and pulled out the contents, frowning as she read the note, then handed it to Holly.

"What's this got to do with you?" Holly asked, glancing at the newspaper story outlined in yellow.

"I sat with that woman on the way back from Boston. Now she's dead. They tried to kill Maddy…." Ronni's voice broke. "I…I…I'm a walking death sentence."

Carrie reached across the table and took Ronni's hand. Holly, her blue eyes turning dark, looked again at the note and quickly reread the article. She waited for Ronni to regain control of herself. Then, looking squarely at her devastated partner, she said: "I don't know who sent you this, but they are about to find out they just messed with the wrong people. Get locked and loaded ladies. We are going hunting."

They began to put together a strategic plan to hunt down her tormenter, but Ronni's ability to concentrate was compromised by grief over the death of Geraldine Girard and her sister's anger. She left the strategy session and spent the rest of the day trying to reach the Richfield Police Department about Maddy's incident. She also tried to call her sister several times, each time getting her voice mail and leaving a "call me" message. On her last attempt she pleaded with Maddy to call her, hoping that it might spur a return call.

After lunch, a Richfield patrolman returned her call, confirming that he had been at the scene of Maddy's hit-and-run. He gave Ronni the name of the witness who had called-in the incident. He had interviewed her, but all she could remember was that a white truck forced Maddy's car off the ramp. They had not turned up additional evidence.

Ronni tried to call the witness, Emily Swenson, but got voice mail and left a message.

Finally, at 3:00 p.m. she gave up and left the office.

She was driving west on Grand Avenue through thin mid-afternoon traffic when a white truck cut across her lane and turned onto northbound Lexington Avenue. Ronni slammed on the brakes and cursed the driver. *Mother....*

White truck! The image of her sister in a car careening toward open water, pierced her brain. ...

...fucker.

Ronni took a hard right at the next corner and circled back, looking for the truck. She looked both ways at Lexington. No truck. She turned right again. Halfway down the block she slammed on the brakes. The truck was parked halfway up the alley. A squat man with no neck was walking around the back of the truck pushing a handcart with boxes on it. Ronni flashed back to the hotel bar in Boston.

Slowly, she backed up and turned into the alley, stopping a car length behind the parked truck. She reached under the front seat and unsnapped the strap that held her Beretta PX4, withdrew the snub-nosed pistol and tucked it in the back of her jeans as she got out of the car. Realizing her teeth had been clenched since he cut her off, she opened her mouth and flexed her jaw, trying to calm herself.

A sign on the back of the building read "Treasure Trove Thrift Store." The man and his hand cart had disappeared through the back door that said "Delivery Entrance". Ronni slid through the door and saw the hulk halfway down the aisle, talking to a sales person.

"Hey! You with the truck!" she shouted, her righthand behind her back, resting on the butt of the pistol. The clerk's head snapped around at the shout, and the block of flesh that was the truck driver turned to face Ronni.

"You cut me off back there," Ronni snapped. Her hand slid off the pistol and resumed a normal position at her side as she realized he was not the man from Boston. "Now you're blocking the alley." The edge in her voice had disappeared.

The man looked her up and down: tight jeans, slim hips, multiple piercings, and a voice oddly deep for the person he was looking at.

"Sorry," he said, a bemused, half-smile on his face. "Almost done here. I'll move my truck in a minute."

"Don't bother," Ronni barked, trying to remain in control. "Just be a little more careful in the future." She turned and walked away. The butt of the pistol was clearly visible above the belt of her jeans.

"Holy crap," she heard the clerk burst out as she exited through the back door.

Ronni backed down the alley out onto Lexington and immediately pulled to the curb, clutching the steering wheel in a death grip. Her entire body shook. After several deep breaths, she freed one white-knuckled hand and took the pistol from her waistband. Shakily she secured it under the seat.

God, it's like I'm back in the Marines. Get ahold of yourself! Before you hurt someone…. or worse.

Toni was picking at the food on her plate, moving it from one spot to another, oblivious to what she was doing.

"What's wrong?" Hamilton asked, unable to wait any longer for his wife to voluntarily tell him what had wrecked her day.

"They took *The Reaper* down today. And they've hired an expert," she sighed without looking up. "We'll probably end up having to hire another lawyer. End up spending thousands more on legal fees."

"Why jump to that conclusion?" Hamilton said, taking on his wife's usual glass-is-half-full attitude. "Maybe their expert will figure out it's the original and we'll be done with this."

"Well, look at you, the optimist," Toni joked. She would have liked to share her husband's outlook but knew that was not the likely outcome.

"I did some research on the guy they hired. Tomas Fabregas. He's from Spain," she continued. "He's always hired by people who are trying to establish a forgery. In the little time I had to check him out, I didn't find a single case where he said the piece of art he was asked to inspect was the original. He found them all to be forgeries."

"How did they find this guy?"

"I don't know, but he definitely looks biased against us."

"You're probably right, so we're going to need more than a lawyer," Hamilton said, agitation rising in his voice. "We're going to need our own expert to testify that *The Reaper* sitting at the Boston Museum of Visual Art is Miro's original."

"I could ask around, but I'm kind of a pariah right now in the art community. The word is already out that *The Reaper* might be a fake."

"Maybe we should call Jim Benson," Hamilton suggested. Benson was a friend of Hamilton's, and an art history professor at the University of Minnesota where Toni had earned her degree. He had served as a character witness for Hamilton in the trial that had established his legal ownership of *The Reaper*. "He might have a suggestion."

After the plates were scraped into the garbage and the dishes stacked in the dishwasher, Toni dialed Benson, put the phone on speaker, and held it so that they could both hear and talk to him. When Benson answered, Barca, who had been lying next to Hamilton's chair, perked up his ears and barked a greeting, obviously recognizing the voice of the man who used to wrestle with him and scratch his tummy.

"Barca says hello. Toni and I do too."

The three friends traded getting-caught-up small talk until Hamilton raised the primary reason for the call. "*The Reaper* is creating problems again," he said.

"How? You sold it.

"Someone has claimed it's a forgery, and now the museum is investigating."

"Investigating the painting, or you?"

"Both, I think," Toni said.

"We need an expert," Hamilton interjected. "One with impeccable credentials who can vouch for the fact that it's the real thing. Do you know of anybody?"

"It's all so damn subjective," Benson replied. "Sorry you're going through this again. Let me think on it a little, and I'll see who I can come up with."

The conversation turned to other things: new wines, Hamilton's painting progress, Toni's job. As they were about to hang up, Benson asked in a whimsical tone of voice: "I've got to ask. You don't have the original *Reaper* stuck in your attic, do you? Tell me you didn't sell the museum a copy."

"Screw you," Hamilton laughed. "Don't even say something like that. For all I know, these phones could be tapped."

Still shaken by her over-reaction to the white truck incident, Ronni sat in her living room half watching the evening news and thinking about Geraldine Girard. Contrary to what Geraldine had said on the plane, the estrogen had not cut down on Ronni's aggression in this case. Her first response was fight, not flight. Maybe that was good for someone in her line of work, but it certainly wasn't feminine. The surgeries had altered her body, but she still had some of the baser instincts of a man. It was frustrating, and sometimes frightening. *After ten years,* Ronni wondered, *is this how it's always going to be?*

A rustling, scraping sound in the hallway caught her attention. She padded to the door and looked out the fish-eye peephole but saw nothing. She opened the door a crack, leaving the safety chain in place. Still nothing. She unlatched the chain and stepped into the hallway.

There was no one there. Only the faint smells of garlic and something else, undefinable but pungent. *Someone's cooking Italian,* Ronni thought. *Bad Italian.* She walked to the end of the hallway and looked down the stairs. Seeing no one, she started to descend and realized the smell was gone. Quietly she finished her descent to the second floor and stopped at the door to the second- floor condo. She sniffed. No smells were coming from that unit.

Hairs on the back of her neck stood up as Ronni's early-warning system kicked in. *Damn. I've got to stop leaving my gun in the car.* Carefully she continued her descent to the first floor, stopping outside the door to the first-floor condo unit. Again, no odor that resembled what she had smelled upstairs. She turned to go back upstairs and saw that the outside door at the end of the hallway was ajar. Quietly, slowly she approached the door. She flattened herself against the wall, reached out with her left hand and pushed hard against the door. It flew open and banged against the side of the house. Ronni caught it on the rebound. There was no one outside, but on the steps that led to the sidewalk the words "Maddy" and "Geraldine" were spray-painted, followed by: "Next?". Ronni stepped back, her hand flying to her mouth at the same time anger boiled to the edge in her brain. Something inside her identified the other smell. Body odor.

SEPTEMBER 20, SATURDAY

Maria stood in the hallway waiting for Isabella to emerge from the elevator. Smells of *carne asada* spilled out of the open penthouse door as if to beckon Maria's luncheon guest.

"Thank you for having me for lunch," Isabella said after the two women had embraced.

"No. Thank *you*," Maria responded, gesturing toward a briefcase that Isabella was carrying. "Please come in."

"It smells really good in here. Oh! Wow! This is spectacular." Isabella stared out the glass wall at blue skies shining down on Boston Harbor. Two sailboats cut through the water, looking like toothpicks and triangles from the height of the penthouse. "So, this is how the rich and famous live."

"Can I get you something?" Maria asked. "A glass of chardonnay?" Maria had purchased a bottle of *Casa Madero*, a Mexican chardonnay recommended by a clerk at a nearby liquor store, for this special occasion. It was the first time Maria had ever purchased wine, and she gulped as she counted out $16.99 for the bottle. It confirmed what she already suspected—that she couldn't afford to become a wine drinker.

"*Sí, gracias.*"

Maria took the bottle from a chiller sitting on a silver platter and poured two glasses. "Make yourself at home," she said, handing a glass to Isabella. "I've got to check on lunch, and then I'll give you a tour."

As Maria disappeared through French doors, Isabella's eyes darted about the room, taking in every detail and nuance. She wandered to a painting of sunflowers, pretending to closely admire it. A glance at the French doors assured her that Maria was still tending to lunch, and she tipped one side of the painting away from the wall and looked behind it. She did the same to another painting, and then leisurely strolled around the room, glancing inside lamp shades and up at light fixtures.

Maria came back into the room. "Ready for that tour?"

"Do we have time before lunch? Would you rather look over the papers first?"

"We can do that after lunch. Let me show you around."

The penthouse, although over three thousand square feet, did not take long to tour. The living room that they were standing in took up nearly a third of the space. To the left was a guest bedroom, guest bathroom, Maria's bedroom and Magnolia's home office. Everything was decorated in shades of white, with the occasional splash of teal. Isabella stayed a long time in Magnolia's office, asking multiple questions about the framed photographs of Magnolia with celebrities and politicians.

To the right rear of the penthouse was Magnolia's bedroom suite, including an enormous master bath and small exercise room. This was the only part of the penthouse where color reigned. Bright vivid blues, soft sea foam greens and accents of magenta replaced the stark whiteness of the rest of the house. Isabella found reason to linger, marveling over the beauty of the bedroom furnishings and the marble tilework in the bathroom.

The center-rear part of the penthouse housed a chef's kitchen, pantry, wine cellar and an intimate dining room, again, all in white except for the cherrywood floor and cabinets. It was there they stopped for lunch: *carne asada*, yellow rice topped with chopped green onions, and slices of avocado.

"This is like a fairytale," Isabella declared, making a sweeping motion with her hand, which held a second glass of wine. The flourish resulted in wine slopping on the floor. "Oh, I'm so sorry," she said. "I think I should have stopped at one glass."

"That's okay. I'll clean it up," Maria said, sounding apologetic even though it was her guest that had made the mess.

"I need to use the bathroom," Isabella blurted, rising from her chair and unstably setting the now nearly empty wine glass on the table. "I know where it is." She hurried out of the room as Maria gathered a bottle of floor cleaner and rags to clean up the spilled wine. Maria had cleared the dining room table and put the dishes in the dishwasher by the time Isabella returned.

"Are you all right?" Maria asked her friend who looked a bit shaken as she came back into the dining room.

"That second glass of wine really hit me. I'm such a lightweight. We should go over the papers for your brother, and then I should leave before I make another mess."

"Oh, no, no, no, no. It's all right," Maria answered. "Please don't worry about it."

Mollified by her host's response, Isabella retrieved her brief case from the living room and laid out three sheets of paper on the dining room table. "These are the signature pages for supporting documents for your brother's application. I've filled out all the documents with the information you gave me yesterday. You just need to sign these. I'll also be sending the actual application to your brother for his signature. If you talk to him in the next day or two, you should tell him to expect the application in the mail."

Maria looked at the three pages, took a pen that Isabella offered and signed them, not sure what she had just signed but trusting that she would soon see her brother.

Isabella put the signed papers back in her briefcase. "I think I'd better be going. Your lunch was superb, but I'm feeling a little woozy from the wine." The statement was again met with apologies from Maria as she guided her friend to the door.

"Can you get home all right? Should I call you a cab?" she asked.

"No. No. I'll be fine. I'll call you later this week."

"Call me when you get home, so I know you're all right."

Isabella nodded. "Thanks for the great lunch, and the tour. Sorry I'm so *fragile*.

Isabella rode down the elevator and waited until she was well clear of the Pier 4 building before taking out her phone.

"No problem," she said in English, behind a hand cupped over the phone. "She has a concealed recording system in the house, but no cameras. The actual recorder is in her office. It's digital. State of the art. There are microphones in every room. I didn't plant any bugs because the place is regularly spit polished and they'd probably be discovered. I did get an imprint of the front door key. There is a doorman, but the building security seems lax. Shouldn't be difficult to gain entry."

Isabella listened to the person on the other end of the line.

"Her campaign schedule should keep her out of her condo most of the time until the election, and I can draw her housekeeper away. If you get your hands on that recorder, you should have all the information you need."

A half hour later, Isabella called Maria. "I'm home, safe and sound. Sorry I had to end lunch so quickly. Call me next week when you know your schedule."

Isabella hung up and looked down at the waste basket beside her desk. Three white pages, all with Maria's signature, rested there, exactly where she had tossed them.

"Maybe you should sit this one out," Holly suggested. Ronni had just finished an impassioned recounting of the white-truck incident on her way home Friday and the late-night spray paint episode at her condo.

"You know me better than that. Someone's going to pay for this, and I'm going to be there when they do with my boot on their throat," she barked.

"Did you report this to the police?" Carrie parried in an attempt to defuse her partner's anger.

"I want to find out who is doing this, not scare them away." Ronnie snapped, shaking her head. "The police will open an investigation, thrash around for a couple of days, maybe put me under surveillance, and then push the file to the bottom of the pile."

"That question mark on the steps seems to be a direct threat on your life," Carrie continued. "I think the police will take it seriously; do more than just thrash around."

"They could have popped me last night," Ronni answered. "They were there. I was alone. They, whoever *they* are, aren't out to kill me. They're trying to intimidate me, scare me off the Blethen case."

"We know they're capable of more than just threats. Making yourself a continual target is too risky. Let Holly and I do the investigating."

"Not going to happen," Ronni shot back, doing a poor job of controlling her exasperation at her partners' suggestions. "If I stay on the case, they are going to keep trying, and we'll catch them…"

"Or they'll decide that they've had enough and you'll end up like Geraldine Girard," Carrie interrupted.

Ronni half rose out of her chair, her face florid: "I….!!".

"Hold it. Stop!" Holly cut in. "We can't be fighting amongst ourselves."

Ronni settled back in her seat. Carrie uttered, "Sorry".

"First," Holly said, taking control of the situation, "we have to remember we don't have a case anymore. I've prepared a report for the Blethens, summarizing where the investigation stands and telling them we've closed our file." Holly pushed copies of a two-page memo across the table. "Review it, add whatever I've missed, and get it back to me by Monday. Also, compile your time and expenses. I'll put together a final invoice to send with the memo."

"Second, we open a new file," she continued, "the Geraldine Girard murder investigation file, if anyone asks. It will give us cover to continue the investigation to find out who's behind Ronni's harassment."

Ronni quickly skimmed the memo. "I don't see anything about the harassment in here. Do you think we should mention it? If the Blethens knew, maybe they'd change their mind and keep us on the case."

"I thought about that," Holly replied, "but decided against it. If we mention the harassment in the memo, there's no guarantee they'll want to continue the investigation even if they're not the ones behind the harassment, and, if they are, they might continue it awhile longer just to divert attention from themselves."

Carrie nodded. "Like they did...might have done...with his assault and hiring us in the first place. I agree with Holly. I don't think we should mention it."

Ronni rocked back in her chair and steepled her nose with her fingers. "If they have someone here breaking into my home and running my sister off the road, they're going to know we're still investigating."

"As far as we know, they're only watching you," Holly responded, looking directly at Ronni. "Let's finish the memo and finalize our bill now; not wait until Monday. I'll email it to them today. On Monday, we'll lay out a plan for continuing our investigation, including Geraldine Girard's murder. For a week or so you'll have to lay low, Ronni; work on other cases. If a week or two goes by and there are no further threats, we can be reasonably sure that Hamilton was behind it."

"I'm not sure we can jump to that conclusion," Ronni answered. "If I stop investigating, the harassment may stop no matter who's behind it. From their perspective, they will have scared me off the case which, it's pretty clear, is their intent."

Holly thought for a moment, turning over Ronni's reasoning in her mind.

"You're right," she finally said, "but we still need to let the Blethens know we've terminated our investigation as they've directed. And I still think it's a good idea for you to keep your head down for a couple of weeks."

Ronni looked neither pleased nor convinced by Holly's last statement.

SEPTEMBER 21, SUNDAY

They should outlaw campaigning on Sundays.

Magnolia stretched on her king-sized bed while considering whether to get up, or have Maria bring her coffee in bed. She discarded the coffee-in-bed idea despite her sensory impulses to the contrary. A luncheon with a group of influential women contributors in less than three hours drove her from the luxury of seven-hundred-thread-count Egyptian cotton sheets.

She shuffled into the kitchen, dressed in white silk pajamas and fluffy slippers, where Maria was making pastries.

"Coffee fresh?" she asked. Maria gave a timid nod, as if afraid to let her head bob fully back and forth. Magnolia poured a cup, eyeing Maria. "Everything okay?" Again, Maria nodded, her body language giving every impression that everything was not okay. Magnolia chose not to pursue it. Magnolia didn't want to get embroiled in Maria's personal life at this juncture. Another couple of months and she'd be gone.

She picked up a pastry, shook off excess powdered sugar over the sink, and ambled into the living room. Setting her coffee and pastry on a sofa table, she clicked on the TV to catch a morning news show. She switched from station to station trying to find any coverage of the U.N. event from the day before. After a half hour, her coffee and pastry both consumed, she gave up. Nothing. No national news coverage. Bean would hear about this.

The United Nations event had actually been quite stimulating. Emma Watson proved to be a sweet, intelligent young woman who spoke eloquently, although Magnolia questioned how someone so young and coming from her background could possibly understand the plight of women.

She had been introduced to U.N. Secretary General Ban Ki-moon and several U.N. Ambassadors. Perhaps those connections would be valuable in the future. She had met other influential people and had gotten minor financial commitments from a few, but without immediate publicity the trip had largely been a waste of her time.

She checked her schedule for the week and then decided to do something she hadn't done since before the primary election, cull and archive recordings. She had a little more than an hour before she had to get ready for the luncheon, giving her ample time to go through two weeks of recordings.

Magnolia refreshed her coffee, took another pastry, and went to her office. She hung the keys laying on her desk back on the hook where they were always kept and turned on the recorder. The first voice she heard was her own, this morning, and then from last night after she had returned from the last campaign event. She deleted those. The next voice was one she didn't recognize, speaking Spanish. Maria's voice followed, and, as Magnolia listened to the conversation between the two women, the corner of her left eye twitched and her expression turned hard.

"Maria!" she roared.

The young woman appeared from the kitchen just as Magnolia stomped from her office.

"Who the hell did you allow in this house?" she snarled in Spanish.

"I...I..." Maria broke down in tears. "She is helping bring my brother to the United States," she gasped between sobs. "Her name is Isabella...."

"You're done here," Magnolia interrupted. "Get your things and get out. You have ten minutes."

Maria froze.

"Now!"

The bellowed command fractured Maria's paralysis. She walked quickly to her room, sobbing, followed by Magnolia who watched as the distraught young woman haphazardly threw clothes in a bag.

"I…I…."

"You broke the rules. I don't want to hear excuses!"

"But…:

"Get out!"

Magnolia stepped aside as Maria, with an overflowing bag in each hand, walked out of her bedroom. Magnolia followed her to the door.

"Empty your pockets!"

Tears began to flow again as Maria turned her pockets inside out. "What will I do?"

"You should have thought of that before you let strangers into my house. I don't care what you do. Get out. And you better not be taking anything with you that belongs to me, or I will hunt you down and put you in jail." Magnolia punched the elevator button.

"My phone…"

"I'll keep your phone. It will be interesting to see who you've been talking to, and about what."

"How will I…"

"I don't care." Magnolia pushed Maria into the elevator and stood, glaring, until the door closed. She paused for a minute, listening to the elevator descending.

Shit, now I'm going to have to get a new maid, and change the locks.

"A quarter of a million dollars down the tube."

Toni had just finished reading aloud the Monet Detective Agency's final memo, and Hamilton was not happy. "At least we get the rest of it back," she said.

"All we learned was that two people in an appliance delivery truck probably killed Gramma. They never found the truck, they didn't identify the two people, and they never came up with any other suspects."

"Don't dwell on it, Ham," Toni said, trying to soothe her husband. "They worked hard on the case. I don't think they ripped us off. Maybe it can't be solved."

Ham grunted. He didn't want to hear it. He wanted to be angry. "Now we can spend it on lawyers to defend ourselves against the forgery claim."

"What about the road sign thing with Magnolia Kanaranzi?" Toni continued, trying to change the direction of the conversation to calm her husband and stop his emotional slide. "That certainly increases the chances that she could be your mother."

"Me? A senator's son? Wouldn't that just be great. Can't you just see the headlines: 'Senator's son charged with art forgery.'"

The conversation was interrupted by the telephone.

"I've got a couple of names for you," Jim Benson said after Toni answered and put the call on the speaker. "The first one is Oliver McColl. He's an art historian with an excellent reputation and extensive trial experience. Plus, he's not far from you. He's a professor at Dartmouth.

"The second, is Elizabeth Sandusky. She works at the Met in New York. She's also frequently hired as an expert witness to establish provenance, and she's written extensively on the subject of forgeries and the art establishment."

"Which one would you recommend?" Toni asked.

"I know McColl personally, so I'd recommend him, but I don't think you can go wrong with either of them." Benson gave them the contact information for both experts, and the threesome chatted for a few minutes about things other than *The Reaper.*

"I've been toying with an idea," Benson said as the conversation was winding down. "How would you like to come to Minnesota for a week and give a series of lectures at the University?"

"Who…which one of us are you talking to?" Toni and Hamilton said, nearly in unison.

"Both of you. Do it as a husband and wife team."

There was a pause as Toni and Ham digested the offer. "What would we lecture about?"

"Please don't get upset when I suggest this," Benson responded, "but I'd like you to do four one-hour lectures on forgeries and the great art forgers." He waited with anticipation for their response.

"When?" Toni asked.

"It would fit perfectly into my class schedule the last week of October," Benson said.

"Do you think it's a good idea in light of what's going on with *The Reaper*?" Ham asked.

"I think it's absolutely perfect," Benson replied. "We know you didn't forge *The Reaper*, but the allegation that it's a forgery makes you a celebrity of sorts. It will stir great interest on campus, and it will give you a platform to advocate your innocence as well as provide insight into a part of art history that is usually ignored in the academic world."

"Let us give it some thought," Ham answered.

"That's as good as a 'yes' in my book," Benson responded gleefully. "And while you're thinking about it, I'll be stocking up on some good wine for when you're here. You can stay with Donna and me. And bring Barca."

"What do you think?" Toni asked her husband after the call ended.

"I think it might be a great idea. I could put together the framework for the lectures in a couple of days and we could flesh them out over the next two or three weeks. You could take vacation time. It would be good for both of us to get out of Boston for a bit, and I wouldn't mind going back to Minnesota when the leaves are turning. It would also give us time to see what the Museum does about the forgery allegation, before we start spending money on experts and lawyers."

And, Toni thought, *it will give you something to get excited about.* She unlocked the footrests from Blethen's wheelchair, allowing them to swing to the sides, then worked her way between his knees and gave him a wet kiss and a big hug.

"I think this might be another great idea," Hamilton said.

SEPTEMBER 22, MONDAY

There were no further incidents during the weekend, but Ronni took a circuitous route with several switchbacks to be sure she wasn't being followed. They had decided to meet early at Holly's condo, rather than at their office, to avoid interruptions.

Carrie and Ronnie were seated at the breakfast bar while Holly set out fruit and biscotti to go with their coffee. Holly left the room and moments later came back carrying an easel and a whiteboard which she set up in the middle of the kitchen.

"Let's start from the beginning," she said. "Your trip to Boston got someone upset. Upset enough to threaten you and your sister and maybe kill Geraldine Girard." Holly turned to the whiteboard and made three vertical columns. "Who are the possible upset people and why? Unknown transphobic thugs; Lorraine Blethen's murderer, or Hamilton Blethen's mother. Any others?" She looked at her two partners.

"Hamilton Blethen," Carrie blurted.

"The list isn't very long," Ronnie said. "Blethen and his wife; the newspaper reporter, Allison Long and two Boston Globe beat writers I interviewed; Magnolia Kanaranzi's press secretary and, maybe Kanaranzi, herself. Those are the only people who knew I was going to Boston besides the two of you."

"And Sandy," Carrie cut in, referring to The Monet Detective Agency's receptionist. "And, maybe, some unknown transphobes."

"Are you sure you didn't mention it to anyone here, before you went to Boston?" Holly asked.

Ronni thought for a minute. "I don't think so," she said. "I bought the ticket online, so I didn't even talk to anyone at the airline. Same for the hotel reservation. I'll ask Sandy if she mentioned it to anyone."

Holly wrote the names on the white board, omitting themselves and their receptionist. Only the names Hamilton and Toni Blethen were in the column headed with the words "L.B. Murder". The rest of the names were under the "H.B.'s Mother" column. Under the "Transphobe" column was a big, red question mark.

She stepped back to look at her handiwork. "Any of these people could have mentioned it to someone else, but this is what we've got for now."

For the next hour the threesome analyzed the motives and opportunity for each of the named suspects. Long and the two *Globe* beat writers were put in the "unlikely" category. Hamilton Blethen and/or Toni Blethen were the primary suspects. Magnolia Kanaranzi and her press secretary were put in a "maybe" category, depending upon whether Magnolia was Hamilton Blethen's mother.

"Let's start there," Ronni said. "We are well down that road already, and we can either eliminate her or elevate her to prime suspect, depending upon what we find."

"Carrie, you and Ronni put your heads together to make sure you both know everything that we've learned so far. I think it's best if you pursue the Magnolia Kanaranzi thread," Holly said. "I'm going to look into Blethen's assault back in 2009."

"I've asked a friend in the St. Paul Police Department to request information about Girard's murder from the Dallas P.D.," Holly continued, turning her attention to Ronni. "While we're waiting for that information, and since you should keep a low profile for the time being, why don't you go on line and see what you can find out about Girard's murder and the murders of the other black trans women in Dallas. See if there's similarity or if Girard's murder was unique. It might give us some leads, but at the very least it will build this file so it looks like it's a real investigation."

"You were going to look into Lorraine Blethen's potential connection to organized crime," Ronni said. "I'll take that off your hands. I have a telephone call today with the Zumbrota police chief to talk about trafficking in that area. I'll see if he'll tell me whether there were any complaints or legal issues with Lorraine before her death. If he asks, who's our client?"

"Our client prefers to remain anonymous, but if any of us have to ever answer that question under oath, the answer is, you are."

Magnolia had scrolled through the contacts and call history on Maria's phone the previous evening and found that her former maid used her phone sparingly. In the past three weeks more than half the calls had been between Maria and Isabella, social chatting and scheduling coffee or lunch. There were calls to her brother in Mexico and to other family members. A few others were from telemarketers. None of the calls contained anything that alarmed her.

There was no smell of freshly brewed coffee when Magnolia woke up the next morning. She searched the house, but the only trace of her housekeeper was her cell phone, sitting on Magnolia's desk. As she stared at it, puzzled, the phone rang. The number looked familiar.

"Isabella?" she answered.

"*Si.*"

"Do not call this number again. Maria has been terminated because of you, and I have confiscated her phone. Do not call this number, and do not ever set foot in my home again."

An hour later, sitting in the back of her limousine, Magnolia flipped through her prepared remarks for yet another campaign event. Her phone went off. *Damn it!* She checked to make sure that the sound proof glass between her and the driver was rolled up, then answered.

"I've got what you're looking for," growled Feldman from the other end of the line. "We need to meet."

"I've got campaign events all day. Come to my place tonight. I should be home by 10:00 p.m." Magnolia said as the limousine pulled away from Pier 4.

Minutes after Magnolia's limo left, a white panel truck parked in the lot across the street from the front of the condominium complex. A workman, "Otto" according to the name on his shirt, got out and entered the building, punching numbers on the access panel. When the inner door didn't open, he went back out to the sidewalk and approached the doorman.

"I'm here to repair a refrigerator in the Kanaranzi place. Is Maria gone?" the man asked.

"I don't know," said the guard. "I haven't seen her leave. Ms. Kanaranzi just left, but Maria must still be upstairs."

The workman went back into the foyer and again punched the security panel buttons, again with no success. He went back outside.

"No answer," he told the doorman. "Could you let me in? It's just a little job. Shouldn't take more than a half an hour. I don't want to have to come back here."

"You sure you have the right code?" asked the doorman.

"I think so. Eight, two, two four."

This time, both men went into the foyer. The doorman confirmed the code for the Kanaranzi unit and punched it in. No answer.

"She must have left before I got here," he said. "Or maybe she went home for the weekend and isn't back yet."

"Hey, man, can you just let me in?" Otto pleaded. "You can come up and watch me fix the refrigerator if you want to."

"There's a lock on the door of the unit. Even if I let you in, you couldn't get in the unit."

"I've got a key." Otto said, pulling a key ring from his pocket. "They gave me one in case of a situation like this. I said I'd give it to you when I got done. You can give it back to Maria."

The doorman paused, then shrugged and unlocked the inner door. "Elevator's over there. It's on the top floor."

The policeman tapped the sole of Maria's shoe with his nightstick. "C'mon sweetheart. Move along."

Maria, lying on a park bench using one bag as a pillow and with the other held tightly to her stomach, woke with a start. She sat up, disoriented, and spilled the bag she had been holding.

"I don't have any place to go," she pleaded.

The cop bent down and helped her pick up her spilled clothes. "There's a homeless shelter on West Street, just off Tremont, about five-six blocks from here. Go that way," he said, pointing south on Park Street. "Take a right on Tremont and it's three, four blocks. It'll be on your left."

Maria thanked him and trudged down Park Street, a bag in each hand. She wanted to call Isabella, but without her phone she didn't have her number and, she realized, she didn't know Isabella's last name.

The call with the Zumbrota police chief had turned up exactly what Ronni had expected: nothing. There were drug issues in Zumbrota in the first decade of the twenty-first century, particularly at the high school, and there had been a few cases of known sex trafficking, but none of them had any connection with Lorraine Blethen. In fact, the chief could remember only one call involving Lorraine, and that was because the neighbor's cows had got out and were eating her Hostas. If Lorraine was connected to organized crime, the local law didn't know anything about it.

Rather than scroll through Dallas newspapers, Ronni took the list of names she'd gotten from Anne Bridgeman and began trying to locate them using online white pages. She got a hit on the third name: Rollie Krebs. He had a St. Paul address and a 651-area code phone number.

An older woman answered the phone.

"He ain't here. He ain't hardly ever here," she said in a voice made guttural by too many cigarettes. "You can probably find the asshole at Neumann's. If he ain't there now, he'll be there tomorrow morning. He can't start his day without beer."

Ronni established that "Neumann's" was Neumann's Bar and that it opened at 9:00 a.m.

She should probably pass on the information to Carrie, but laying low wasn't part of Ronni's modus operandi. She'd talk to Rollie Krebs herself.

The amber liquid splashed over the ice cubes and settled in the crystal lowball glass, sending sparkling reflections across the room.

"Where's your girl?" Feldman asked, watching Magnolia pour them each a cognac, neat.

"I had to terminate her."

"Too bad. Did she steal something?"

"She let someone in the house while I was gone. I have a strict no-visitors policy."

Feldman shrugged and took a crystal glass from Magnolia.

"I knew Metzger had skeletons in his closet," she said as the two raised glasses clinked together.

"Here's to lust," Feldman responded. He tilted the glass, swirled the cognac in his mouth and shook his head in admiration. "Fine stuff."

"So, tell me why we're celebrating," Magnolia said.

"Her name's Amber Fizer. Worked as a page in Metzger's office in his first term. She was a student at Radcliffe, daughter of some big supporter of Metzger. Spent a summer in Washington I think 2004 or 5. That's when she got together with Metzger. Works for the FCC now. Some kind of information systems specialist."

"What do you mean 'got together with Metzger'? Give me the gory details."

"She was nineteen or twenty when she worked for Metzger. According to her roommate back then, she saw her with Metzger multiple times. Fizer and Metzger were together in Fizer's bedroom one time. According to the roommate, judging by the sounds they weren't having an intellectual conversation."

"You haven't talked to Fizer?"

"No, just her roommate," Feldman replied. "There was a third roommate, but I'm not going to wait. I'm giving the information to a couple of friendly news sources later tonight."

"That's it? One bimbo ten years ago. Metzger will deny it, and the press will dwell on her sex history instead of his. It will be out of the news cycle in forty-eight hours." Magnolia threw back the last of her cognac and poured herself a second. She didn't offer to refill Feldman's glass.

"Simmer down," Feldman said, comfortably in control now that he was in his wheelhouse. "Forty-eight hours after the Amber Fizer story breaks another woman will come forward claiming that Metzger paid her for sex."

"How do you know that?"

"Let's just say I'm well acquainted with the sex trade in the Capital," Feldman said.

"That puts the sex story in the news cycle for at least another two, three days. Also gives the media another reason to revisit the Fizer allegations. If it's in the news for a week, it's possible someone else will come forward. And I'm still looking. I found Fizer. I might find more."

"When will the story come out?"

"Not sure. I'll know more after I meet with my news sources later tonight, but it could be as early as tomorrow's evening news.

"What does she look like? Fizer. Do you know?"

"All I've seen is a picture. Every teenage boy's wet dream."

"Every fifty-year-old's as well." Magnolia's smile was brittle. She refilled Feldman's glass.

SEPTEMBER 23, TUESDAY

"Turn on channel four. There's a new poll."

Magnolia scrambled to locate the remote in response to Samantha's phone call. "Is it good?"

"It's not bad," Samantha replied just as Magnolia turned on the TV in her bedroom. "It should be on right after this commercial." There was silence as talking heads touted the newest eye liner. As music signaled the end of the commercial, Samantha said, "Here we go."

"A new poll released this morning by Wellesley College shows that challenger Magnolia Kanaranzi has increased her lead over incumbent Senator David Metzger by two percentage points. According to the poll conducted by Wellesley College, Kanaranzi leads Metzger 44 percent to 39 percent with 17 percent still undecided. The poll of six hundred likely Massachusetts voters taken between September seventeenth and September nineteenth has a margin of error of plus or minus three percent. In other news...."

"That's lovely," Magnolia said, switching off the TV. The poll had been taken after Metzger's attack ad featuring her disgruntled former employees, and Magnolia's press conference response. The poll implied that she had won that battle, but she wondered if the jump was actually due to her remark about his cloak room escapades. *We'll know soon enough,* she thought.

Sam and Magnolia reviewed the day's schedule and agreed to meet at campaign headquarters at eleven a.m.

Samantha wore a puzzled look as they hung up. *Lovely. I've never heard her say anything was lovely.*

"I just remember she liked to fuck." The scraggly, gray-haired biker sat among his tattoos, swilling morning beer and looking sideways at Ronni. "How 'bout you?"

"I'm not that desperate," she said. "Let's stick with Mary Blethen. Tell me what she looked like."

"What's in it for me?"

"Another beer."

"How about a little…" The hand that was reaching for her thigh suddenly was wrenched behind the biker's back, creating a great deal of pain in his shoulder and a surprised yelp from his lips.

"Listen, asshole. I bought you a beer. That's all you get. Try that again and I'll break it off and shove it up your ass." Ronni said the words calmly, even as she struggled internally with the situation which required her to sound and act like a typical male. She knew she could take him if it became necessary, but it was a constant struggle to live in the world in which she identified, while continually being drawn back into the role of her previous gender.

The other bar patrons instinctively looked away from the altercation. She let his arm go.

"Fuck you!" Krebs started to slide off the barstool.

"Sit the fuck down and talk to me," Ronni said, her voice elevated, commanding this time. He sat.

"Now, all I want you to tell me is what you remember about Mary Blethen back in high school."

She signaled to the bartender to bring them each another beer.

He started slowly, recalling sketchy details. Ronni pulled out her phone and showed him the two photos she had taken of Mary Blethen at age fifteen or sixteen.

"She was little. Cute. Pretty smart."

"Did you date her?"

"Me? Shit no."

Ronni would've bet her last dollar that this dick-head never had a date in high school.

"Well, where did you come by the information that she liked to screw?"

He looked down at the bar, wagging his head back and forth. "Guess I don't know that," he said.

"Tell me what you do know."

"That's about it. Cute. Smart. Ready for anything. Like all the rest of us, she was kind of a rebel, but I always thought she'd make herself into something. Too smart for the rest of us."

"Did you see her after high school?"

"No. Far as I know she left Zumbrota the day she graduated. Never saw her again."

Ronni left Krebs sitting at Neumann's Bar in North St. Paul. If she needed to talk to him again, she knew where to find him.

As she worked the Dakota through midday traffic, Ronni considered whether it was worth looking up the other person she had located from the Zumbrota High School class of '71. She decided to wait. She stopped at the Burger King on Seventh Street to get a burger and fries before her meeting with Eldon Koskinen, the resident artist at the St. Paul police department. Koskinen, respected in law enforcement circles for his suspect sketches based on witness descriptions, had free-lanced for Ronni in the past. She popped a breath mint into her mouth as she walked up the steps of the Grove Street police headquarters.

"Jail entrance is over there," the woman behind the desk said, pointing to her left.

"I'm here to see Eldon Koskinen," Ronni said.

"Oh. Have a seat. I'll try to find him."

Ronni knew that people, like the sergeant behind the desk, drew assumptions from her appearance, and she knew that her job and life would be easier if she grew out her hair, got rid of the piercings, and wore different clothes. But she had gone through the physical pain of multiple operations, and tremendous emotional challenges to become a woman, and felt she'd earned the right to be the woman she wanted to be. She could deal with the wrong assumptions of other people. They would have to learn to deal with her.

Koskinen was a short, bald little man in his fifties with an over-sized, droopy mustache and a *Caspar Milquetoast* personality.

"Thanks for seeing me, Eldon," she said after sitting down in the army surplus chair opposite his desk. "I've got a little job for you if you have the time."

"I can try to find the time," he said.

Ronni laid her phone on his desk and scrolled to the two photos of Mary Blethen. "She was a sophomore in high school at the time of these pictures," she said. "That would make her fifteen or sixteen. I would like you to draw her as you would see her at forty, and, again, at sixty."

"That's an interesting project." Koskinen sat up straighter in his chair. "Can I assume that she wasn't in any way physically disfigured after these photos?"

"Yes. And I'd also like you to assume that she colors her hair black so that there is no gray." Koskinen nodded. "What's her name?"

"Call her Jane Doe. She's a small person, if that makes any difference when you consider the aging process. About five feet, one hundred pounds."

"This doesn't relate to an open law enforcement investigation does it?"

Ronni assured Koskinen that it didn't. They agreed on a price and a timetable. Ronni would have her drawings by the weekend.

Back in her truck, she once again dialed Maddy and once again left a message, pleading with her sister to call her back. As the Dakota eased through the parking lot toward the exit, Ronni did a double take at a rusty Mercury Marquis with a weathered vinyl top parked facing the jail entrance.

Was that same car parked outside Neumann's Bar?

It had been a good day. The poll energized the staff, fifty-thousand-dollars in campaign contributions had been deposited, and offers to volunteer had streamed in all day long. Bean was happy that all three campaign events had gone smoothly, and even Magnolia had been in good spirits, passing out compliments and flashing a well-pleased smile.

Bean suggested she go home early and get a good night's sleep to rest up for what promised to be a grueling Wednesday. To his surprise, she agreed.

"Who was that person?" Bean asked after Magnolia left, "and what has she done with our candidate?"

"She actually used the word lovely," said an equally incredulous Samantha.

A wan smile rested comfortably on Magnolia's face, reflecting her fatigue and her feeling of contentment. The limo pulled up to the entrance of Pier 4, and the doorman dashed to the rear door.

"Welcome home Ms. Kanaranzi," he said, offering his hand.

Magnolia gratefully took it. "Thank you, Byron," she said, holding on as he walked her to the front door.

"Oh. I almost forgot. I have your key," Byron said. The doorman quickly walked to his desk and brought back a single key. "The man who came to repair your refrigerator yesterday asked me to give it back to you."

There was a split second between a tic in the corner of Magnolia's left eye and her explosion.

"What?! What man? I didn't authorize any repair. There's nothing wrong with my refrigerator. What the hell are you talking about!"

"I..I..I..," the back-pedaling doorman sputtered.

"I sure as hell didn't give anyone a key!"

"Maria…"

"I fired Maria yesterday! What the hell did you do?"

The limousine driver came sprinting to the door. "What's going on?"

"This stupid asshole let someone break into my condo!" screamed Magnolia. "I'll have your head on a platter. You'll never work in Boston again!"

A search of the penthouse failed to disclose anything missing. Exhaustive analysis turned up four sets of fingerprints, only one of which was thought to be a male. The male prints were found only in the living room and entryway.

Feldman. They have to be Feldman's prints, Magnolia thought. She sure as hell didn't want the police thinking Feldman was a suspect. She offered her opinion that the three sets of fingerprints believed to be female belonged to her former housekeeper, a friend of the housekeeper and Magnolia, herself.

She gave the police Maria's name. "I think she may have been in on this. The burglar probably got a key from her. I think her friend's name is Isabel or Isabella. She might be involved with immigration in some way. She was helping Maria get her brother here from Mexico. Her brother's name is Jesus, and I don't know where to find either of them.

"I'm guessing that the male fingerprints belong to a campaign staffer, Aaron Feldman. He was here sometime last weekend, I think on Saturday, to discuss foreign policy issues. He's my foreign policy advisor."

Byron had already informed the police that, according to the repairman, he had received the key from Maria. The repairman, "Otto" by the name on his shirt, was described as being of medium height, one hundred eighty to one hundred ninety pounds, brown hair, no distinct identifying marks. "Ordinary" was the way Byron described him. It was midnight before the police left.

Exhausted, Magnolia crawled into bed but sleep eluded her as her mind churned through lists of what could have been stolen. Her last look at the clock said 2:12 a.m. before she drifted off.

SEPTEMBER 24, WEDNESDAY

Her eyes flew open. *The recordings. I never erased the recordings!*

In the midst of her panicked awakening, Magnolia tried to remember: had the forensics guy said anything about fingerprints on the recorder? She threw back the down comforter and struggled to unwrap the tangled sheets from her legs. Finally freeing herself, she slid out of bed and realized she was sweating.

Her hands trembled as she pressed the button on the recorder. Overlapping conversations of the previous evening made it difficult to hear specific conversations, but, as she heard the voice of the forensic investigator she concentrated, listening, then rewinding and listening again. When she finally turned off the recording replay, she was sure that he had not said anything about fingerprints on the recorder.

The clock on her desk blinked 4:52 in red numbers. *No sense trying to sleep now.* Magnolia padded to the kitchen and put a pod in the Keurig, waiting while it gurgled and hissed its way to a fresh cup of coffee. Back in her office, she set the cup on her desk, sat stiffly in her office chair and began scrolling through recordings.

She skipped the recordings of the previous evening, leaving them intact. As she scrolled back through earlier records her jaws clamped hard enough for the muscles to bulge and for beads of sweat to form on her forehead:

- September 22-Feldman talking about Amber Fizer and the prostitute.
- September 18-She and Feldman talking about finding women to testify against Metzger.
- September 18-Her telephone call with Hawke spelling out how she wanted him to dispose of Feldman and blame Metzger.
- September 13-Another phone call with Hawke about terminating Feldman, and the *Reaper* forgery plot.
- September 12-Feldman talking about how the Minnesota private investigator would be neutralized.
- September 12-Hawke talking about the hacking that had buried her past, and also about Feldman being collateral damage.

My God. If these became public… Magnolia's first instinct was to delete all of the recordings, but she recalled something about being able to recover deleted stuff. She decided to save them to the cloud instead.

Still running on adrenalin and caffeine at 7:00 a.m. she called the Boston Police Department and asked for the forensic investigator. To her surprise, he was in.

"Did you check my office for fingerprints last night?" Magnolia asked when he came on the phone.

"Yes. We found two sets. One was yours. We've checked the others in our data base but didn't come up with anything. Won't be able to tell if they were your housekeeper's, or her friend's, until we locate them."

"I have a recording machine located in a desk drawer. Was that checked?"

"I'll have to check the log. Let me get back to you on that."

Magnolia spent the next hour checking on everything that she thought might be of interest to a burglar, but everything was in its proper place. Her anxiety level crept toward full-blown panic. *It has to be the recordings.*

Morning fog hung over St. Paul like a spongy white blanket. Swirling mist was all that was visible through the conference room window of the Monet Detective Agency, rendering the mood in the room equally morose.

"I combed the Blethen assault file yesterday," Holly announced. "Not a very good job of investigating in my opinion. From little things I picked up from the file it appears that the investigating officers saw him as the prime suspect in Lorraine Blethen's murder and thought he got what he deserved."

"I'm sure his skin color didn't help," Ronni interjected.

"I didn't see anything racist in the file, but I wouldn't expect to," Holly continued. "They had only one other suspect, a lawyer who thought Blethen was screwing his wife, but he had an alibi. The incident report wasn't helpful and the interviews were pretty cursory. I'm trying to set up an interview with one of the investigating officers, Adam Sylvester. The other officer, he was the lead, is retired and living somewhere in Florida. Right now, I've got nothing. How about you?"

"I've got Eldon Koskinen doing a couple of sketches for us, using the photos of Mary Blethen when she was a sophomore in high school," Ronni said. "Should have them by Friday. We can compare it to the campaign photo we have of Kanaranzi and see if there's any resemblance."

"What if Kanaranzi has had work done on her face?" Holly asked.

"Then I just wasted a couple hundred dollars, but I think it's worth a try. Mary Blethen and Magnolia Kanaranzi have two things in common. They're both drug addicts and small in stature. It's worth pursuing a little further. I'm going to go back to Zumbrota today to look through more newspapers and library archives."

A chair creaked as Carrie leaned forward, taking a swallow of her coffee and eyeing another of the donuts that lay in a box on the table. "Anything new on your front?" Holly asked.

"They have a real problem in Dallas," she said. "There appears to be some sort of feud between the Latino and the Black communities. It started as a turf war between a couple of gangs, but it's gotten a lot bigger than that and more violent. In the last few months, the victims of the war have been the transgender members of both communities. The first two deaths were trans Black women. They've charged two different Hispanic gang members in those deaths. The third death was a Hispanic trans woman, and the fourth was Geraldine. No arrests in either of those. I've accumulated a lot of paper to go in the file and have sent letters requesting copies of the incident reports for each of the cases. I doubt I'll get anything, but the letters will look good in the file. What else do you want me to do?"

"I thought you were going to investigate the Dallas murders," Holly said, looking at Ronni.

"We agreed to switch assignments," Ronni responded. Holly shook her head, exasperated with her partner.

"Well, as long as you're doing this, see if you can get anyone from Dallas P.D. to talk to you on the phone about these cases," Holly said to Carrie. "Specifically, see if you can get someone to talk about Geraldine. An interview memo would look good. If you can't get the police to cooperate, make a note of that in the file, and try to reach a newspaper reporter who's working the case.

"While you're at it, see if you can research Geraldine's family history. Maybe there's a family member we could contact to see if they'd be interested in hiring us."

Carrie looked at Ronni. "You find anything else?"

"Yeah. A biker asshole that was a classmate of Mary Blethen's. One of the bad boys, but he wasn't much help. Pretty much a drunk who's still trying to be a rebel at sixty. When I go to Zumbrota tomorrow, I'll try to track down the other person from the Class of '71 that hung out with Mary Blethen in high school."

The sun was glowing through the fog as the meeting broke up, promising a beautiful fall day.

The call Magnolia received from the forensics investigator brought bad news. There were no fingerprints on the recording machine. That meant the machine had been wiped clean. That meant that the burglary had been done by a professional. That meant that Magnolia was about to go down.

"You look a little pale. You okay?" Bean asked as he walked into Magnolia's campaign headquarters office.

"My condo was broken into yesterday. I was up all night with the police."

"Oh my God!" It was Samantha, who had just walked into the office. "Are you all right?"

"Just tired. I didn't get any sleep."

"I'm sure the press will pick this up," Bean said. "We may want to get out in front of it. See if we can get a little sympathy bounce. What did they take?"

"Nothing that I could see."

"Nothing? What were they looking for?"

"I don't know."

"Maybe it's campaign related," Samantha jumped in. "Watergate?"

"Let's get out a press release," Bean said. "Drop an innuendo that it may have been campaign related. Make it subtle, but not so subtle that Metzger won't recognize it."

"Should we schedule a press conference?" asked Samantha. "Could be an opportunity to roll out an anti-crime program."

"I want it to be about how women are more vulnerable to crime," Magnolia added, snapping out of her doldrums. "Have it transition into domestic violence."

"We don't want you to be seen as vulnerable," Bean countered.

"I'll talk about the cowardly crime. How they were afraid to confront me. All hundred pounds of me. Don't worry. I won't come off as vulnerable."

But she knew she was. If Metzger was behind the break-in they would know soon enough.

The press conference was scheduled for 4:00 p.m., in time for it to hit the evening news cycle.

Warm sunshine felt good on her shoulders as Ronni walked the long sidewalk to the main entrance of Zumbrota High School. Inside the large, meandering building, she located the school office, ignoring stares along the way from the handful of students that were in the hallways.

Ronni flashed her P.I. credentials to the woman behind the desk and was directed to the school librarian who, Ronni was assured, was the person in charge of school records.

Bertha Warren was, indeed, in charge. The size of a linebacker and the age of an oak tree, she had been the school librarian for over forty years. A spinster, the archives of Zumbrota high were her only children, which she protected like a pit bull. She was unimpressed by Ronni and her credentials.

"We do not open our records to just anybody who asks," she informed Ronni. "Privacy matters, you know."

"So, you're telling me I have to get a court order?"

"Well. No. Maybe."

"Let's start over," Ronni said. "All I'm trying to find out is whether a person named Mary Blethen was in the Class of '71. Can you look that up for me? Then I won't have to look at your records."

"Oh, I don't need to look that up," she said smugly. "Nineteen seventy-one was my first year here. I was twenty years old. Not much older than some of the kids. I remember Mary Blethen. She was a senior. Pretty little girl. Very smart, but always in trouble. She spent a lot of time in the library because she didn't like to go home and there really wasn't any place in Zumbrota for teenagers to hang out back then."

Ronni showed Bertha the pictures of Mary Blethen on her phone. "Is that her?"

"Yes. That's Mary," she said.

"Does she still live around here?"

"Oh, no. She left here right after high school. You know, her mother lived here, but she died five years ago. Murdered. They've never solved the crime."

"Really?" Ronni gave her best impression of sounding surprised.

"She was smothered with a pillow. Everyone thinks her grandson did it, but they never convicted him."

"Was there a trial?" Ronni asked.

"Oh, no. They never charged him with the crime."

Ronni shook her head, trying to look disgusted. "Did you ever hear from Mary Blethen after high school?" she asked.

"No, but I heard she got into drugs. Up in the Twin Cities. Got in trouble with the law. Far as I know she never came back to Zumbrota."

"Do you think you'd recognize her if you saw her now?"

"Oh, I don't know."

"I'm going to get a picture out of my truck. I'd like you to take a look at it. You think you might be able to look at the records for the Class of '71 while I'm getting it? See if there's any information about Mary Blethen in your records?"

"Oh, sure."

It took fifteen minutes for Ronni to get back with the photo of Magnolia Kanaranzi. She waited another fifteen for Bertha to reappear, now with a stricken look on her face.

"I must have misfiled the class of '71 records," she said. "I can't find them. I…I don't know where to look?"

Ronni thought for a moment. "Have you tried looking in the other ones? You know. 1961, 81, 91? Maybe you accidentally filed them there."

"I didn't think of that. I'll go look."

"Before you go, would you look at this picture for me?" Ronni held out the 8x10 photo. "Is that Mary Blethen?"

Bertha took the picture and laid it on her desk. She placed her thumb over the nose and cocked her head. Then she placed her right hand on the photo so that the hair was blocked and only the face could be seen.

"It could be. But if this is Mary, she's had a nose job. Her nose was bigger than this woman's."

As Bertha left to check the "ones", Ronni looked at the pictures on her phone again. Bertha was right. Mary Blethen's nose was wider than Kanaranzi's. She dialed Koskinen and left him a message: "call me before you start. The subject may have had plastic surgery on her nose."

Bertha was shaking her head as she came back into the library. "I don't make those kinds of mistakes," she was saying, more to herself than to Ronni.

"They weren't in the ones," she said after sitting down at the desk.

"Does anyone else file records or have access to the records?"

"The principal. He has access. He doesn't file. I'm the only one who files."

Ronni felt sorry for the distraught woman. Clearly, this was a major catastrophe in her world.

"Do you remember another member of the Class of '71: a guy named Ken Olson?" Ronni asked, trying to distract Bertha from her anguish.

"Um. There have been a lot of Olsons over the years. I don't specifically remember one named Ken."

"Is there anyone else that still works here that was here in 1971?"

"No. I've been here the longest."

"How about a retired teacher or someone in administration? Anyone like that still live in the area?"

Bertha named three teachers, a custodian and a bus driver. She wrote the names on a slip of paper and gave it to Ronni. I'm pretty sure you can find them all in the phone book."

In response to Ronni's look of surprise, Bertha added, "Yes. We still have phone books." She dug into her desk and handed one to Ronni. "You can have it," she said.

The burglary and Magnolia's press conference got twenty seconds on the evening TV news, shunted aside by the real news of the day: Senator Metzger was accused of having an affair with a teenager!

Amber Fizer was everything Feldman had promised: honey blonde, big blue eyes, pouty lips. When ambushed by a TV reporter, who shoved a microphone in her face and asked her about her affair with Metzger, she at first denied knowing Metzger, then, when confronted with the fact that she had been a Senate page in 2004, admitted she did know him, but "couldn't remember having an affair with him."

An admission wouldn't have been nearly as effective.

Metzger, of course, couldn't be reached for comment. Magnolia could only imagine the scrambling that was going on at Metzger headquarters as they tried to figure out a way to spin the bombshell.

"I've got to hand it to you," Bean said. "You were right about Metzger."

Magnolia took no pleasure in being right. She explained her somber attitude toward the news story by saying she felt sorry for the woman who now, ten years later at age twenty-nine, would have her character torn to shreds in a very public way in the most public of all places, Washington, D.C.

"Her whole life is going to be defined by this," she told her staff. "Every time there's another affair in Washington in the next ten years, her picture will be on television. So, while you're celebrating the good news for our campaign, remember that a life is being destroyed." Her sermon squeezed the giddiness out of the room.

Bean stepped in. "If anyone asks you about this, and I mean *anyone,* your answer is 'no comment'. The official position of the campaign will be just what Magnolia said: there is no joy in this news, only sadness for a young woman whose life will be forever tainted, and sadness that our current Senator had no better judgment than to have sex with a teenage employee. Sam, put together a press release and make sure it gets to the TV and radio stations before the 10:00 p.m. news. And, remember to keep your pants on and your zippers up everybody, or you could be the next one on the evening news."

The news was full of the Metzger sex scandal. All the TV stations picked it up, and WFXT had an interview with Amber Fizer's former roommate. A WBZ-TV reporter caught Metzger leaving his campaign headquarters.

"Until we find out what these allegations are all about, I have no comment," he said. "I suspect it's a hoax perpetrated by my opponent. We'll have more to say about that later."

Metzger was a pro. He handled the question perfectly and his final comment sent chills down Magnolia's spine. Tomorrow, she was sure, would be her turn in the news cycle with the disclosure of the tapes.

A disclosure that would be the end of her campaign.

SEPTEMBER 25, THURSDAY

The chatter in campaign headquarters was lively as the campaign staff waited for Metzger's press conference. Magnolia elected to watch it from home. She and Feldman sat in her living room watching the ninety-eight-inch television screen.

"Ten minutes," Feldman said, looking at his watch. His attendance had been demanded by Magnolia. No one else in the campaign had received an invitation, nor did they know that Feldman had been invited. Since his demotion, he was seldom in the office. His absence would not raise any questions nor even, for that matter, be noticed.

"Do you know Maria's friend, Isabella?" she asked. The question, coming out of the blue, was calculated to get an emotional response from Feldman.

"No." He gave his head a shake, a puzzled look on his face. "Why do you ask?"

"Just wondering."

"You don't 'just wonder'," Feldman snapped. "Why?"

"What's Maria's last name?"

"How the fuck would I know?"

Feldman passed the test. Judging by his reaction, Magnolia was confident he wasn't involved in the break-in. The test was one of the reasons for his presence in her penthouse. The other? If Magnolia was going to go down, she was going to take Feldman with her.

"Who do you think was behind the break in?" she asked.

Feldman didn't appreciate the test, but he grudgingly nodded his acknowledgment of her strategy. He would have done the same thing under the circumstances.

"Got to be Metzger," he said.

"If it was Metzger, he has all our recent conversations. Everything since the primary."

Feldman's ordinarily slack jaw dropped open. "What the...."

"All conversations in this house have been recorded," Magnolia explained. "Ordinarily I go through them every week, saving the important ones and deleting the rest, but I've been so busy I hadn't done it since the primary. I think that's the reason for the break-in. To listen to the recordings."

Feldman looked at her, somewhere between amazement and disgust, trying to recall their conversations.

"You know that even the ones you save or delete can be recovered, don't you?" he said.

Their conversation stopped as Metzger approached the podium, accompanied by his wife and two staff members.

"This will be short, and I won't be taking any questions," Metzger announced. "There have been allegations made that I had an affair in 2004 with a page, Amber Fizer. I stand before you today to admit that those allegations are true. Ten years ago, my wife, Amy, and I were at a low point in our marriage, and I am ashamed to admit that I gave in to temptation. Amy has forgiven me..." At this point, Amy stepped forward in a carefully choreographed move and Metzger put his arm around her.

"...and I am happy to say that those hard times have made our marriage stronger than ever.

"To the people of Massachusetts, I want you to know that my lapse in judgment ten years ago was a one-time event, that the affair was consensual, and that it did not affect how I represented you then nor how I will represent you in the future. I have apologized to my wife, and now I apologize to each of you. I am only human, and all humans are flawed. The real test, I believe, is how we deal with our flaws. I admit mine and promise it will not happen again.

"I wish to continue to represent you in the U.S. Senate. I ask for your continued support. Thank you."

Metzger and his wife stepped away from the podium in unison, ignoring the questions being shouted by the media.

Magnolia and Feldman sat in stunned silence, only the babbling of the TV commentator filled the room. Metzger had outsmarted her. She had expected him to deny the affair, but, unlike every other sleazeball in Washington, he had admitted it and threw himself on the mercy of his constituents. His spineless, fearful wife had backed him up. He had turned a potential disaster into an opportunity to show his humanity. The voters would eat it up.

"We'll see how he deals with the hooker when she comes out Friday," Feldman snorted, breaking the stillness between them.

"Find another one! We need to bury the arrogant son of a bitch," Magnolia raged. "Did you see his wife? She's an abused woman. I want his balls on a plate! I want a dozen women to tell the world this asshole is a lecher, an abuser. I want him destroyed!"

Feldman flinched, a stunned look on his face. He leaned back in the chair, which groaned under his bulk. "Okay. Okay. I get it. I'll get right on it."

He heaved himself out of the chair and waddled to the door. He turned. "Get rid of the damn recorder."

She already had.

"Only the nose knows."

It was Koskinen's attempt at humor.

Ronni had made a tracing of Magnolia Kanaranzi's nose from the 8x10 photo, and then had printed one of the Mary Blethen pictures and made a tracing of her nose. Back at the St. Paul Police Department, she handed them to Koskinen.

"This is Jane Doe's nose from one of the photos I gave you, but I want you to use this one when you do your drawings," she said, pointing to the Magnolia tracing. "I think Jane had a nose job somewhere along the way, and now her nose looks something like this."

After his lame play on words, Koskinen assured Ronni that she would still have her drawings by the weekend. She left and was relieved to again see the old Mercury Marquis in the police parking lot.

Must belong to one of the cops, she thought.

Her next stop, at the Ramsey County Clerk of Courts office, turned up nothing. She got the same result when she crossed the river to Hennepin County. There were no criminal court records for anyone named Mary Blethen, nor for Magnolia Kanaranzi. On a hunch, she checked county marriage licenses, but again came up empty.

Bertha Warren had said that Mary Blethen had gotten in trouble with the law in the Twin Cities after high school. There were seven counties in the Minneapolis/St. Paul metro area. That left her five more to check, but Ronni's instincts told her she wasn't going to find any records of Mary Blethen there either. Maybe Bertha was wrong, just repeating an unfounded rumor, but....

Back at her office, Ronni called Bertha.

"Did you ever locate the records for the class of '71?" she asked.

"No. I just don't understand it. I looked some more after you left. They're just not here."

Bertha sounded defeated.

"When was the last time you saw them?"

"Let me think. Hmm. I can't remember. I do have a vague recollection of someone asking about them years ago, but I don't think I showed them the records."

"How long ago was that?"

"Maybe five or six years ago. I'm sure I didn't give them the records. Not even to look at."

"Was it a man or a woman who asked?"

"A woman, I think."

It was Ronni's turn to go, "Hmm".

"Have there been any thefts at the school? Could they possibly have been stolen?"

"Why would anyone want to steal the records of the Class of '71?"

"I don't know, but have any thefts been reported at the school?"

"Oh, occasionally there's the theft of a laptop or someone's jacket, but there's been no theft of school property that I recall."

"Okay. Thanks," Ronnie said. "One more thing. Are you sure about Mary Blethen getting in trouble with the law after high school?"

"I don't know anything about it first hand, but I do remember some conversation about it in the teachers' lounge. It's not so rare to have our students getting in trouble with the law nowadays, but back then it was."

Ronnie spent the rest of the morning trying to convince county court clerks to look for criminal records for Mary Blethen. Only two of the five counties agreed. She would have to make the trips to Anoka, Washington and Dakota counties to search for herself.

"Frustrating morning," she complained to Holly as the two of them ate sandwiches at Mickey's on West Seventh.

"Maybe you're looking at it the wrong way," her partner suggested. "Maybe it's what's not there that's significant."

Ronni slowly turned her head to look at Holly, realization spreading across her face. "You're brilliant," she exclaimed.

"No, you are."

"I didn't mean it that way." Ronni rolled her eyes and laughed. It felt good to laugh.

"You're right," Ronni said, wiping away a tear, settling back on her counter seat. "It feels like someone wiped the slate clean of Mary's identity. Her high school records are gone. There are no court records, either here or in Goodhue County where she grew up. If it wasn't for the Zumbrota newspaper, and the library, we would have thought Mary Blethen disappeared in 1967 after eighth grade."

"Let's not forget Magnolia Kanaranzi," Holly said. "She popped out of a road sign, and there is no record of her in Sturgis until after high school, and that's where she supposedly grew up."

"It's like someone has been rewriting history. They wiped out one life and created another."

"Or at least they tried to," Holly said. "I'll buy you a drink at The Commodore tonight if you find any records for Mary Blethen or Magnolia Kanaranzi in any of the seven metro counties."

"I don't think I'll take that bet. You're probably right, but I've still got to go look. Anyway, I can't tonight. I have a date."

"A date?"

"Yeah. Don't get excited. It's not a man. I'm having dinner with some old friends, a lesbian couple."

Ronni spent the afternoon driving around the perimeter of the metro area looking at court records, and trying to reach retired Zumbrota High School employees on her cell phone. As predicted, she found nothing at the courthouses, but she did stop at the Richfield Police Department and picked up a copy of the accident report from Maddy's hit and run. She tried Emily Swenson, the witness, again, and left another message. She did reach one retired teacher and a bus driver, but neither of them remembered Mary Blethen. She learned that the retired custodian was in a nursing home with Alzheimer's disease.

"The real test is how we deal with our flaws. I admit mine."

The last words of Metzger's news conference had played in a loop in Magnolia's head all day. He had looked contrite, sincere. Damn, he was good. Tomorrow his campaign would release her tapes. Her campaign would be over. She might be arrested. She would definitely be disgraced.

Should I tell Bean? For what purpose. He can't do anything about it, and there's no way to spin it that would save her or her campaign. Let him sleep in peace.

For the third night in a row, Magnolia didn't sleep.

SEPTEMBER 26, FRIDAY

Ronni buried a left hook into the bag with a grunt, bobbed back, rat-a-tat-tat, left-right-left, another left hook and an overhand right that would have brought the heavy bag to its knees if it hadn't been hanging from a two-inch chain. She stepped back, bent over, her gloved hands on her knees.

Sweat flowed from every pore in her body. Her chest heaved.

"You ever think of going pro?" It was Marcus, the gym manager and sometimes trainer.

Ronni shook her head.

"You got fast hands. I could set up a sparring partner for you."

Ronni cocked her head sideways and looked up at Marcus, her chest still heaving. "Too old," she said.

Marcus strolled away toward the ring that stood in the middle of the floor, shaking his head. Two fighters wearing over-sized gloves and head gear were pawing at each other. No chance of any damage there.

"Don't drop your shoulder," Marcus yelled at one of the fighters. Ronni watched him instruct one of the youngsters as she cooled down. Trying to keep the kids off the streets. Give them something besides gangs and drugs. She admired Marcus.

A shower and a drive-thru breakfast got Ronni on the way to the office. Her phone buzzed. Caller ID said it was Carrie.

"Hi. What's up?"

"Can you meet at the office? Half an hour?"

"On my way there now. Something going on?"

"Your friends are back. They didn't like me digging into Geraldine's death."

Carrie tried to stand up straight as she lifted her blouse to show a bruise on her rib cage just below her left breast. "I think my rib may be broken," she said through gritted teeth.

"We need to get you to the hospital," Holly said.

"I will. Maybe one of you could drive me, but I wanted to get this on the record first. Somebody please record this because I may not remember it tomorrow."

Holly laid her phone on the conference table and tapped the recording app.

"I was stopped at a light on Robert Street. Not sure the cross… street." Carrie stopped to let the pain subside. "I can find it again if I need to. Some guy came out of nowhere, jerked open my door and hit me. He said something like, 'Keep your nose out of Dallas and tell your fucking queer partner to stop this investigation or the next time it will be a bullet'. I'm not sure that's exact." Carrie stopped and bent over, trying to ease the pain, "but it was something like that."

"What did he look like?" Ronni asked.

"I don't know. It happened so fast."

"Big, small? Black, white?

"He was white. I think he was big. That's all I remember."

"What was he wearing?"

Carrie tried to concentrate. "I don't know. Some detective I am."

"C'mon. Let's get you to emergency," Holly said, picking up her phone.

"He was white," Holly said, repeating Carrie's words as she and Ronni sat in the emergency waiting room. "So, the assault didn't come from the gang war in Dallas."

"They wouldn't have known about me anyway," Ronni chimed in. "This has to be the same bunch that ran Maddy off the road and broke into my condo."

"Maybe Carrie will remember more after they give her something for the pain."

"Not likely. But maybe *she* could be hypnotized after she recovers. Maybe that would help her remember what this guy looked like."

They sat without speaking further, waiting for Carrie to come back from x-ray. Ronni got a return call from Emily Swenson, but she was unable to add any information about Maddy's hit and run.

"What do you think we should do?" Holly asked after Carrie was back with her broken ribs wrapped.

"Abandon Dallas for the time being," Ronni said. "We can get back to Geraldine later. Keep investigating, but keep our heads down."

"Or," Holly offered. "We could openly dig deeper into Geraldine's murder. Smoke them out to find out who is behind this..."

"And find Lorraine Blethen's murderer in the process." Ronnie finished the sentence.

"One of us would have to become the target," Holly said.

"That would be me, I'm already there," Ronnie conceded.

"She's exhausted!"

Samantha fairly shouted the words at Bean. "This break-in has completely consumed her. She hasn't slept in three days. We can't send her out looking haggard. She's likely to make a mistake, and say something wrong."

"She just had a couple days off last week," Bean groused, "but you're right. Get her some Ambien and cancel everything today and tomorrow. You'll need to fill in for her at tonight's fundraiser. Just tell them that she's a little under the weather. Slight case of sniffles."

This may cost us the race, Bean thought as Samantha left his office. *Maybe she doesn't have the stamina to be a Senator.*

The new doorman at Pier 4 eyed Samantha with suspicion.

"Where's Byron," she asked.

"He no longer works here. I'll buzz Ms. Kanaranzi." There was no answer.

"She might be sleeping," Samantha said. "Will you deliver this to her?" She handed him a white paper bag with a plastic vial of Ambien inside. "It's a prescription."

He held the bag at arm's length, opened it and looked down his nose at its contents. "Are you from a pharmacy?"

"I'm her press secretary," Samantha said, trying to keep the agitation out of her voice.

"I will make sure it gets delivered," he said, turning his back on Samantha and setting the bag on his desk.

Magnolia sat in a daze, staring blankly at the TV. She would doze, then wake with a start when her nightmares started: images of hulking cops with dangling handcuffs; of Metzger's face contorted into a maniacal grimace, laughing; of vertical iron bars. The Ambien only added to the gruesomeness. Purple and yellow and red and black colored her intermittent dreams. She woke up nauseated, barely making it to the bathroom before vomiting.

She forced herself to take a shower, then ate a toasted bagel. A glass of water washed down two more Ambien, and Magnolia crawled into bed. If Metzger was going to release the tapes, he would have to do it without her watching.

She finally fell asleep.

Two cracked ribs and a bruised lung.

"This wasn't part of the job description," Carrie said with a painful laugh.

"I suppose you'll want hazardous duty pay," Holly teased, then, seriously, "You should take it easy for a couple of days. Don't come in, maybe until Monday."

"I'm not going to fight that," Carrie replied. "Think I'll go home, get drugged up on painkillers and binge watch *House of Cards* with my cats. "

They watched Carrie painfully slide her feet over the side of the bed and struggle to stand up.

"I'll give you a ride home," Ronni said, placing a hand under Carrie's arm to help her stand. "We can get your car home."

Several hours later Ronni and Holly were riding back to the office after dropping off Carrie's car, Suzie Subaru.

"Why doesn't she buy a new car? That one's a wreck."

"You know Carrie," Ronni responded from behind the wheel of the Dakota, "She's not into material things, and the car has a lot of nostalgia. They've been through a lot together."

"But that one's going to fall apart around her," Holly said.

"Maybe we should all get new cars with bullet proof windows and steel-plated doors," Ronni said sarcastically. Holly nodded, acknowledging the irony of Ronni's comment.

"While you were running Carrie's car back to her, I got confirmation from Carver and Scott Counties," Ronni said, changing the subject. "Neither of them has any criminal records or marriage certificates for anyone named Mary Blethen."

"How about Kanaranzi?"

"Her neither."

"As we expected," Holly said. "We need to find a hacker who can tell us if someone hacked the county records. Know anyone?"

"No, but I'll ask around. I talked to one of the teachers who was at Zumbrota High School in '71," Ronni continued, changing the subject again. "She vaguely remembered the name, but she didn't have any recollection of Mary Blethen. She did tell me that the other teacher, the only one I haven't talked to, is in assisted living. I think I have to take another trip to Zumbrota. I'd like to take another pass at the newspaper, and maybe the library again. I could talk to the teacher in person."

"Tomorrow?"

"No. Koskinen is supposed to deliver his drawings tomorrow. I want to be here when he does.

SEPTEMBER 27, SATURDAY

The clock on her bedstand read 8:13 a.m. as Magnolia Kanaranzi woke up, refreshed. It took only a nanosecond for her to realize that twenty hours had come and gone since she had fallen asleep, perhaps the most important twenty hours of her life. She switched on the TV, first to local morning news, then to the national news networks. There was nothing about her campaign, or about her. The proverbial "other shoe" hadn't dropped.

She dialed Samantha. "I'm ready to get back at it," she said. "I'm feeling great. Anything happen yesterday that I should know about?"

A successful fundraiser. An endorsement from the local teacher's union. The Metzger affair had disappeared off local media but, generally, it had been a good day for the Kanaranzi campaign. *What is he waiting for?* she thought while, at the same time, feeling relieved. She hung up and called Feldman.

"When will this hooker make her announcement?" she asked.

"I don't know," Feldman said. "That's in someone else's hands, but it will be made in time for the evening news. I know that."

"Have you found anyone else who Metzger abused?"

"Still looking. Might have another possibility, but she lives on the West Coast. I'm going to try and get ahold of her today."

"Why do you think Metzger hasn't released the tapes?" Magnolia asked, finally getting to the real point of her call.

There was silence on the other end of the call.

"Could be he's trying to dig up more of the story, or he's waiting to release it at a more critical time in the campaign," Feldman finally answered. "Or, maybe the little bitch doesn't have them."

A cold fury swept over Magnolia.

"The private detective from Minnesota!" Her words were like razor wire. "Could she have stolen them?"

"Not likely, she...."

"Not likely!" she screamed. "You said you had taken care of her!"

The phone was silent.

Magnolia's words came, hard and passionless: "Kill her."

Holly's suspicion about the 2009 investigation of Hamilton's Blethen assault was reinforced by her interview with Adam Sylvester.

With more hair sprouting from his ears than covering his head, and a waist line that long ago rendered his belt invisible, Sylvester was right out of central casting for the fat cop: too lazy to be efficient, too close to retirement to care.

"Two Thousand Nine?" he queried. "That was a long time ago. Probably handled a hundred assaults since then."

"Really? When was the last one?" Holly asked sweetly.

"Ah.... ah....um," Sylvester stammered.

Holly put on her best vivacious smile. "It really doesn't matter. Could you get the Hamilton Blethen file from back then so I can look at it? Then maybe we can talk about it over a cup of coffee or a beer."

Sylvester grinned back at her. *Stupid bastard,* she thought. He dialed his phone and ordered the file from archives.

"I know you're busy," Holly cooed. "I'll just sit over here until they bring the file up."

"You just do that. I'll be right here if you need me...anything." The grin was stuck on Sylvester's face.

The squad room was well worn and outfitted in shades of gray. Walls which may have been white or tan once upon a time, were now a dingy yellow-gray from decades of cigarette smoke, even though there had been a smoking ban in place since 2007. Holly sat on a straight-back office chair with aluminum legs and a cushion that long ago lost its cush. Smoke curled from ashtrays on desks that looked like they were left over from the Korean War. The glare from overhead fluorescent lights caused her to squint. This part of police work she didn't miss.

Twenty minutes later the file arrived on Sylvester's desk. He made a big deal of carrying the file across the squad room and presenting it to Holly.

"There's an interrogation room open," he said. "Why don't you go in there and look at the file. You can spread it out on the table. I can come in later and interrogate you."

The inflection in Sylvester's voice made her want to puke but, instead, she beamed her best smile and said: "Thanks. That would be great."

Holly flipped through the file, looking for the blue incident report. She found it on the bottom of the stack. Sylvester had been the junior officer in the investigation and, accordingly, been tasked with writing the report. Neither his organization or his grammar would have passed a high school English test.

She searched for anything that would identify the weapon, but all she found was "blunt force object". The report identified the victim as a black male. The description of the scene was brief, without detail. Not something she could rely on.

Holly read the report of Sylvester's interview with Toni Blethen nee Chapereaux. He had not pressed her for information that might have been helpful and there were no notes of a follow-up interview. Holly jotted down the name of the nurse who had happened upon the incident scene, a bit of serendipity without which Blethen would not have survived the beating. The notes from the interview with the nurse were only a paragraph long.

On the other hand, the notes from the interview with George Ravalo, the lawyer who suspected Blethen was having an affair with his wife, was lengthy. It was clearly not written by Sylvester.

It detailed the attempted assault by Elaine Ravalo on her husband when she learned of the assault on Blethen. She had been convinced her husband was the perpetrator. A nephew of the Ravalos, Todd D'Anselmo, was identified as the person who had informed Mr. Ravalo of the affair. Ravalo's statement that provided an alibi was set forth in quotes.

An hour and a half later Sylvester opened the interrogation room door. "I've come to interrogate you," he snickered. He plopped down in the chair across the desk from Holly and took out a pack of cigarettes, smacking it several times on the table top.

"Why do smokers do that," said Holly in her best innocent voice.

"To pack the tobacco so it smokes better."

"Hmm. I've got a couple of questions for you. And would you please not light that. I have asthma," she lied.

Sylvester fumbled with the cigarette, jamming it back into the pack. "Um. Sure."

She picked the incident report out of the documents strewn on the table top. "You wrote this, right?"

"Yeah. That's my signature."

"Something I'd like to clear up," she said. "Here you state that the victim was a black male. Hamilton Blethen is of East Indian descent, not African, as the reference to black would suggest."

"It was dark out that night, and he was all bloody."

"So, you *do* remember." Sylvester looked like he'd been caught with his hand in the cookie jar.

"Um, sure. I thought about it while you were in here."

"Good," Holly said. "Did you do any follow up interviews with either the nurse who found Blethen or with his wife—then his girlfriend—Toni Chapereaux?"

"I don't remember. If we did, the notes would be in the file."

"There aren't any, but I do see a lot of communication with the Goodhue County Sheriff's office about the murder of Blethen's mother, Lorraine," Holly continued. "Did you get involved in that investigation?"

"No, and it was his grandmother. The old lady got killed... murdered...about a week before Blethen got his brains beat out. The locals handled that. Blethen was their primary suspect, but they could never pin it on him."

"Because he was a suspect, did you kind of back off your investigation?

"No. No way."

"So, your investigation was thorough?"

"Yeah, but we just couldn't find anything. The only person that had a motive had an alibi. It was just a random act of violence. He was in the wrong place at the wrong time."

"The person with the motive. That was George Ravalo?"

"Yeah."

"He's a very prestigious attorney in Minneapolis, right?"

"Yeah. What are getting at?"

"He thought Blethen was fucking his wife."

The word, coming out of the mouth of the beautiful, demure Holly, stunned Sylvester. "Uh. Yeah. By the way she blew up at him, I'd guess he was right."

"I don't see any statement in here from Elaine Ravalo."

"We didn't see any need to take one. We already knew she thought her husband did it."

"According to the notes of the George Ravalo interview, he thought his wife was having an affair with Blethen because a nephew told him. Did you question the nephew?"

"I don't remember. I think we couldn't find him."

Holly paused.

"Is Elaine Ravalo white or black?" she asked.

"What the hell has that got to do with anything?" Sylvester barked.

"Just curious."

"She's white, but she likes black men. Anything else?" His stupid grin had long disappeared, replaced with a nasty scowl and a testy tone of voice.

"One more thing," Holly said. "Was there ever any consideration that Blethen's injury might have been self-inflicted? I mean, that he might have hired someone to beat him, to deflect suspicion from himself?"

Sylvester looked stunned. "Uh. Sure, we thought of that. Uh, but we couldn't prove it."

"That would be real justice, huh?" Holly baited him. "Hire someone to assault you and end up paralyzed."

"Fucker got what he deserved."

Holly drummed her fingers on her desk, waiting for Ronni to come back from Koskinen's office with the drawings of Mary Blethen. She had been shocked by her interview with Sylvester. It was apparent that they had stuffed the investigation of Hamilton's assault for multiple reasons, and none of them were legitimate.

The question for Holly, and the rest of the Monet Detective Agency, was whether they should pursue this any further. Finding the perpetrator of the assault might link Blethen to his Grandmother's murder, but it might not, and it would definitely be a time-consuming and expensive undertaking. *Maybe if we show Hamilton that Magnolia Kanaranzi is his mother, he'll pay us to find out who assaulted him. Or maybe his wife would.*

Ronni stood in Holly's office doorway, a large manila envelope under her arm.

"What have you got?"

"Koskinen went above and beyond. He did four drawings for me. Two with a nose like Mary Blethen's from her high school photos, and two with a nose like Magnolia Kanaranzi's, all twelve-by-eighteen. Let's go look at them in the conference room."

Ronni slid the photos out of the envelope and laid them in a square pattern, then took the eight-by-ten campaign photo of Magnolia Kanaranzi and put it in the middle. "What do you think?" she asked Holly.

Holly took the two drawings that were intended to depict Mary Blethen at age forty and turned them face down on the table. She then moved the campaign photo between the two "sixty-year-old" drawings. She nodded. "It sure could be her."

"Another woman has come forward, alleging she had a sexual affair with Massachusetts Senator David Metzger. Dawn Rogers, a woman from Washington D.C., alleges that she and Metzger had numerous sexual liaisons over a period of two years, from 2007 through 2009.

"Just two days ago, Metzger admitted having an affair with a Senate page, Amber Fizer, in 2004, but claimed that it was his only sexual transgression while he has been in office."

The CNN anchor cued up the video of Metzger's news conference. The picture of Dawn Rogers that had been behind him was replaced by Metzger, and then his wife.

"Metzger, a Republican, is a two-term Senator who is locked in a close race with media mogul Magnolia Kanaranzi. In the most recent poll, Kanaranzi led Metzger by five percentage points. Efforts to reach Metzger for comment were unsuccessful."

"It made national news. Can you believe it? This race is over!" Becky Lindstrom and the other members of the Kanaranzi campaign staff were, literally, dancing in the aisles, elated by the news of Metzger's most recent indiscretion. "I wonder what his wife will do now?"

Jim Bean watched the celebration, letting it go on for several minutes, before stepping out of his office.

"All right," he growled loud enough to be heard above the din. When he didn't get immediate attention, he turned off the TV. The room quickly came to order.

"Let's not get our cart before our horse," he thundered. "This race is far from over. Stick to your tasks. We may have our foot on his throat, but now is not the time to take it off. Now is the time to step down harder. Think of it as an MMA fight. We're on top. We've got our opponent down. We don't let him up. We go for the choke hold. We go for submission. How do we do that? By doing exactly what we have been doing, and doing it harder and better."

If anything, Bean's speech added fuel to the ballyhoo. He stepped back, allowing himself a small smile of satisfaction and beckoned several staffers into his office. Magnolia and Samantha would be back from their event soon, and he wanted to have a strategy ready for them when they returned.

SEPTEMBER 28, SUNDAY

"Our guest today on *Meet the Press* is Massachusetts Senator David Metzger," announced newly-minted host Chuck Todd. "Senator Metzger: getting right to what everyone is talking about, this past week three women have come forward alleging that you had sexual contact with them while serving in the Senate. One of those women said the contact was unwelcome and forced upon her. You have admitted to having an affair with one of those women, a nineteen-year-old Senate page. Are the allegations of the other women also true?"

"Absolutely not," the Senator sputtered. "I have never met Dawn Rogers. That is an absolute fabrication. It appears that my opponent…"

"What about Lois Bennett? The woman who worked in your Boston office and claims you groped her."

"That's an outright lie," Metzger exclaimed. "As I was saying, my opponent…."

"That's a good boy," Magnolia chuckled, turning off the television. "Now you're playing the game the right way." Her appearance tomorrow before the Women's Leadership Institute was perfectly timed. Metzger had all but written her speech for her.

She took the burner phone out of her desk and dialed Hawke. To her surprise, he answered.

"Feldman's usefulness is about done. Women have come forward, accusing my opponent of cheating on his wife. Feldman has one more task to accomplish, and then we'll leak that he was connected to at least one of those women. I'll let you know when that happens."

"Everything is in place," Hawke responded.

"One other thing," Magnolia said before hanging up. "I don't want you to be alarmed, but someone stole some recordings. They included some of our phone calls. Don't worry, it's being taken care of." There was a long silence from Hawke.

"Who did it?" he hissed.

"A private investigator hired by my son. It's being handled."

"It better be."

SEPTEMBER 29, MONDAY

Carrie was still walking stiffly on Monday morning but, with the help of a loose-fitting blouse and painkillers, she hobbled into the office and listened to Holly recount her interview with Adam Sylvester. Fifteen minutes later Ronni joined them and laid out Koskinen's drawings on the conference room table.

"What do you think?" Ronni asked, placing the Kanaranzi campaign photo among the drawings.

"You guys have been busy," Carrie said, her gray eyes darting back and forth from drawing to photo and back. "Give me a minute." She gingerly lowered herself into a chair, looked once more at the pictures before her and closed her eyes."

"Séance," Ronni whispered out of the side of her mouth to Holly.

"Shut up," Carrie said good naturedly, her eyes still closed.

A minute passed. Two. Five. Carrie's breathing had visibly slowed. After ten minutes Carrie started to stir, as if coming out of a sleep. She sat up and winced, the pain bringing her back to the present.

"It's her," she declared. "Magnolia Kanaranzi is Mary Blethen, Hamilton Blethen's mother."

"How do you know that? Ronni asked.

"I don't know. I just do."

"Is this part of your psychic thing?"

"I can't explain it," Carrie said. "It just comes to me, like in a dream, but not really a dream. I'm awake. Just not here. Like I said, I can't explain it. But I'm sure Mary Blethen and Magnolia Kanaranzi are one and the same.

"So, what do we do with it?" Holly asked. "Do we confront her?"

"No," was Ronni's quick response. "Not until after the election."

Holly looked at her, puzzled.

"Because we need people like her in the Senate, and this could affect her election."

"Shouldn't we tell our client, and ask him what to do?" Carrie intervened.

"We don't have a client," was Ronni's curt answer.

"I think we should give this information to him and let him decide."

Holly rocked back in her chair, her chin cradled between her thumb and forefinger, gazing at Monet's *Water Lilies*. Her partners recognized Holly's "thinking pose" and stopped their argument. They waited.

"Let's be smart about this," Holly said finally, sitting up. "We are being threatened, apparently because we are close to finding out something that someone doesn't want us to know. The most likely person behind those threats is Hamilton Blethen, still the prime suspect in the murder of his grandmother. So, one possibility is that we are close to uncovering evidence that would incriminate Blethen in that murder.

"Now we have uncovered something else, that Magnolia Kanaranzi is Blethen's mother. We now have at least a second plausible reason we are under siege. Blethen is dark-skinned and an alleged art forger…"

"What?" Ronni interrupted.

"I saw it on the internet yesterday. Blethen and his wife sold a painting to a Boston museum a couple of years ago, and now there is a claim that the painting is a forgery."

"As I was saying," she said, resuming her audible thought process, "Blethen is an alleged art forger. Having a dark-skinned, illegitimate son with a shady past is the last thing a Senate candidate in a white bread New England state wants. So, there is our second plausible reason."

A faint smile of recognition crossed Ronni's face. "And we're going to use these drawings to set a trap," she said.

"Two traps, actually," Holly responded.

Toni sat in the director's office, her head bowed, her bushy orange hair swaying back and forth as she shook her head in disbelief.

"I'm being put on leave?" she said, incredulously.

"This has gone viral on the internet," Meredith Glenn said from the opposite side of her desk. "Someone leaked this to a blogger, and now everyone is talking about it. I'm really sorry, Toni, but I've got to put you on leave until this is sorted out."

"Leave with or without pay?"

"Without, I'm afraid."

Toni again dropped her head. She knew that this was a risk, but she never thought it would really happen. She took a deep breath and sat up straight.

"This is just unfair. You won't tell me where the forgery claim comes from. You hire one of the most biased 'experts' in the world, and now I'm fired?"

"This is just a leave of absence, Toni," Meredith said, attempting to sooth the assistant curator.

"You know I'll never be able to come back to this job or this museum," Toni said, tears welling in her eyes."

"We don't know that," Meredith said. "If the investigation determines that the painting is authentic and the claim has no merit, the door will be open and your job will be waiting."

Toni got up to leave, not believing a word she had just heard. "You could at least tell me who is saying it's a forgery," she pleaded.

"I can tell you that they are not related to you," Meredith said, looking more and more uncomfortable as the conversation continued. "You could hire your own expert. Please let me know if you do,"

Toni nodded as she walked away, unable to speak for fear that she would break down.

"I've been fired," she told Ham by phone. "I've got to box up the stuff in my office. I'll be home in an hour. I'll bring lunch."

"I'm sorry." While the words were heartfelt, Toni could hear the anger in Ham's voice.

They spent the afternoon calling lawyers, including the French lawyer who handled the litigation started by Toni's uncle challenging Ham's right to *The Reaper*. He would be happy to consult but recommended finding a local lawyer to handle the dispute with the museum. "Our case didn't really deal with the authenticity of the painting," he reminded them. "It was about whether Aunt Monique's will was valid."

His statement wasn't entirely true. The trial had also been about whether Ham and Toni had exercised undue influence over a vulnerable elderly woman. The court found they had not, and that Aunt Monique was of sufficiently sound mind when she executed her will and left a multi-million-dollar painting to Hamilton.

"Scruples! You don't even know the meaning of the word." Magnolia's derisive retort had come from deep within her, involuntarily propelled by Feldman's revelation that there were some heinous acts in which he was not willing to engage.

Heads turned at Magnolia's exclamation. Business at Cheers, Beacon Hill was typical Monday night slow, the weekend tourists having gone home resplendent in *Cheers* memorabilia. A handful of regulars, seated around the square bar made famous by Cliff and Norm, gave the diminutive woman and the obese man a second look, but soon refocused their attention on the beer in front of them.

Magnolia had chosen the storied pub for the meeting, expecting that the crowd would be sparse on a Monday night, and it would be the last place she would likely be recognized. She was right on both assumptions, but what she wasn't prepared for was Feldman having cold feet.

"I do a lot of dirty political shit," Feldman muttered after he was sure no one was listening. "But I draw the line at murder."

Magnolia glared at him.

"You don't know for sure that the private dick stole your recordings," he continued. "We don't even know if she's been back in Boston. I could be killing the wrong person."

"Who else would have stolen them? We know it's not Metzger. He would have released them by now to divert attention from his own troubles."

"Could be anybody," Feldman answered. "Maybe for blackmail. You're a rich woman. Makes you a target for every greedy motherfucker."

"Don't you think I'd have heard from the blackmailer by now, if that was the reason?" Magnolia asked.

"Maybe. Maybe not. Could be waiting for a better time. Maybe he wants you to be a senator first."

Magnolia made little circles on the wood table with her Singapore Sling glass. She looked down at the red tile floor and stretched her neck, turning it from side-to-side, trying to relieve the tension. She exhaled slowly.

"You're right," she said, looking up. "I was angry. I didn't mean it. Forget the private investigator."

Feldman drained his beer, finishing with a loud "aaahhh" of satisfaction and relief. "You want me to keep making her life miserable? She's still poking around, looking into stuff about you according to my guy in Minnesota."

"She hasn't found anything, so let's let her be for now. We've got more important things to do. Have you found anyone else to come forward against Metzger?"

"No. There are three already. Do you think we need more?"

"We could always use more," Magnolia said, her tone oddly pleasant. "How did you find Lois Bennett?"

Feldman bit the inside of his lip, hesitating. "I didn't. She came out of the woodwork."

"There have got to be more like her. Have someone get in touch with her to see if she can lead us to others. I want Metzger's sex scandal to follow him all the way to Election Day."

Magnolia sat in the back seat of the taxi as it eased past City Hall toward South Market. She'd give Feldman the rest of the week to see if he could come up with more women. She'd have to talk to Hawke about dealing with the private detective, but she was too tired tonight. That would have to wait until tomorrow.

Or maybe, she thought as the taxi pulled up to the front entrance of Pier 4, *maybe I should take care of it myself.*

SEPTEMBER 30, TUESDAY

What the hell is his campaign manager thinking, Bean thought. *The man looks like death warmed over. How could they let him go on television looking like that?*

"I have never paid that woman for sex," Metzger was proclaiming to a local morning news reporter. "I have never paid any woman for sex. This is outrageous. She's after a big pay day. Get some magazine to pay her a million dollars. These are all lies."

"So, you're saying you never had sex with Dawn Rogers," the reporter said, pressing the issue.

"I've never even met her," Metzger responded.

"Well, there you have it," the morning news anchor of Channel 25 intoned as the live feed switched back to the studio. "Investigators have confirmed that Dawn Rogers, a Washington, D.C. prostitute, travels in influential circles and appears regularly at Capitol Hill fundraisers. Yet Senator Metzger, a fixture in Washington for twelve years and known to be one of the most prolific fundraisers in his party, claims he doesn't know who she is."

As the story droned on, Bean turned down the volume and looked at Samantha. "How's our candidate holding up?"

"She was in good spirits when I talked to her this morning," Samantha answered. "She's got a meet and greet at Converse later this morning and two coffee klatches this afternoon. Tonight, she speaks at Wellesley. In between all that, we've got to find some time to prep her for the debate."

The debate, scheduled for October 8, had been a seminal event on Magnolia's campaign calendar when she won the primary. In August, The League of Women Voters had proposed a debate between Metzger and the winner of the Democratic primary. At the time, Magnolia was just one of several potential opponents for the incumbent Senator. Things had changed radically since then. Not only had she won the primary, but she was now leading Metzger in the polls; polls that were taken before the sex scandal that was rocking his campaign and dominating the current news cycle.

"The debate comes two days after the next poll is due out," Bean said. "If we have a double- digit lead, we'll tone down her approach. She won't need to be nearly as aggressive."

There was on-going negotiation between the two camps for a second debate later in October, hosted by New England Public Radio, but Bean was slow-walking those discussions now. If Magnolia's lead continued to build, a second debate would not be in her best interest. It would only be an opportunity to make a mistake and let Metzger back in the race.

Caller ID identified the caller as the Monet Detective Agency. Toni frowned at the phone, then reluctantly answered.

"Toni, it's Holly Bouquet."

"I saw the caller ID."

"Listen, I know we're not representing you and Ham anymore, but I thought you should know that we think we've found evidence that will either identify, or lead to, his Grandmother's murderer."

Toni was silent.

"Are you still there?" Holly asked.

"Yes. So why call me? Are you looking for more money?"

"No. No. I just wanted to put you on notice so you didn't hear it first from some reporter."

"Oh. Thanks.," Toni said haltingly, her voice not reflecting gratitude. "Can I ask what kind of evidence?"

"I can't say. Don't want to take a chance that someone might be listening."

"Hmm. Well, good luck. Will you let me know?"

"When Ronni gets back from Zumbrota tomorrow, you'll be the first to know if an arrest has been made." Toni thanked her and hung up.

Oh, God. Now what. Toni took in a deep breath and exhaled. *Should I tell Ham? It will only get him upset, and he never answers the phone so he won't get ambushed by some reporter asking questions.* She chose not to tell him.

"I need a gun. Nothing big. For personal protection. Because of the break-in. Can you arrange to get one for me?"

Magnolia's request caught Hawke off guard. He knew she had supported the new, restrictive gun law that had passed the state legislature a month ago. For her to want a gun was an anomaly, and, more importantly, in Hawke's opinion, with her temper the last thing she should possess was a gun.

"I don't think that's a good idea," he said, thinking quickly. "Not right now. To own a hand gun you need to be licensed, and licenses are public records. Can you imagine the fun your opponent would have with that? I'd wait until after the election, if I were you."

"I suppose you're right," Magnolia said. Her quick capitulation surprised Hawke, and he quickly took advantage to change the subject.

"Have the missing recordings been recovered?" he asked.

"No. There's a problem. Feldman was supposed to take care of it, but he backed out."

"And I assume you need my help."

Magnolia related the details of the break-in and her belief that the recordings had been stolen as part of an investigation perpetrated by her son.

"If you're right," Hawke said, "you have a larger problem than just the private detective. You have to assume that Hamilton has the recordings in his possession by now. There's only one way to be sure that the problem is taken care of."

Hawke's unspoken solution disturbed Magnolia. Confronted with the prospect of her son's death, some instinct welled up from deep within her, repelling the proposal.

"Let's not go there," she said. "Let's find out if he actually has the recordings."

"I can do that."

"But you can't contact him. I don't want any traceable connection between Hamilton and me."

"I'm well aware of that, madam," Hawke said with sarcasm. "This is not, as you say in the States, my first rodeo."

"And what of Feldman?" he asked, breaking an uncomfortable silence.

"He will be leaving my campaign staff next week."

"Ah. Then I will need to pay him a visit." Hawke hung up. A line from a Sir Walter Scott poem came to him: *O, what a tangled web we weave when first we practice to deceive.*

OCTOBER 1, WEDNESDAY

The two-vehicle caravan left the parking lot of Holly's condo where the three women had been staying since the attack on Carrie. They sped south on Highway 52 out of St. Paul, Ronni and Carrie riding in Ronni's Dodge Dakota, followed by Holly and Bob Decker, an off-duty cop friend of Holly's, in Holly's car. A twenty-year veteran of the St. Paul police force, Decker had outfitted them with two-way radios that clipped to their belts.

"If there's any sign of trouble, press this button," he'd said, pointing to an oblong button on the side of his own unit. "If you press the top of the button, you can talk. When you release it, you can hear what the other person is saying. If you press the bottom of the button, it will lock the radio open until you press it again. In the open configuration, you can both talk and hear. I've put all your radios on channel 61. Don't change channels. We'll test them on the way to Zumbrota."

By the time they rolled through the village of Coates, all radios had been tested and proven workable.

"You never know where the threat might come from," Decker warned them. "So, don't wait to make sure there's trouble before you let the rest of us know. If you suspect anything, push the bottom of the button."

"Be vigilant," were his last words.

They barreled down Highway 52, crossing the Cannon River and skirting the edge of the village of Cannon Falls, lost in their own thoughts, until Carrie broke the silence. "Is your radio on?"

Ronni ran her fingers over the oblong button on the side of her radio. "No. Why?"

"What do you think of Decker?" Carrie asked.

"You mean as a cop, or otherwise?"

"Otherwise."

"Let's see. Six-two, zero percent body fat, a little distinguishing gray at the temples, looks kind of like George Clooney with a crewcut. I haven't really noticed. What do you think?"

"Hottie," was the only word Carrie could get out between convulsions of laughter as both women cracked up.

"Holly's hottie," Ronni gasped, wiping the tears from her eyes with her sleeve.

"When he said 'be diligent' I don't think this is what he was referring to." Carrie's retort triggered more shrieks of laughter.

"I don't think he and Holly are a thing," she continued after the hilarity subsided. "She told me he's been a friend of her family for a long time, knew her dad when he was on the force. I didn't get the impression that there was any attraction there, just a friendship.,"

"So, we can still dream," Ronni said.

"Yup."

The inside of the Dakota lapsed back into silence as both women got lost in their respective fantasies. Ronni's was not so much fantasy as lament. *God, it would be nice to have someone like him lay beside you, touch you, make you warm, keep you safe. No way that is going to happen. Scraggy bikers and drunks. That's my only hope for a sex life. Nobody like Decker is ever going to want to be with a woman who's a T.*

"Anything going on up there?" The radios crackled with Holly's voice. Ronni looked in the rearview mirror. She couldn't see Holly's Toyota.

"No sign of trouble," Carrie said, then realized she hadn't pressed the button. She did and repeated herself. "How about you?" she added.

"No. Nothing. Just wanted to see how everyone was doing."

"Doing fine. We'll be in Zumbrota in ten minutes."

"When we get to Zumbrota we'll split up and retest the radios to make sure there's no interference." Holly said. "Are you going to the nursing home?"

"Yeah."

"Bob and I are going to swing past Lorraine's old farm," Holly said. "We'll test from there."

"These are good up to sixteen miles," Decker's voice chimed in.

Carrie made sure her radio was turned off. "Even his voice has muscles," she said with a grin.

"Vigilant," Ronni reminded her. "I just hope he's as good as he looks when the shit hits the fan." She got out of her truck and looked around the parking lot and adjacent street. Nothing seemed out of place. "Let's go." She and Carrie walked into the nursing home.

Bertha Warren had identified three teachers from the Class of '71 that were still alive. Mildred Frank was the last of the three to be interviewed, and she was happy to have visitors. She looked at them through watery, opaque eyes that were once blue and said in a crackly voice, "It's so nice to have company."

Ronni sat on a wicker chair next to Mildred's bed and explained the reason for their visit.

"Of course, I knew Mary." Mildred's voice was like crumpling cellophane. "She was a cheerleader. Beautiful girl."

"Can you describe her?"

"I remember one homecoming…" Mildred's mind wandered off.

Ronnie let her ramble, then brought her back to Mary Blethen, again asking for her description.

"Tall, blonde, very athletic," Mildred said. "I think she married that Tostrud boy."

Ronni took out her phone and pulled up a picture of Mary Blethen. "Do you recognize this person."

"Yes., dear. That's…that's…that's…. uh…. aren't those lovely pictures on my wall?"

Ronni agreed, then turned to Carrie who had been standing by the door of Mildred's room. "Do you think hypnosis would help?"

She cocked her head with an "I doubt it" look on her face. "I'm not sure she can concentrate long enough to be hypnotized." Ronni agreed, and they wished Mildred a warm good-bye with hugs and thanks.

"Well, it was worth the effort," Ronni said as they walked down the winding open spaces toward the front door of Bridges of Zumbrota. "I've talked to everyone except one of her classmates, who I haven't found yet, and the custodian with Alzheimer's."

Carrie stopped so quickly that Ronni almost ran into her. "What?"

"Is the custodian in this facility?"

"Let me look," Ronni replied. She sat down in a green, wing-back chair, one of several that dotted the serpentine hallway, and flipped through a file she was carrying until she found the custodian's name, Albert Freeman. Freeman was, indeed, a resident of the memory care unit.

"Are you relatives?" the woman at the nurse's station asked.

"No," Carrie answered. "We're trying to locate a missing person. Someone Mr. Freeman may have known when he was a custodian at the high school."

"So, you're police."

"No," Ronni jumped in. "But we're assisting the St. Paul police department."

"I'll need to see some credentials," the woman said. "We can't have random people coming in and bothering our residents."

Ronni bristled at the "random" comment, but rather than lash out she called Holly. "Where are you?"

"Sitting at Bridget's Café drinking coffee," Holly said. "I take it there's been no action on your end."

"Not the kind we were expecting." Ronni confirmed. "We talked to the teacher but she wasn't of any help. Now we're trying to talk to the former high school custodian, but we've run into a road block. Could you ask Decker to come over here and flash his badge, and tell this resident gatekeeper that we're helping him locate a missing person?"

"Just a minute." Ronni could hear Holly talking with Decker. "We'll be right over," she said, coming back on the phone.

As she sat and waited for Decker and Holly, Carrie's thoughts went back to the first time she had communicated with an Alzheimer's victim. It had happened quite by accident. Carrie's mother had just transitioned to memory care because of early-onset dementia. They were having lunch at a community table with two other women, both of whom had not uttered a word. Suddenly, one of them, a woman named Irene, looked directly at Carrie and asked, "Can you talk to my sister?"

"Um. Sure," Carrie answered. "Where is she?"

"Dead."

How does she know I'm a medium, Carrie had wondered? But apparently, she did.

"Tell me about your sister."

In great detail, Irene told Carrie about her sister, Doris, two years older. Doris was the favorite, got whatever she wanted, thought she knew everything. She was always telling Irene what to do. At Carrie's urging, Irene described how Doris looked, what she liked, what she hated, her favorite saying, what she liked to eat, what happened to her when she left home.

"How long ago did Doris pass on?"

Ten years ago, was the answer.

"And how old was Doris when she died?"

"Seventy-one"

When Carrie felt she had a grasp of who Doris was, she asked: Why do you want me to talk to Doris?"

"I want you to tell Doris it wasn't her fault," Irene said, and then went on to relate a story. When Irene was a senior in high school, her sister had interfered in a budding relationship between Irene and a young man named John who was in his twenties. John joined the military and had gone to fight in Europe. He was killed there. Doris never forgave herself. "Tell her I had a fight with John that night," Irene continued, "and that's why he went off and joined the Army the next day. Tell her I'm not mad at her."

Carrie took her Mom back to her room, and then she and Irene found a quiet corner at the nursing home. Carrie held Irene's hands as the two sat with knees touching. She had no idea how long they sat that way. Without warning, there was clarity in Carrie's mind. Doris was there.

Silently, Carrie conveyed Irene's message, then listened as the reply came.

Her eyes opened and gradually she withdrew her hands from Irene's grip. "I spoke with your sister," she whispered.

"Did you tell her?"

"I did."

"Did she say anything?"

"She said thank you. Your forgiveness gave her peace. And to tell you she loves you."

Holly and Decker walked through the nursing home entrance and snapped Carrie out her reverie.

Ronni nodded her head toward the woman behind the desk. Decker introduced himself and showed her his badge. "These women are helping me with a missing person's case and she," he said, pointing at Carrie, "Would like to interview Albert Freeman."

"He has Alzheimer's," the woman said.

"We know that," Decker said. Again, referring to Carrie, he continued, "but this woman has a special gift that enables her to help them recover their memories, at least temporarily."

The woman frowned. "I'll have to ask the head nurse."

Decker smiled, and in a friendly voice, said: "You wouldn't want me to tell the head nurse that you're obstructing a police investigation, would you?

"Um. No. I guess not."

"Then why don't you just let Carrie talk with Mr. Freeman for a few minutes. If you want someone there to observe, I'm sure that would be okay."

Carrie nodded her head. "It should take only about a half hour. If he gets upset, I'll stop."

"You have a half hour," the woman grumped, and then gave Carrie directions on where to find Freeman.

As Carrie left, Ronni approached Holly. "Could you go over to the library and see if they can help you locate Ken Olson? He was in the class of '71 with Mary Blethen. I tried to look him up in the phone book but he's not there."

"Phone book?"

"Yeah. They still have phone books in Zumbrota."

Albert Freeman didn't look like a nursing home resident. Average height, brown thinning hair, wearing khakis and a plaid, corduroy shirt, he looked like any other retired octogenarian. He was sitting on the cushion of a bay window in a large, open room, gazing out the window.

'Mr. Freeman?"

"Who are you?" His voice was a little gravelly but pleasant.

"My name is Carrie Waters, Mr. Freeman. You and I have never met, but I would like to talk to you. Ask you some questions. Would that be all right?"

"Do I know you?"

Carrie ignored the question, knowing it would be repeated time and again if she engaged in that conversation. Instead, not waiting for permission, she slid a straight-backed chair in front of Freeman, and sat on it, close enough so their knees touched. She reached for his hands, but he jerked them away.

"Are you a nurse?"

"I'm kind of a therapist," she said, her voice soothing. "Can I hold your hands? Maybe we can remember together."

Shyly he put his hands in his lap. Carrie leaned forward, reaching out gently, taking his hands in hers. They were strong hands that dwarfed hers. She guessed Freeman was a farmer or laborer. They sat quietly, the passing time of no importance. Ronni had followed Carrie, purposely ignoring the glares of the woman at the nurse's station. She sat on a rose-colored couch across the large area, her legs crossed, watching and keeping watch. People passed through the room, paying no attention to the two people sitting close together next to the bay window. None of the passers-by appeared to be a threat.

"What was the best thing about your work?" Carrie asked, her voice just above a whisper.

"When I laid the perfect seam. When the horizontal seam and the vertical seam made a perfect T." Freeman's words were dream-like.

"Were you a bricklayer?"

He nodded.

"How did you learn to be a bricklayer? How old were you?

"Mr. Milliken taught me, but then I got drafted."

"Who is Mr. Milliken?"

Freeman didn't answer. After waiting a few moments, Carrie tried a different approach.

"Tell me about high school. What was your favorite subject?"

"Math," he intoned, and then started gently swaying back and forth, "but I really like to dance."

"Did you dance in high school?"

"Some of the boys made fun of me, but the girls liked it."

"Did you like high school?"

Freeman smiled, still moving to the music in his head, far, far away. Carrie waited. His movements became more intentional. The music must have changed.

"What song are you listening to?" Carrie asked. No answer. She looked at her watch. Ten minutes had passed and she had made little progress. She needed to press forward.

"Where did you serve in the military?"

The smile vanished. "Korea." They sat in silence as Carrie watched Korea play out on Freeman's face. She was afraid she had lost him.

"Mr. Freeman?" she said softly after several minutes, stroking his hands. He looked up, a stricken look in his eyes, tears welling on the rim. "It's all right. The war is over."

"They died. They all died."

She was tempted to ask who died, but if she went down that rabbit hole with him, he might never come back. Instead, she tried to ease him past the memory. "Tell me about going back to school after Korea."

"There were no jobs," he said, the pain disappearing from his eyes. He wiped them with the heels of his hands. "There was a recession. No jobs. I couldn't be a bricklayer."

"So, you went back to school."

Freeman rocked gently back and forth, like he was nodding with his whole body. "School wanted a janitor. I got the job because I was a vet."

"Zumbrota High School?" Carrie asked. This time only his head nodded as his eyes again took on the faraway look.

"What year is it Mr. Freeman?"

"1954."

"Tell me why you love your job."

"I'm with kids. I can dance again."

"Tell me about the dancing."

Again, Freeman started to sway and the story poured out.

"I'm not much older in years than the kids, but way older in experience because of what I've been through in the military."

"Did you dance in the military?"

Freeman ignored her question. "It's January, and I'm sweeping the gymnasium floor, watching Mr. Sharpe trying to teach his class how to dance. He's really frustrated. He's trying to demonstrate using one of the boys in the girl's role: one and two and one and two. It was really awkward and uncomfortable. The other boys snickered, but they obeyed because they had to. They move like puppets on a string. A cafeteria worker, Marlene, comes through the kitchen door. She watches the boys moving like wooden soldiers and chuckles. She walks across the gym floor and there's a bounce in her step, in rhythm with the music. I lay my broom handle against the wall and intercept her as she passes me. We whirl around the gym floor, and I see that the class has stopped and they're all watching us, even Mr. Sharpe. Marlene is laughing. We dance to the gym doorway. I let go of her hand and give a deep bow. She says thank you and curtseys. She walks out of the gym with a smile on her face and her step as light as a feather. I turn around and the class hadn't moved. 'Girls love it when you know how to dance,' I say. They start calling me the dancing janitor after that. I love it. The next time it was time to teach the students to dance, they asked me to help."

"Do you still dance?" Carrie asked him.

"What?"

She had made a mistake by asking a question about the present. Freeman no longer lived there. Again, she checked her watch. Her allotted time was almost up. She decided to go for broke.

"Did you ever dance with Mary Blethen?"

Clouds crossed his face. Dark, dangerous clouds. Freeman seemed to shrink, as if cowering from an impending storm.

The woman from the nurse's station entered the room, and Ronni got up to intercept her.

"Just a few more minutes," Ronni whispered. "She's right at the critical point in the interview. It should only take another minute or two."

The woman scowled in the direction of Carrie and Albert Freeman. "But...," she started.

Ronni raised her index finger to her lips with a hushed "shhh."

"Mr. Freeman," Carrie resumed. "Mary Blethen?"

"She didn't deserve it," he said.

"Deserve what, Mr. Freeman?"

"I couldn't do anything about it. The bastard's father was a doctor." Lightning crackled in the dark clouds. "He ran everything. Couldn't buck him."

"Tell me what happened?" she asked softly.

"Little prick beat her up. Raped her. Tore her." For the first time, Freeman's voice rose. "I found her. Tried to help her." Again, tears welled in his eyes, one escaping down his cheek. Carrie waited.

"I took her home. Her mother blamed me. She blamed Mary too. She never held her, never hugged her."

Again, there was a pause that lasted several minutes as Freeman battled with the demons that had locked him into the past.

"He ruined her. Her mother ruined her too. She was never the same. She was only a freshman."

"Who raped her?"

Freeman didn't answer.

"Can you tell me who raped her?" Carrie repeated.

Freeman's face disintegrated, his eyes pools of sadness as tears ran down.

Carrie knew he was gone. She squeezed his hands and leaned forward, kissing the tears on both of his cheeks. "I'm sorry I've caused you pain," she whispered, then kissed his forehead, "but you have helped me a great deal. I will try to rescue Mary Blethen."

Freeman's breathing slowed and he withdrew his hands. Despite his sad eyes, he smiled.

Carrie recounted Freeman's story to Holly and Decker over a beer at the Covered Bridge. Visibly shaken, she downed her glass and ordered a second. "It's times like these when I wish I didn't have this...this *ability.*"

"That was brutal," Ronni agreed. "I can understand why she couldn't get out of Zumbrota fast enough."

"And changed her name." Holly added.

"That would explain why I didn't find anything in Boston about Kanaranzi's early life," Ronnie added.

"It feels like the pieces of the puzzle fit together, except for the math." Carrie rejoined the conversation. "There's a five-year gap. Mary Blethen left Zumbrota in 1971. Magnolia didn't show up in Sturgis until '76."

"That's a long road trip," Decker interjected, a twinkle in his eye.

"I don't know if Holly told you," Ronni said, turning to Decker, "but there's a road sign on I-90 that says the town of Magnolia is one way, and the town of Kanaranzi the other. I went to Sturgis and there are no records of a Magnolia Kanaranzi. We believe she changed her name and the name she came up with came from that road sign. She was probably on the way to the Sturgis road rally. That's where her story starts, according to the news and campaign stuff I've read."

"But we still have that five-year gap," Carrie said.

"If Magnolia Kanaranzi is her legal name, she had it changed some place," Decker said. "Have you checked court records?"

"We've checked, but there are no records in any of the counties we can connect either her or Mary Blethen to," Ronni said.

"How about Boston? Did you check there?" Decker asked. Ronni shook her head.

"Usually, in order to change your name, you have to have lived in the same place for six months," Decker continued. "Check Boston and, if you don't find anything there, find out where she lived before Boston."

"Guess I'll have to make another trip to Boston," Ronni said.

"You're not going alone," her partners said in unison.

"Nobody stepped in the trap, so do we write off Hamilton Blethen as a suspect?" Carrie asked on the trip back to St. Paul.

"We're not home, yet," Ronni said. "And even then, we can't be sure that something won't happen tonight or tomorrow."

Carrie gingerly touched her ribs. "So, what do we do now? We can't all live together forever."

"I don't know," Ronni said. "Let's talk about it when we get back."

They stood in the parking lot of Holly's condo complex, saying good-bye to Decker, thanking him for riding along and apologizing for wasting his time.

"Not a waste at all," he said as he shook Ronni's hand, engulfing hers in both of his. She was sure she felt a little extra squeeze in that handshake.

Magnolia called Feldman into her office.

"I need a gun. Can you get one for me?" she asked.

"What do you need a gun for? You planning on killing that private dick?"

"No." She looked disgusted by the thought. "I'm just not feeling safe at home since the break-in."

Feldman nodded, accepting her explanation. "I can get one for you."

"Nothing big."

"Nah, I've got just the thing in mind for you."

"And it can't be registered to me. At least not until after the election. I don't want Metzger calling me a hypocrite."

"Got it. I'll loan you one of mine. Nice little Glock G26, nine-millimeter. You can carry it in your purse if you like. After the election, I'll help you buy one of your own."

"That's very kind of you," Magnolia said.

"See," Feldman grinned. "We can play nice. Next thing you know I'll be calling you Maggie."

The smile drained from Magnolia's face.

"No one calls me Maggie!"

OCTOBER 2, THURSDAY

They stayed together one more night. Decker arranged for a cruiser to drive past a couple of times, but there were no problems.

"Well, that didn't work," Holly said, as they sat in their pajamas around her kitchen counter, eating toast and drinking coffee.

"If Ham isn't behind the threats," Ronni said, "Then it's got to be Kanaranzi. This all started when I started digging into her past. There's something she wants to hide enough to try and scare us off."

"If she *is* Ham's mother, would the fear of it becoming public be enough for her to assault us?" Carrie asked.

"If she thinks it would cost her the election," Holly answered, pouring each of them more coffee.

"Maybe, we should hold off doing anything further until after the election," Carrie said, reaching for another slice of toast. The reaching reminded her of the bruise on her rib cage that was turning purple and yellow.

"I think I should go back to Boston," Ronni said, redirecting the conversation. "I can check county records to see if Kanaranzi changed her name there. Dig a little more into her past."

"We can hire somebody to do that," Carrie said, concerned for her partner's safety.

"We could use the trip to set a trap," Holly said, a sly look crossing her face.

"And how'd that work for us yesterday?" Carrie fired back.

"We eliminated one suspect and learned more about Kanaranzi's background," Ronni argued.

"Mary Blethen's background," Holly corrected her.

"Another trip to Boston might *prove* that they're one and the same," Ronni said.

Ronni called Allison Long at the *Globe*, asking her for access to the archives again and inquiring whether Kanaranzi had any upcoming campaign events that were open to the public. Meanwhile, Holly called Toni Blethen.

"It turned out to be nothing," she told her. "I'm sorry to have gotten Ham's hopes up."

"I didn't tell him," Toni said. "I didn't want him to get upset if, as you just said, it turned out to be nothing."

Holly hung up, stunned. No wonder nothing happened on the trip to Zumbrota. Ham didn't take the bait because he never knew about it.

Using voice-command software, Ham scrolled through web sites about art forgery and forgers, making oral notes in his voice-activated recorder. He began formulating an outline for the presentation he and Toni would make at the University of Minnesota at the end of the month. He was watching a documentary on notorious forger, Mark Landis, when Toni came into the room.

"I need to tell you something," she said. "The detective agency is still investigating your grandmother's death."

"Why? I thought you told them to stop," Ham said.

"I told them that we were terminating their services. They sent a final report and the balance of the money we had on retainer, but they're continuing to investigate. I just wanted you to know."

"How did you find out they're still investigating?"

"I talked to Holly. She called me. She said that they thought they had a lead, but it turned out to be another dead end."

"So, just like before."

"Yes. Pretty much."

"Why would she call about another failure," Ham said. "Something about that doesn't feel right."

"She called me last week to tell me they were about to solve the case. She just called now to tell me that it didn't happen. It was a courtesy call."

"Huh. It just doesn't make sense to me that they are still digging around in Grandma's death without being paid. It's really none of their business."

Toni could hear the anger rising in Ham's voice.

The Metzger scandal had lost momentum as other events pushed it to the bottom of the news cycle, but for the Kanaranzi campaign it was number one on the list of Magnolia's debate preparation.

"The subject is sure to come up," Samantha insisted. "You need to have a response ready. Like what you said when the news first came out. About the tragedy of a life destroyed. You can take the high road. Make it about the victim without saying anything negative about Metzger."

"No." A media consultant sent to Boston by the national party for the specific purpose of helping Magnolia prepare for the debate, butted in. "Call him out on it. Amber Fizer was 19 years old. Doesn't matter if it was consensual or not. Call him a scum bag, a pervert. Label him a dirty old man. What people will remember when they walk into the polling booth is that he screwed a teenager, not whether you took the high road." The consultant, clearly accustomed to having his advice followed, stared down Samantha.

As much as she disliked having Samantha embarrassed by the arrogant prick, Magnolia had to agree with him. *Unless, I wait until after the debate to feed them Feldman. Then it might be better for me to take the high road in the debate.*

Magnolia walked back to her office after the prep session, considering her options and listening to the hum of activity. Volunteers manned every available phone. Voters streamed through the storefront, stopping to take literature or register for a lawn sign. She felt confidant: *Only a month to go. I've got this thing.*

She was contemplating possible choices for her chief of staff when Feldman lumbered through the door.

"Knock next time," she scolded him.

"I brought you a present," he said, ignoring the rebuke. He laid a small pistol on her desk. "It's small, but it'll do the job."

"Close the blinds," Magnolia hissed.

Feldman obediently walked to the corner and pulled the blinds across the windowed wall. "Let me show you how it works."

"I know how it works," she snapped. "You put the bullets in here. You pull the trigger here. The bullet comes out there. Bang. You're dead."

OCTOBER 3, FRIDAY

The headline, in seventy-two-point type, shouted "JPMorgan Chase Hacked. 83 Million Exposed." The announcement of the cyberattack that affected two out of every three households in the U.S., relegated political news to the inner pages of every newspaper in America, and shoved it off radio and television altogether.

That was unfortunate for Lois Bennett and the Kanaranzi campaign.

Bennett's scheduled news conference was sparsely attended. Her announcement of a sexual harassment lawsuit against Senator David Metzger, and her appeal for other women to join her legal cause, largely went unnoticed. Unless, of course, it was brought to the attention of someone such as a discontented former employee of Kincaid Media, who learned of Bennett's lawsuit thanks to a Metzger campaign worker who dangled the news like a carrot. "Maybe you should start a lawsuit against Kincaid Media and Kanaranzi. I may be able to find someone to pay the legal bills."

The revelation that Hamilton Blethen had not known of their carefully planned trap in Zumbrota cast a pall over the Monet Detective Agency office and cast doubt on the wisdom of a trip to Boston. While the trip could provide another opportunity to expose Hamilton, if he was behind the attacks (this time they would make sure he knew of the trip), Ronni had already talked to Allison Long, so it was possible that Kanaranzi already knew they would be coming.

If both Blethen and Kanaranzi knew Ronni was in Boston, there would be no way to determine, if a threat (or worse) was made, who was behind it, unless they could catch the perpetrators in the act and force them to rat out their employer. They argued the pros, cons and probabilities throughout the morning.

Ronni was putting on her jacket to run some errands and have lunch when her phone rang. She didn't recognize the number. "Hello."

"Ronni? It's Bob Decker." Goose bumps rose up on Ronni's arms. "Got time for a quick lunch?"

"I was just heading out to do that," Ronni said, clearing her throat to dislodge the frog that had just set up residence there.

"Can you meet me at Frost's? Fifteen minutes?"

"That's pretty fancy for a quick lunch."

"Well, maybe we can make it a little longer than quick," Decker said, a smile in his voice. "I've got some information about the guy you're trying to find, Ken Olson."

"Okay. I'll see you there in fifteen."

Ronni stopped in the bathroom and looked at herself in the mirror. *It's only business. But why did he call me and not Holly? And, W.A. Frost?* She turned her head from side-to-side. She ran her hand through her hair. *There. Perfect.* She loved her short hair, a haphazard, layered razor cut. She took a spritzer from her purse and sprayed on a mist of perfume. Damn. Why hadn't she worn a dress? She turned up the collar of her jean jacket to cover the feather tattooed on her neck. *This is stupid. It's only business.* But she couldn't deny the tingle she felt as she drove up Cathedral Hill.

He was waiting for her by the hostess stand, dressed in his police uniform. Her tingle morphed into full-out chills. After greetings, he let her pass in front of him to follow the hostess. When they reached the table, he glided smoothly past them both and pulled out a chair for Ronni.

"I've located an address for Ken Olson," he said. They were still holding the menus which the hostess had handed them. "He lives in McAllen, Texas." He took a business card out of his shirt pocket and pushed it across the table to her. "I've written his address on the back of my card."

"Clever," Ronnie said.

"What?"

"Clever pick-up maneuver," she said. "Your card with your phone number, disguised as business." *Shut your mouth, Ronni,* she thought. *You just blew it.*

He looked at Ronni with a bemused smile. "Do I need to pick you up?"

"No." The word was barely audible.

Twice the waitress came to take their order only to learn they hadn't yet looked at their menus. The third time, with some luncheon patrons already come and gone, they ordered. It was 2:15 p.m. by the time they left the restaurant.

"That was fun," Ronni said.

"I'd like to do it again some time."

"Me too."

They hugged in the parking lot. Decker got in his cruiser and rolled down the window. "If you go to Boston, I think I should go with you." There was no romance in his voice. The suggestion was all business. "You're swimming into dangerous waters. You should have a shark with you for protection."

I can protect myself was Ronni's first reaction, but she didn't say it. It would be good to have extra muscle, especially when the muscle was as pretty as Bob Decker.

OCTOBER 4, SATURDAY

On the third try, Ken Olson answered the phone. His words, slow and hoarse, made him sound older than his sixty-one years. His memory, however, was sharp.

"Those were crazy days," he said, referring to his high school years in Zumbrota. "A bunch of us ran around together, always looking for trouble. We usually found it, too." He chuckled, like someone who hadn't seen trouble in years, but wished he had. "I remember Mary. She came along later. I think she was a junior when she became part of the gang. Somebody brought her in because she had drugs."

"No, we didn't date. Not in high school. None of us dated back then. We just all hung out together. She wasn't very friendly, at least not to the guys, unless she was stoned, which was a lot of the time."

"We all moved on after high school. I went into the Air Force. I did run into her once, in Las Vegas. I was stationed at Nellis Air Force Base. She was dealing at some casino. She'd changed her name. Wasn't into drugs anymore. We went on one date, but we didn't click."

"Her name? Don't remember. Something, name of a flower. I still called her Mary."

"Yeah. That's it, Magnolia."

"What year? It was after I re-upped. Maybe '76- '77."

Ronni thanked him for his time and hung up. She looked up the number for Clark County, Nevada, court records and dialed the number, then realized it was Saturday. She was sure the court records held the final piece of the puzzle that would prove Magnolia Kanaranzi was Hamilton Blethen's mother, an order changing Mary's Blethen's name to Magnolia Kanaranzi. She'd call on Monday.

She needed to call someone to share the exciting news. She started to dial Holly, then stopped. She picked up the business card with Ken Olson's handwritten name and address. She turned it over. There was Bob Decker's cell number. Should she call him? *Oh, what the hell.*

She dialed. He answered.

"You solved the case," she said.

"Ronni?"

"Yes. I just wanted you to know that I talked to Ken Olson. I know where Mary Blethen changed her name. I know she's Hamilton Blethen's mother."

"We should celebrate," he said. "How about dinner tonight at the *St. Paul Grill.* I'll pick you up at seven."

Magnolia looked out of place at the Suffolk County Jail, dressed in a Burberry trench coat and four-inch stilettoes.

Maria, sitting at a table in the visitor area, burst into tears at the first sight of Magnolia. "I'm sorry," she gasped between sobs. "I didn't know."

Magnolia reached out and took Maria's trembling hand. She listened as her former housekeeper poured out her grief and the story of how she met Isabella.

"She promised to bring my brother here from Mexico. I signed papers. But she's gone. She's not at the address she gave me. Her phone's disconnected." Maria broke down again.

"It's okay," Magnolia purred. "I'm not going to press charges. I'll get you out of here."

"Can…can I…come back to work?"

"No. I've already hired someone. She starts Monday. But I will give you a month's pay and a good recommendation. And I'll give you back your phone."

Magnolia left as Maria sobbed her thanks.

Outside the jail, she called her personal attorney to arrange to have the charges dropped. She climbed into the taxi that she had paid to wait for her. "Harvard Club, please."

Samantha was waiting for her as the taxi pulled up to the private club in Boston's Back Bay. They made their way through the dark wood and the opulence to the President's Room where two dozen business executives, all male, were waiting to hear what Magnolia had to say about taxes, tariffs and other economic matters.

"That went well," Magnolia opined as they left the club, "for a hostile environment."

"I think you won them over," Samantha said. "They understand you're one of them, as much concerned about the economy as they are."

"Thanks, Sam, but they're still Metzger supporters. Maybe I swayed a couple of them. At least now they know I'm not a tree hugger."

Her usual limousine awaited outside the club. As they rode back to campaign headquarters Samantha said: "Remember the Minnesota detective that was here a month ago, looking into your past?"

Hackles rose on the back of Magnolia's neck.

"I got a call yesterday asking if I could get her a ticket for the debate."

"Give her a ticket," Magnolia said. "I think it's time I meet her."

Four a.m. was his favorite time in Barcelona. The club action was at its crescendo. La Rambla was packed with tourists, young professionals and the occasional veteran clubber like Hawke. By this time, his evening buzz firmly in place, Hawke would be dancing with some lithe twenty-something at The MOOG or Marula Café. Barcelona, or at least Hawke's part of it, didn't sleep until after 6:00 a.m. Little wonder that he didn't hear his phone ring until he sat at a café table, his shirt wringing wet under his blue blazer and sweat oozing from every pore from his exertion on the dance floor.

"Hawke," he answered. He listened. "I'll be in Boston Monday. I'll call you when I know what time I'll be in."

He hung up, wiped his forehead with a napkin, took a sip of Pernod and scanned the room for potential dance partners. Hawke was a legend in the Barcelona clubs. Despite his short stature and rotund shape, he was a superb dancer, and the generosity with which he occasionally rewarded a partner added an air of mystique and anticipation. On any night, by 4:00 a.m., he could have his pick of partners, woman or man.

Tonight, he had a tennis bracelet of white sapphires in his jacket pocket. He had not yet found the evening's deserving partner upon which to bestow it. The DJ spun another disc. Hawke took a small mirror from his purse, patted down his slicked back hair and dabbed away the sweat.

A woman he guessed to be in her thirties, clearly a tourist by her dress, was standing with two younger women.

"American?" he asked as he approached the trio.

"Canadian."

"Shall we dance?"

"How did you know I wasn't from here?" she shouted above the music as they gyrated on the dance floor.

"Your dress is not so short nor so tight as the local women," he shouted back. "You are much more sophisticated; shall we say urbane. You are a woman among children."

She blushed but did not walk away when the music changed. They continued dancing until they were both breathing heavily. Hawke walked her to the table where her two companions awaited.

He made a deep bow and kissed her hand. "What is your name, fair lady," he asked.

"Marta."

"Marta, as the great Martha Graham once said, 'Great dancers are not great because of their technique, they are great because of their passion.' You have that passion. For you, I have a gift." He took the bracelet from his pocket and placed it in her hand.

"For honoring me with a dance, I give this to you. And for you," he continued, turning to her two companions, "another bottle of wine." He signaled to a nearby waiter.

"I can't accept this," said a shocked Marta. "This is beautiful, but…"

"You have just danced with the great Henri Hawke," the waiter said, arriving at the table. "You cannot turn down a gift from Mr. Hawke. His reputation, and the reputation of The MOOG, would be tarnished. Surely you don't want that."

Hawke looked at Marta, his head cocked, smiling.

"Thank you," she said, breathlessly.

"My pleasure," Hawke bowed his tilted head. "A bottle of *Poggione Brunello* for ladies," he said to the waiter. "My tab."

So, now there are two jobs, Hawke thought as he picked his way back to his table. *I wonder what my American benefactor has in mind this time?*

OCTOBER 6, MONDAY

A new Boston Globe poll had Magnolia leading by nine points with only eleven percent of the electorate undecided. The poll had plus-minus accuracy of three percent. With less than a month to go before the election, a professional handicapper would have made Magnolia at least a five-to-one favorite to be the next Senator from Massachusetts.

The revelations of Metzger's infidelity had definitely affected the race, but not in the way Bean expected. Metzger had actually gained one percentage point from the last poll. Magnolia had picked up the largest chunk of the "undecideds" who had now made their choice, pushing her to a forty-nine percent, but Metzger's support had not eroded.

"This race is not over, people," Bean announced to the paid staff assembled at campaign headquarters. He had called in staff workers from around the state in anticipation of the new poll, to lay out strategy for the rest of the campaign. "The news is good, the campaign is solid, but there is a lot of work still to be done, starting with Wednesday night's debate."

For the rest of the morning they plotted strategy, laid out the candidate's calendar all the way to the end of October, and analyzed their get-out-the-vote logistics in the days leading up to the election. At 11:15 a.m. Magnolia made her entrance as the staff stood and cheered.

"Please sit, and thank you," she said as she stood in the middle of the room. "We're almost there, thanks to all of you. The people are listening to our message of equal opportunity, equal rights and equal pay. We've been at this for over six months. Only one more month, one more push, will put us over the top and take us to Washington where we can really make a difference in the lives of people who need a voice in the halls of power, whose own voices need to be heard."

The staff rose as one, giving Magnolia a loud, long ovation.

"Where to now," she asked Samantha as they left the room.

"A meeting with the archbishop at Cathedral of the Holy Cross. There will be other priests there too. I'll prep you on the way."

"So much for the division of church and state," Magnolia smirked.

"The private detective from Minnesota. Have you had a chance to look into her theft of the recordings?"

"I have not. I was about to, when you called and summoned me. As long as I was coming to the States, I thought I would handle it myself."

"That is precisely what I had in mind," Magnolia said, sitting down with her second drink in hand. "And, as part of handling it, I would like you to make sure that she will no longer have any reason to investigate me."

"I completely understand," Hawke said. "But we must discuss my fee for this endeavor."

Magnolia agreed to pay Hawke a six-figure sum that was larger than usual. In hindsight, she blamed it on the Absinthe.

OCTOBER 7, TUESDAY

Allison Long called. The Kanaranzi campaign had cleared Ronni to attend the debate Wednesday night. It threw the Monet Detective Agency into chaos.

"We're not ready," Carrie argued. "We haven't resolved the Mary Stumpf issue."

"Maybe we don't need to," Ronni contended. "We could confront her with the drawings, with her connection to Ken Olson. Maybe she'd admit she's Mary Blethen."

"She's a politician," Holly chimed in. "She will have anticipated being questioned about her past and have pat answers. I agree with Carrie. We need to have our case iron-clad so she can't spin her way out of it."

"I thought you didn't want to do this until after the election anyway," Carrie said.

Ronnie rubbed her forehead with the fingers of both hands. "I keep going back and forth on that," she admitted. "I want her to be elected, but I also want to reveal she's Hamilton's mother."

"So, let's reveal it after the election," Holly said. "It's less than a month away and that gives us time to close the Mary Stumpf loop. Meanwhile, we can continue to try and solve Lorraine Blethen's murder.

Have you had any luck trying to find a relative of Geraldine Girard?" she asked Carrie.

"I haven't had time to look, but if you don't need me to help track down Mary Stumpf, I can start on that today."

Ronni was still rubbing her forehead, with a pained look on her face.

"Is that okay with you?" Holly asked her.

"Yeah. I can take care of it."

"Is something else bothering you?"

"I've never been to a debate," Ronni said. "Since Long went to all the trouble of getting me a ticket, it would be rude not to show up. I'd really like to go."

"It's going to cost you two thousand dollars, at least," Carrie said. "Last minute plane ticket, hotel room, all that."

"What about the threat last time you were in Boston?" Holly added. "What if Kanaranzi was the one behind the threat, and now she knows you're coming again?"

Ronni looked at the floor and spoke without looking at her partners. "I'm not worried about the threat," she said, sheepishly. "Bob Decker wants to come with me."

"What!!?" Both Holly and Carrie shrieked at the same time.

"We went out Saturday night and had the greatest time. He said if I went to Boston, he wanted to come with me. He said that I was swimming in dangerous waters and I should take a shark along to protect me."

"Oh, hell," Carrie beamed, "You don't care about the debate. You just want to go to Boston and screw Bob Decker."

Despite repeated denials, Ronni's blush and ear-to-ear smile gave her away. It took an hour of congratulations and teasing until the happy women returned to productive tasks. Ronni called Decker and left a message, then called Long to express her thanks and get the logistics of attending the debate.

"I hate to even ask," she said as the conversation with Long wound down, "but is there any possibility of getting a second ticket? I have a plus one on the trip who would also like to go."

"Not a chance," Long responded. "It was a miracle I got this one. Sorry."

Ronnie checked online for airfares. She was surprised that she could get a round trip ticket for just over $350 dollars. Her hotel room would cost another $150 dollars. Not bad.

She filled the rest of the morning making Mary Stumpf inquiries, starting with Clark County. Neither an internet search nor a series of phone calls turned up any birth, death or marriage records for Mary Stumpf. She tried to search the Nevada Motor Vehicle Division to see if Mary Stumpf had a Nevada driver's license but was told that the information could not be divulged without a search warrant or court order.

She went to lunch, still awaiting Decker's call. Instead of eating, she stopped at Target and browsed the women's section. If Decker did come with her, she would need something to wear. She picked out a lilac dress with a pencil skirt that reached mid-calf and a v-neckline. Her black strappy heels and black shawl would look nice with it. *This dating thing is really expensive* she thought as she checked out.

Decker called as she was driving back to the office.

"Wow. Short notice," he said, momentarily plummeting Ronni's heart to the basement, "but I'll figure it out. I can take a couple days of vacation and get someone to cover my shift tomorrow." Her heart soared out of the basement and into the clouds.

She told him what she'd found for airfares. They agreed she would book for both of them.

"What about hotel rooms?" she asked.

"Do we need more than one?" His tone made it clear that he hoped they didn't.

"Not as far as I'm concerned," she said. "You can sleep on the couch."

There was silence on the other end.

"That was a joke," Ronni said, while thinking *STUPID! STUPID! STUPID!*

He chuckled. "I was trying to think of some clever comeback, but you beat me to it. Let me know when we have to be at the airport and I'll pick you up."

"Are you sure you want to do this?" she asked, suddenly self-conscious of the sound of her voice. "I understand if you don't."

"I've always wanted to date a girl whose voice was deeper than mine," he quipped.

"Is that what I am, an experiment?" She was hurt.

"That was my joke," he said. "I'm sorry if it was a bad one." The phone was silent.

"Listen," Decker continued, "You are the most intriguing woman I have met in a long time, maybe ever. Yes, I really want to do this. Go to Boston with you. I apologize."

"I'm sorry for being defensive," Ronni said. "I'm just learning how to do this relationship thing. I'm probably overly sensitive."

" This is new to me too," he said. "Sometimes I try too hard to be funny. I need a little slack if I make mistakes. I will make them, but they aren't intentional. I like you. I like you a lot. Just tell me when I say or do something out of line. I'll try not to make the same mistake twice."

At the moment, Ronni felt like she could fly to Boston without the plane. "I'll make mistakes, too. And I like you a lot, too."

"Say that again. The 'I like you a lot' part."

"I like you a lot."

"Again. A little lower."

"I like you a lot."

"Perfect," he said. "Now, if we find a couple who sing lead and tenor, we can start our own barbershop quartet."

OCTOBER 8, WEDNESDAY

"What are you going to do when I'm at the debate?" Ronni asked. Decker, sitting next to her, smiled. "Doing what I'm doing now, sitting right beside you."

"Really. You got a ticket?" Her excitement at the prospect of having Decker with her at the debate was in full view for the rest of the Minneapolis-to-Boston passengers. "I tried but was told there weren't any."

"I have connections," he said, doing his best to look mysterious.

She arched her neck and looked at him with an "are you kidding me" look.

"I called Boston P.D. They helped me out. Professional courtesy. Actually, they had a bunch of tickets. There wasn't much demand for them in the department. They endorsed her opponent."

Ronni slowly shook her head in disbelief, a broad smile on her face. She looped her arm through Decker's and squeezed, snuggling as close as the airplane seat would allow.

Magnolia recited her answer to a question that Bean had posed about the threat of an Ebola pandemic, an issue that had bolted to the top of the news when a nurse traveling from Spain to the United States had been diagnosed with the deadly virus.

"You're going to be great," Samantha said. "There's nothing Metzger can throw at you that we haven't prepped for."

"Just concentrate on staying composed," the Washington, D.C., consultant said. "Your biggest problem is your temper."

And yours is that you're an asshole, Magnolia thought. The national party's man had gotten over his hissy fit and was back giving directions. Magnolia wished he'd gone back to Washington. She didn't need another irritant at the moment.

Her mind wasn't on Ebola or the other issues for which she'd prepared. She was distracted by what they, and she, didn't know. Did Metzger have the recordings? Was he waiting to make them public tonight at the debate?

She was sure she could handle herself, and Metzger, on policy issues. She was confident that she would come across as senatorial. To the public and the press, Metzger was the one with the baggage, not her. She had a comfortable lead in the polls. Her message was being heard by the voters. Samantha was right, she was going to be just fine. Unless Metzger released the recordings. If he did, what would she say?

That's what Magnolia was thinking as she paced, tuning out the others in the room.

She concentrated on what was on the recordings. Her conversations with Hawke were sufficiently vague, and only her part of the conversation could be heard. She could pass those off as reflecting her reservations about Feldman. It was the Feldman conversations that were the problem. The recordings contained both sides of her conversations with him. They would show that she was the one who suggested digging into Metzger's sexcapades. But look what they had found. That was proof that her intuition about Metzger had been right. Maybe it wasn't so bad after all. There was also her tirade at Maria, but that could be justified by bringing up the subsequent break-in.

That's it! The break-in. It struck Magnolia like a lightning bolt: if Metzger brought up anything that was in the recordings, she would turn it on him, charge him with the burglary. She would call it another Watergate.

Magnolia exhaled and tuned back into the conversations going on around her. She sat down.

"I'm ready," she said.

Ronni was nervous as she unpacked her suitcase. *Terrified* was the word that kept going through her head. It was her first time in a hotel room with a man since she had become a woman, and she was scared. She carried her toiletry bag into the bathroom, her insides clenched, hoping she wouldn't wet herself or throw up. The hotel room seemed so small. The bathroom closed in on her.

Decker was the perfect gentleman, giving her ample time and space to put her things in order, bantering in a breezy fashion intended, she was sure, to help her relax. He was amazing. But he was a man. Would she be enough woman for him? All the counseling she had gone through before, during and after her transition had not prepared her for this.

"All in order?" Decker asked as Ronni came out of the bathroom.

"I think so."

"C'mon. Let's go downstairs and have a cocktail. We can stop at the concierge desk and make dinner reservations."

The lounge at the Freepoint Hotel was a combination of art deco and earth tones, in keeping with the décor of the rest of the hotel. Decker ordered a Rusty Irishman. Ronni demurred, saying it was too early. She ordered a glass of prosecco. Decker ate bar snacks. Ronni tried, but they didn't taste good. Nerves.

On the way back to their room they made reservations for six-thirty at an Italian restaurant, Giulia, on Mass. Ave., halfway between the Freepoint and Sanders Theatre, the site of the debate. They had just enough time to go back to their room, change and get to the restaurant. Ronni was relieved. As wonderful and handsome as Decker was, she might need more alcoholic fortification for the night ahead, even though it was a night she very much wanted to happen.

Feldman stood on the corner of Dexter Row and Warren Street, in Boston's Charlestown neighborhood, waiting for his Uber ride to Sanders Theatre. A black Cadillac Escalade with an Uber sign in its dark, tinted windows pulled up. The front passenger window rolled down. "Mr. Feldman?"

He nodded and climbed in the back of the vehicle, settling his mass in the comfortable seat in preparation for the twenty-minute ride to the theater.

The opposite door of the Escalade opened and a short, round man slid into the back seat.

"Mr. Feldman," he said in an oily voice thick with accent, "we have business to discuss."

"What the...who are you?" a surprised Feldman blurted as the Escalade pulled away from the curb.

"I am your executioner or your savior, depending on your answers to a few questions."

"You little fuck, I'll squash you like..."

"Tut. Tut. Mr. Feldman." Henri Hawke's head tilted left. Feldman's eyes followed, to the barrel of a Ruger Standard, complete with silencer, held by the Uber driver. It was pointed directly at Feldman's forehead.

"Let me assure you, Otto can both drive and shoot," Hawke said. "And he is very accurate."

Feldman eased back into his seat.

"Now, if you will be so kind as to listen for a moment, I think you will find my proposition interesting."

"Who are you?" Feldman asked again.

Hawke held his finger to his pursed lips. "Ssshhh. That is not so important. The real question is, who are you, and who will you be in seventy-two hours. Allow me to explain. You are going to die on Saturday."

Feldman's first reflex was to attack, but a twitch of the gun barrel kept him in place.

"It may not be so dire as it first sounds," Hawke went on. "Or it might. It depends entirely upon how reasonable you are."

They were crossing the Charles River on I-93, traveling south, away from the Sanders Theatre.

Ronni sat in the middle of the Sanders Theatre, her left arm looped through Decker's, waiting for the candidates to take the stage. Decker, whose head had been on a swivel all night, surveyed the crowd. Satisfied, he looked at Ronni. "If we're hungry when this is over, let's go to the Union Oyster House." They had been late getting to the restaurant and had only eaten appetizers so that they would not be late for the debate.

"I was there once a long time ago," Decker said. "It's the oldest restaurant in the United States. Lots of history and good seafood."

"That sounds like fun," Ronni answered. "Can we get a drink there?"

Decked nodded: "And the best oyster stew you've ever had."

The announcer introduced the candidates who came out on the stage and took their places behind podiums placed ten feet apart. From their angle, Ronni could see Magnolia Kanaranzi step up on a riser that gave her the appearance of being the same height as Metzger.

For an hour-and-a-half the two candidates sparred, fielding questions from the panelists and from the audience. Ronni found herself cheering some of Kanaranzi's answers. When it was over, she was sure her favorite had won the debate.

"I'm so glad we came," Ronni said. They shuffled toward the exit and an opportunity to shake hands with Kanaranzi in the theater lobby. "I think she was awesome."

"Yeah. Me too. Kind of surprised there were no questions about his indiscretions." There was no enthusiasm in Decker's voice.

"Is something wrong?" Ronni asked, giving him a concerned look.

"No. Nothing. Just this feeling."

"What?"

"I felt all night like we were being watched."

Ronni's eyes swept the room. "At dinner, or just here?"

"Just here. May be just my imagination, but I'd feel better if you didn't stop to shake Kanaranzi's hand."

They were quiet, vigilant until they were outside the theater. Decker hailed a cab.

"Oyster House or hotel?" he asked.

"Oyster House," Ronni replied. "I need a drink."

The place was packed, and they got seated just in time to order before the kitchen closed: oyster stew and a Rusty Irishman.

"Where is the ladies' room," Ronni asked the waitress, who directed her to the back of the restaurant.

"See the sign? Turn left down the hallway," she said.

Ronni sat in one of the stalls. Someone else came in the restroom and went into the stall next to her. A second person came in. When Ronni came out of the stall, a woman was standing at the sink, her mascara smeared, looking like she had been crying.

"Are you all right?" Ronni asked as she washed her hands.

"I'm okay," the woman said, turning and knocking her purse off the counter, scattering its contents on the floor. "Oh," she said, looking like she was going to cry again.

"Here, let me help you." Ronni kneeled and started picking up the scattered items. She heard the stall door behind her open and felt a sharp pain where the needle pierced the muscle connecting her neck to her shoulder. Paralyzed by the shock, within seconds Ronni's world went black.

OCTOBER 9, THURSDAY

"I knew something was going on. I could feel it. It's my fault." Decker poured out his guilt and grief as he told Holly of Ronni's abduction. He had waited for Ronni to come back from the restroom. At ten minutes he had become concerned. At fifteen he had asked a waitress to check the restroom. At twenty he had called Ronni's cell phone and gotten no answer. At twenty-one, twenty-two, twenty-three and twenty-four he did the same with the same result. At twenty-five he called the police.

Because he was a policeman, Decker got the immediate attention of the Boston P.D., and a full investigation was launched. A dusting of the women's restroom at the Union Oyster House found Ronni's fingerprints in a stall, but the door handles, counter and sinks had been wiped clean. There was no sign of a struggle.

"Maybe she just ran away," one of Boston's finest had suggested, and Decker had grudgingly admitted to himself that it was a possibility.

"If you could have seen how excited she was when she told us that you were going to Boston with her, you wouldn't even think that," Holly told her friend. "Bob, she is in love. For the first time since I've known her. Probably for the first time ever. She wouldn't just run away. Even if she had a panic attack, she would have called you."

"We know one thing for sure," she said in parting. "Hamilton Blethen is not behind this. He didn't know that Ronni was going to be in Boston. It's got to be Kanaranzi."

Holly promised to be on the next plane to Boston.

"I can't believe nobody asked him the question," Bean said. "The whole fricking debate, and not one question about his affair." To his surprise, Magnolia didn't seem upset.

"Frankly, I'm glad that the subject didn't come up," she said. "Is Feldman here?"

"He hasn't come in yet, why?"

"Because, after the debate last night I learned that Feldman may have been behind the Metzger sex scandal."

"Where did you hear that? Who told you?"

"I can't tell you the source, but it's reliable."

"Damn. Metzger will find out, for sure. We need to get in front of this," Bean said.

"Have Samantha set up a press conference. I'm going to disclose what I've learned and fire Feldman. Set it up for 3:00 p.m. so it will make the evening news."

A pleased smile crossed Bean's face. *Damn, she's good. She'll deflect any blame and will keep the sex issue in the news at the same time.*

Slowly the world came back to Ronni. Her head thundered in waves, making her wince with each roller. She was lying on a concrete floor, curled in a fetal position, her hands tied behind her back, causing her shoulders to ache from the stress. Her hip hurt. Her neck hurt. Her ankles were bound together with duct tape. The dim light hurt her eyes.

Like the slime trail of an indolent slug, her memory of the previous evening emerged. She tried to picture the woman at the sink. Hispanic. Maybe five-foot-eight. Well dressed. She tried to think of specific facial features, but nothing stood out. Her mind went back to the debate, and she tried to put herself there, looking around the room. Bob had thought someone was watching them.

Bob. Poor Bob. He's got to be worried sick. He probably blames himself. Thinking of him made her heart hurt, along with all the other parts of her body. She closed her eyes, hoping to ease the pounding in her head. Under the lingering effect of the drug, she drifted between sleep and anesthetized lethargy.

"The pundits said she either won the debate or it was a draw," Samantha said as she watched Magnolia walk to the podium. "I hope this doesn't change their mind." Bean didn't respond, intent upon watching what was about to happen.

Magnolia adjusted the microphones and cleared her throat.

"I wish to thank everyone connected with last night's debate," she said to the half dozen assembled members of the press corps. "I am energized by the response of the people to our message and firmly believe it will carry us all the way to Washington.

"But today I come before you for a different reason. I come before you with a heavy heart, and with an apology. It has come to my attention that a member of my campaign staff, Aaron Feldman, is connected to the unfortunate sex scandal in which my opponent is involved. We have learned Feldman is an associate of Dawn Rogers, a Washington, D.C., prostitute who has claimed that she had multiple sexual liaisons with Senator Metzger. I have learned that Feldman was responsible for Ms. Rogers making those allegations public. I want you to know that Mr. Feldman has been terminated from my campaign. We have zero tolerance for this kind of behavior. I also want to apologize to Senator Metzger and his family and to let them know I am sorry for any pain that a member of my campaign staff caused them. A memorandum setting forth what we know about this unfortunate and unforgivable action is being prepared and will be given to Senator Metzger's campaign and to the authorities when it's done, to determine whether any legal action should be taken against Mr. Feldman."

Questions were shouted at Magnolia, but she held up both hands. "I have nothing further to say at this time. Thank you."

"Metzger is going to go ballistic." Samantha said.

"Let's see how they spin the story tonight and what the headlines read in the morning," Bean counseled. "Magnolia's apology will be on all the national news channels. Metzger's response won't, but it will keep the sex scandal issue alive in the local news. When anybody raises the issue, all we've got to point out is that he admitted to having an affair with a teenager while he was serving in the Senate. We're going to come out the clear winner on this one."

Feldman sat in a locked room in his underwear, somewhere in Boston's suburbs, staring at the large TV screen attached high up on the wall. Magnolia's press conference had just ended.

The oily, accented voice came over the speakers mounted in the room's ceiling. "Was I right, Mr. Feldman?"

"That fucking witch. The whole sex scandal thing was her idea, and I'm the one that gets hung out to dry."

"Such is the way of the world, Mr. Feldman. Soldiers in the trenches die. Generals survive." Hawke let his words sink in for a minute. "But I'm giving you a chance to survive, and, perhaps, get your revenge, too."

Feldman was silent, contemplating options. He had already made an inch-by-inch inspection of the windowless room in which he was a captive. Heat, light and water supply were all controlled from outside the room. The toilet and sink in the corner were completely encased in steel, no place to grab a handhold or insert a pry bar, even if he had one. The faucets were embedded in the sink and were motion operated. The door had no handle and the hinges were on the outside. A slot in the bottom of the door, covered by an outside steel flap, allowed the passage of a food tray. There was no furniture except a mattress on the floor and an orange beanbag chair. The television screen was flush-mounted as high as the twelve-foot ceiling would allow. He could not reach it. Two cameras embedded in opposite corners of the room kept him under constant surveillance. Communication, when there was any, was through the speakers from which Hawke's voice now came.

His only window to the outside world was the TV. His only possessions: the remote that operated it, a roll of toilet paper and his underwear.

"Saturday you will rent a boat." The voice came through the speakers again.

"Why would I do that? I have a boat."

"There are reasons. It is not important that you know or understand them. You will take that boat out into Cape Cod Bay. Whether you leave that boat dead or alive is entirely up to you. You have until tomorrow to decide."

Decker met Holly at the airport with a big, tearful hug. He looked haggard.

"Nothing," he said in response to Holly's question. "They haven't found anything. She just disappeared."

"It has to be Kanaranzi," Holly said. "I have some ideas, but let's talk about them tomorrow when we've got clear heads. I'm exhausted and so are you."

As much as he didn't want to stop, Decker knew she was right.

OCTOBER 10, FRIDAY

They sat over steamy lattes at Simon's Coffee Shop on Mass Ave. The weather had turned bitter, the Montreal Express making an early visit to New England. Neither Holly nor Decker had brought clothes warm enough to fend off a drop of the temperature into the twenties, accentuated by a stiff wind.

Even with both hands wrapped around the hot cup, Holly shuddered from the fifteen-minute walk from the Freepoint Hotel. "We're from Minnesota," she chided herself. "This shouldn't bother us, but man it's cold." She took a sip, watching Decker's troubled eyes over the rim of her cup.

"All I can think of is Ronni lying some place in this," he said, gesturing toward the paper and debris being blown around outside the coffee shop window, "freezing."

He had checked with Boston P.D. The lieutenant-detective in charge of the investigation, Dan Boyle, had said there were no new developments. Staff at the restaurant had all been questioned, but no one had heard or seen anything. They were in the process of going through the credit card slips from Wednesday night. They would contact the people who had been there around the time Decker and Ronni were there. If anything came up, he would immediately let Decker know.

They called for a taxi, and ordered a second latte to go. The driver, from East Boston with a classic "Bahston" accent, was more than happy to drive them around for the day.

"It's not open," he said in his nasally twang, when asked to take them to the Union Oyster House. "Doesn't open until eleven."

"Drive us there anyway," Decker said. He directed the cabbie to the parking lot behind the restaurant.

"That's the door from the hallway where the restrooms are located," Decker pointed out as he and Holly stood in the parking lot, turning their backs on the wind that whistled between buildings.

"She had to come out there. She couldn't have gone out through the front door without being seen by a dozen people, including me."

They paced up and down the alley that ran between the back of the restaurant and the parking lot, studying the ground for any sign that Ronni may have been there. If there had been anything, the wind had blown it away.

"From here, it's an easy shot down the alley either to Union Street or Fitzgerald Parkway," Decker said. "After that......" He let the sentence dangle. Shivering, they got back in the taxi.

"Six-twenty-one Boylston Street, please" Holly said. "It's right across from Copley Square."

Boston traffic was crazy busy on Friday morning, and it was 10:50 a.m. by the time they walked through the front door of Kanaranzi Campaign Headquarters.

A cheery, college-age woman emerged out of the hustle and bustle of campaign activity. "How can I help you?"

"Who's in charge here?" Holly asked.

"That would be Jim Bean, the campaign manager."

Decker flashed his badge just long enough for her to realize it was a police badge. "Tell him there are a couple of cops here that need to ask him some questions," he said.

A few minutes later, Ms. Cheery was back. "Follow me," she said, and led them back to Bean's office.

"I'm Sergeant Bob Decker and this is Holly Bouquet, a private investigator working with me on a missing persons case," Decker said. "We're looking for a woman who disappeared right after the debate

Wednesday night." Decker bent the truth, hoping that it would short circuit any reluctance Bean might have to cooperate. "We'd like a list of everyone who attended the debate."

"You'll have to get that from The League of Women Voters," Bean said. "They sponsored the debate and took care of credentials and tickets."

"Did each candidate have a certain number of tickets that they were allowed to distribute?" Holly asked.

"We had two-fifty. Metzger's campaign probably had the same."

"Do you have a list of who got your two-hundred-fifty tickets," Holly persisted.

"I'm sure we do, but…"

"Could we please get a copy?" Holly pleaded in her best persuasive voice. "The woman who is missing is a friend of mine. It would give us a chance to get started while we're waiting for the full list from The League of Woman Voters."

Bean hesitated. "Sure." He buzzed, and Ms. Cheery came into his office. "Make these nice people a copy of our guest list from Wednesday night's debate."

"Thank you," Holly said as she took the stapled sheets of paper from the volunteer's hand ten minutes later. She and Decker headed back out to their waiting taxi. It hadn't gotten any warmer.

"Back to Oyster House for lunch?" Decker asked. "I think I saw a sign that they have Wi-Fi." Holly agreed.

Ronni shook uncontrollably, her teeth chattering. Her thin dress was little protection against the cold that seeped into every part of her body. She could hear the wind howling outside. She fought to stay awake. From somewhere, she remembered that you fell asleep before you froze to death. She focused on the stain on the front of her dress where she had wet herself when she could no longer hold her bladder in check. She was sure the spot was frozen.

It seemed like the second day since she had come out from under the drug-induced coma, but she couldn't be sure. For a time, she rolled on to her back, then to her other side, then back again, transferring the pressure from the concrete floor to alternating body parts when the pain got unbearable. Eventually the pain had given way to cold and now she lay in a fetal position, freezing to death.

Through the shaking, she thought she heard a door open. Ronni was convinced she was hallucinating until someone lifted her by the armpits. She tried to twist her head to see who it was, but her head was suddenly inside a bag and a drawstring was pulled loosely around her neck. She heard a sound she thought was scissors, and her ankles were suddenly free.

The hands lifted her to her feet and dragged her across the floor. Ronni tried to make her legs work, but they refused. She felt her feet bumping over something and realized it was the threshold of a door. She was being dragged through the doorway and out of her dungeon. Someone untied her hands. The pain in her shoulders was excruciating as she slowly moved her hands from behind her. They lifted her into a chair. She heard a ratcheting sound as her wrists and ankles were lashed to the chair. *Zip ties*, she thought.

Footsteps, two people, walked away. Then, silence.

The air was warmer, gloriously warmer. After a while, her teeth stopped chattering but her body continued to convulse, even as her core temperature crept slowly upward.

In a few minutes, footsteps returned. Her hood was removed and Ronnie turned her head away from the bright light that glared at her. When her eyes were able to focus, she saw a spoon in front of her, filled with liquid. Instinctively, she pulled her head back, away from the spoon.

"It's just soup," a kind female voice with an Hispanic accent, said. Ronni opened her mouth and tasted the warm chicken broth. Then, she gratefully accepted each spoonful until the bowl was empty.

"I'm sorry," the woman said, starting to put the hood back on Ronni's head.

"Wait," Ronnie said. "I need to use the bathroom." The woman looked unsure of what to do. She left the room, then came back a minute later and put the hood on Ronni. A second set of footsteps approached and the zip strips were cut from her wrists and ankles.

Someone, Ronni was sure it was the woman who fed her the soup, took her hand and led her into another room. The second set of footsteps shuffled along behind them. A door closed and the hood was removed.

Ronni was in a bathroom with the woman who had fed her the soup. The woman gestured toward the stool and backed away, giving Ronni room.

Sitting on the stool, Ronni dissected the room. It was old and cramped, a typical bathroom in an old house, maybe a farmhouse, with a sink, a small bathtub, a window too small to crawl through and no means of escape except the door through which they had come.

She finished and stepped out of her soiled panties. "Can I wash these out in the sink?" she asked. The woman nodded. Ronni washed her underwear with hand soap and dried them as best she could with a small hand towel. She stepped back into them and pulled them up, uncomfortably damp but at least they were clean.

The woman approached her with the hood. For a moment, Ronni thought about taking her out, and taking her chances with the person on the other side of the door. She decided against it. She had no idea if the other person, whom she suspected was a man, was armed or if there was anyone else in the house, or even where she was.

Ronni looked at the small Mexican woman who had been kind to her and lowered her head so the woman could put on the hood.

If Ronni's abductors were to be found in the registered attendees of Wednesday night's debate, Holly and Decker guessed that they would come from the Kanaranzi list. They perused the ten pages of names as they ate clam chowder.

"I'm not sure what we're looking for," Holly said. "I can't imagine we'll recognize any of these names."

"Here's Ronni," Decker said, pointing to her name on page ten. There were only two names listed after hers.

"It looks like they just kept adding names as they came in," Holly said, flipping back through the list. "The first part, maybe two-thirds of them, are in alphabetical order. The names that came after are not alphabetized. The first part probably came from some fundraising roster."

"If you're right," Decker said, "then only the names that come after Ronni's would have been added after Kanaranzi knew Ronni was coming to the debate." He dialed Lieutenant Boyle. "Could you check out a couple of names for me?" he asked. After explaining the situation, he gave the lieutenant the two names from the list.

"Now what?" Decker said after hanging up.

"I think we should pay Hamilton Blethen a visit," Holly said.

"Why? How will that help us find Ronni?"

"I'm not sure," she replied, "but we've got nothing to lose and no place else to look." Decker had to agree.

Holly scrolled through her contacts and found the number for Toni Blethen. She dialed but got no answer. She was leaving a message when Toni called back.

"I'm in town," Holly said. "Can I come see you?"

"We're not in town," Toni answered. "We're on a train headed for Lowell. We're going skiing for the weekend."

"When will you be back?"

"Sunday, late."

"If I'm still in Boston, could I come and see you on Monday?"

"Sure. Why?"

"I've got some news."

"Can't you just tell me over the phone?"

"It would be best if it were in person."

They were at a dead end, at least until the Boston P.D. ran the names from the debate guest list. They finished their lunch and walked back to the hotel. The temperature had crawled over freezing, the sun had come out and the wind was at their back, but Holly was still frozen by the time they got there. Decker, trying to catch up on the sleep he'd lost since Wednesday night, went to take a nap. Holly checked in with Carrie.

"I'm having no luck finding Geraldine's relatives," Carrie said. "I've tried to trace them back through where she went to college. I thought they might have a record of parents' names, but I didn't get anywhere. They weren't anxious to talk about a gender-switching ex-basketball star. Claimed that they couldn't give out information because of some security policy."

Holly suggested she take a break from her Geraldine search.

"Do me a favor and follow up on Maddy Brilliant's accident," she said. "Get in contact with the witness, her name's on the police report, and see if she remembers anything more now that she's had a little time to think about it. Check Richfield P.D. and see if they've done anything further. Also, I've been thinking, check the Twin Cities body shops and see if any of them have had a white delivery truck in for repair or paint since the date of the accident. The truck left a smear of white paint on the side of Maddy's car, so there must have been some damage to the passenger side of the truck. Maybe we'll get lucky."

They had fed Ronni, again, and brought her a generic gray sweat suit. No socks, no shoes, no underwear. The Mexican woman took her dress, saying she would clean it and bring it back. The zip strips that had been applied after she changed clothes were pinching her wrists, causing tingling in her hands. Her circulation was being restricted.

She fretted about it the next time someone came in the room.

"Certainly, mademoiselle, we are not barbarians," a new voice said, dripping with honey and heavily accented. *French,* Ronni thought, *but not quite. Something else. Maybe a different dialect.* The zip strips around her wrists were cut off.

"Comfortable now?" the voice asked.

"It would be better if I could see," she said.

"Ah, but that is not possible for the moment," the man responded. There was silence in the room.

"What do you want?" Ronni finally filled the void.

"Well, that is very complicated," the voice said. "We do not mean you any harm. At least that is not our first intent. But the rest is very complicated." Again, the voice stopped. Ronni listened, trying hard to hear something: breathing, the scrape of a shoe on the floor, anything. Only her own heartbeat and the wind howling outside were audible. Ronni vowed not to be the one to break the silence this time.

"You see," the voice finally said, "it is like this. You have been making yourself a nuisance. My client wishes you to stop. There is a simple way to make that happen but, as I just said, it is not our intent to do you harm. That is why it's complicated."

"Are you the person that threatened me and tried to kill my sister?" Ronni tried to keep the emotion out of her voice.

"Oh. No. No. No.," the voice said. "You and I have never met before and probably will never meet again. But it does seem you have a penchant for getting into trouble--even when you were in the military police before becoming a private detective."

The words cut through Ronni like a knife.

"How do you know about me!" She lost the battle to stay calm.

"It is my obligation to know about all those with whom I come in contact. Especially those with whom I must transact business."

"And you have to transact business with me?"

"I do."

Ronnie waited. Time ticked by. Only the wind howled. Finally, she couldn't stand it anymore. "Are you still there?" she asked

"I am, indeed. Perhaps you are not ready to discuss business?" She heard him stand up and take steps in the direction from which they'd come.

"Wait," she said.

The steps stopped.

"What business?"

The steps returned and she heard the groan of a wood chair.

"I know that, in addition to being a nuisance to my client, you are investigating a five-year-old murder case, an elderly woman from a small town in Minnesota. Your investigation has been unsuccessful."

Again, silence. They played at cat and mouse. Unfortunately, Ronni knew she was the mouse and finally gave in. "You're right, but I don't understand how that translates into business between us."

"I am prepared to deliver to you the executioner of the old woman."

"What! Why would you do that?"

"Because I want something from you."

"What?"

"In exchange for the executioner, you and your colleagues will stop all of your current investigations and disband your private investigation firm. You and your colleagues will surrender your private investigator licenses and will never practice that craft, or any craft involving law enforcement-type work, again. Upon surrender of your licenses, there will be placed in a bank account, for each of you, the sum of one hundred thousand dollars to provide financial support until you settle on a new occupation."

"What the hell. I won't agree to that. Besides, I'd have to talk to my partners before I could make that commitment."

"Furthermore," the voice continued, ignoring Ronni's comment, "you will not communicate with anyone regarding any investigation in which your company is involved. If any of you provide any information about any of your current investigations to anyone, all three of you will suffer a most unpleasant death, which I will see to, personally. You may think my demands are excessive and my methods unorthodox but, I assure you, they are very effective, and, in light of the alternative, the demands do not seem extravagant at all. I will give you time to think about it."

"And if I say no?"

"As I said, our *original* intent was to do you no harm."

Samantha was right. Metzger did go ballistic, shouting and pounding his fist, threatening lawsuits and electoral investigations, insinuating that Magnolia, herself, had been behind the scandal or, at the very least, was responsible for the misdeeds of her campaign staff.

When reached for comment, Magnolia's response was cool, measured: "I've fired the person responsible, and my campaign has turned over all the information we have on the matter. I've personally apologized to Senator Metzger and his family. I don't know what more I can do. I'm sorry he refuses to accept my apology, but I do think we should remember, among all this, that he did admit to having an affair with a teenager while he served in the Senate, so these aren't just rumors."

OCTOBER 11, SATURDAY

They left Boston in the black Escalade for the ninety-minute trip to Northside Marina in East Dennis, Feldman and Hawke in the back seat, Otto driving. Hawke had chosen this particular marina because of its isolated location--and because it was where Senator David Metzger moored his boat.

Hawke kept up a steady stream of chatter about fine art; his love for Boston, second only to Barcelona among his favorite cities; how a prehistoric ice block had formed Cape Cod, even about the American League baseball playoffs between Baltimore and Kansas City. Feldman, dressed in dungarees, a blue-and-white striped sweatshirt, a Gill foul-weather jacket, heavy socks and deck shoes, sat sullenly. A zip tie wrapped around his neck and the Escalade's headrest restricted his movement. His hands were fastened to his knees, his ankles tied together.

They crossed Sagamore Inlet on Highway 3, then turned east on 6A.

"The time has come Mr. Feldman," Hawke said, taking wire cutters from a small duffle bag on the floor. "Do you accept my proposal?"

"How can you be sure I won't get more than ten years?" Feldman asked, sweat rivulets running down the sides of his head over his fat cheeks. He tried to shift his bulk to get more comfortable, causing the zip tie to momentarily cut off his air supply.

"Minnesota sentencing guidelines," Hawke said. "Do you know what they are?"

"I can guess," Feldman rasped.

"Let me explain. First, there is an ambitious county attorney. Second, you are about to hand him the keys to solve a case that will fuel his highest aspirations. Third, in exchange for that, he will reduce the charge against you to third degree murder and fourth, the sentencing guidelines for third degree murder are one hundred and twenty-eight months. Ten years and eight months. With time off for good behavior, you'll serve seven years."

"And how do I know Kanaranzi'll go down for this?"

"I can control many things, Mr. Feldman, but I cannot guarantee a conviction," Hawke said. "I can only guarantee that she will be arrested and charged with conspiracy to commit murder. I also guarantee that it will ruin her, regardless of the outcome of a trial."

Feldman was quiet, deep in thought as the Escalade passed through Barnstable and then Yarmouth.

"And when I get out?" Feldman broke the silence.

"You will join my organization, somewhere outside the United States, where your time in prison won't matter," Hawke answered, "but where your skills will be put to good use."

"Shit. I'm done here anyway," Feldman railed. "Fucking bitch. Let's do it."

"So, we are agreed?"

"Yes."

Hawke cut the ties from around Feldman's wrists and ankles. He slid the jaws of the wire cutter between Feldman's neck and the zip tie. "Do not disappoint me, Mr. Feldman," Hawke said, his syrupy voice turning to ice. He turned the wire cutters to tighten the zip tie, prodding a response from Feldman.

"I won't," he croaked.

Otto and Feldman came out of the marina office, trailing a third person who led them to a dock where a twenty-six-foot cruiser was moored. After a short primer on boat operation, the boatman unhooked the lines from the dock and tossed them on the boat's deck. "Just have her back by six, or I'll have to charge you extra," he shouted as Feldman backed the idling boat out of its slip.

He steered the cruiser out into Cape Cod Bay at twenty knots. A light drizzle fell from a thick, overhead blanket of gray. Feldman pulled up the hood of his jacket against the damp, mid-fifties temperature. A half-hour out, he slowed the boat to an idle and began circling.

Otto scanned the horizon. He couldn't see a shoreline in any direction. "You know I'm going to have to hurt you," he said, matter-of-factly.

Feldman nodded. "Just not my face."

Otto kicked a wall in the bridge, leaving scuff marks. He put the boat in neutral, broke off the shift lever and used it to beat dents into the dashboard and break the glass in one of the gauges.

"Now, it's your turn." He turned to Feldman who was white as a ghost. "I want you to remember this every time you think about double-crossing us. Remember this because it will be a thousand times worse if you do."

He swung the shift lever. The jagged, broken end took a two-inch chunk of skin and hair off Feldman's skull. Feldman staggered back, stunned, blood running down his neck.

"Sit down," Otto ordered. He wiped the blood from Feldman's neck with his gloved hand and smeared it on the steering wheel and dashboard. Within minutes, a runabout appeared out of the mist and pulled alongside the drifting cruiser.

"Take off your right glove," Otto said. "Throw it on the deck. Now wipe the cut on your head with the palm of your hand."

Feldman recoiled at the touch of his fingers on the gash. Otto grabbed Feldman's wrist and dragged his hand over the wound as Feldman yelped.

"I said the *palm* of your hand," he snapped. "Now get in the boat." He motioned toward the runabout. "Put your right hand on the gunnel."

Feldman staggered to the side of the cruiser and placed his right hand on the gunnel, as directed. With effort, he lifted his leg over the gunnel. Otto gave him a hard shove, propelling his bulk over the side and into the runabout, head first.

Feldman groaned. "You didn't have to do that," he whined.

"Had to make it look real," Otto replied with a sneer as he admired the blood smear left on the gunnel by Feldman's right hand.

Holly finally convinced Decker that he might as well go home. The report from Boston P.D. had come back. The two names on the

Kanaranzi guest list were not in the system and further inquiry showed no reason to suspect they might have been involved.

With no leads to follow, and with the Blethens not available until Monday, it made little sense for Decker to stay in Boston. Reluctantly, he agreed, catching a five-forty-five flight on Delta back to Minneapolis-St. Paul.

Back at the Freepoint, Holly checked in with Carrie. She had been unable to reach the witness to Maddy's accident, "But I did call Maddy," Carrie said. "I told her about Ronni. She kept referring to her as Ron. It was kind of uncomfortable. She didn't seem all that upset. I told her I'd keep her informed."

"Ronni told me that her sister never accepted her gender change," Holly said. "It's been really tough on Ronni."

"Anything I can do from this end?" Carrie asked.

"Any luck tracking down Mary Stumpf?"

"There's no record of a Mary Stumpf in any of the metro counties. I'll start looking at the other counties on Monday."

"I'll check out here, too" Holly said, "but right now I'm trying to think of anything that might lead me to Ronni."

"You still think it's Kanaranzi?"

"I haven't found anything that changed my mind."

"Maybe you should just go ask her?"

"She doesn't have the recordings."

"You're absolutely sure." Magnolia quizzed Hawke, sitting in the front seat of the Escalade, parked just off Jamaicaway in Mission Hill.

"Absolutely."

"Well, then who has them? I don't believe it's Metzger or he would have released them by now."

"Who are the possibilities?" Hawke asked. "Your son? Your daughter-in-law? A competitor? A blackmailer? Perhaps no one. As you have explained it to me, there is no actual proof that the recordings were actually taken."

"But the recorder was wiped clean," Magnolia countered.

"Perhaps you did it absent-mindedly. It's the kind of thing I might do if I were talking on the phone."

Magnolia didn't look pleased with Hawke's suggestion. She gazed coldly out the passenger-side window, staring into the night.

"What do you want me to do with her?" he asked.

"What do you *think?*"

"Is that really necessary? She has never seen me; has no idea who I am. I have given her nothing by which she could connect me with you," Hawke said.

"She's been investigating me. That's enough reason."

"I understand she is a big fan of yours. She flew out here with her boyfriend just to see you in a debate."

"Where did you hear that?"

"Feldman."

Magnolia did a double take. "When did you talk to him?"

"Today."

"And?"

"I suggest you keep an eye on the news," Hawke said. "And the P.I.?"

"Do what I paid you for."

OCTOBER 12, SUNDAY

The cruiser was spotted by a couple on an early-morning beach walk, run aground in Herring Cove just east of Provincetown.

"If the wind'd been a little more outta the south, she'd a missed the point and be out'n the Atlantic," the old salt towing the boat back to Northside Marina said. "Nevah woulda found her."

"Nah. I think they got drunk and beached it. Prolly walked to P'town," his mate said.

"That boat came in sideways. Blown in. 'Twarn't beached. Woulda come in bow first ifn it was beached."

Abandoned rental boats happened a few times a year on the Cape, usually because the renter got inebriated, or stayed out too late and didn't want to pay the extra. It was always reported to the authorities, but very little effort was made to catch the runner unless there was damage to the boat. No harm, no foul, was the attitude of the local police. So, there was no urgency when the cruiser was pulled into the marina and tied up on Sunday morning. While the mate untethered the towboat from the cruiser, the old salt went into the office to deliver his invoice.

"Looks okay from the outside," he said. "Didn't go aboard, though. Just another runner I'ma guessin'"

"My boss'll check it out tomorrow," the weekend dock boy said.

Ronni sat on the toilet stool, working a screw holding the return-air vent in place. She had spotted it the second time they let her go to the bathroom. It looked loose, and she had been working it with her thumbnail each time she was alone in the bathroom.

Since Friday night, when The Voice had offered her The Deal, Ronni's captivity had become less restricted. She was allowed to go to the bathroom without the Mexican woman in attendance. Her hands were freed when she ate, although her feet remained tightly tethered to the legs of the heavy chair in which she sat. Food, such as it was, was served on paper plates. A plastic spoon was her only utensil.

She continued to work the screw with her thumbnail until a shout from the other side of the bathroom door asked her what was taking so long. "Be right out," she said flushing the toilet. She tried the screw one last time. It wiggled. She turned on the faucet and tried the screw again. It turned. Quickly, she unscrewed it and put it in the pocket of her sweatpants. She turned off the faucet and opened the door, drying her hands on her pants leg.

"It would be nice if there were some paper towels, or something," she said. The man, Hispanic like the woman who had been nice to her, said nothing.

Ronni walked back to her chair. Her breakfast, a piece of unbuttered toast and a container of yogurt, was on a paper plate on the floor. The man zip-tied her ankles to the chair and watched as she ate.

"Would it be possible to get another piece of toast?" she asked. She pointed at the crumbs on the plate in case the man didn't speak English. He nodded, apparently understanding her gesture, and left the room.

The screw in her pocket was about an inch long with a flat head. The point was sharp enough to draw blood as Ronni explored the screw with her fingers. She extracted it from her pocket and raked the screw across the zip strip around her ankles. Given enough time, enough repetitions, she was sure she could cut the strip. She stuck her bleeding finger in her mouth and waited for the man to return, hiding the screw in her left hand.

He handed her a paper plate with a piece of toast on it. "*Gracias,*" Ronni said, taking the plate with her right hand. The man nodded, backing away. Ronni ate the toast in small bites, slowly chewing as she absent-mindedly folded the paper plate in quarters, all the while watching the man. He looked away for a moment. She slid the screw between the folds of the plate, standing it on end. By the time she had finished the toast, she had worked the point of the screw through the top layer of the folded plate. She turned it over and laid it on her lap.

"I'm done," Ronni said as she chewed the last bit of toast.

The man walked forward and Ronni picked up the plate as if to hand it to him. As he reached for the plate, Ronni's right hand shot out and grabbed his arm, jerking him toward her. She slammed the plate and the point of the screw into the side of his head with her left hand. The man, off-balance and falling forward, screamed, grabbing the side of his head, just as Ronni brought up her right hand with all the force she could muster. The heel of her hand caught the man under the nose, snapping his head back and driving the cartilage back into his brain. He went down like a sack of cement, the scream cut off in mid-crescendo.

Ronni launched herself on top of the fallen man, tipping over the chair on top of her. Frantically she ran her hands over him, hoping for a gun, expecting any moment that someone would come running in response to his scream. She felt something in a pocket and dug her hand into it, coming out with a jackknife. She opened it and sawed at her ankle bindings until she was free of the chair.

Staggering to her feet, she held the knife in front of her in a defensive stance, waiting for someone to burst through the door.

No one came.

Ronni backed up until she was next to the fallen man. She kneeled, keeping an eye on the door, and put two fingers on his neck. There was no pulse. She started to shake. After a minute, drawing on all the self-discipline left within her, she willed herself to stop shaking. She patted down the dead man more thoroughly but found nothing that would help her. Moving quickly, she went into the next room which turned out to be a kitchen.

Sitting on the counter was a cell phone. She tapped it to activate. She needed a passcode. *Shit!*

She stuck it in her pants pocket. Carefully she peeked out a kitchen window. She could see no one. Slowly she opened the door that led outside and slid through the opening onto a wooden stoop with peeling white paint. A dirt driveway that ended just short of the house was empty. The driveway disappeared into a wall of tall trees that grew to within twenty yards of the front of the house where she stood. She was in the middle of a forest.

Ronni went back into the house, searching through two small bedrooms and the kitchen, hoping for a gun and shoes. She found neither, except for the shoes worn by the dead man, and they were at least two sizes too small. She stuffed part of a burrito she found in the refrigerator into her mouth and went back outside. There was only one out-building, a small shed that contained a few old tools, nothing of any use to Ronni.

Now what? She sat on the stoop thinking about fight versus flight when the decision was made for her, the sound of a truck coming up the driveway. She leaped off the stoop and ran to the shed, slipping inside before the truck came into view, realizing, too late that she had trapped herself if someone came looking for her. She took the jackknife from her pocket and opened the blade.

A rusty pickup rolled to a stop at the end of the driveway and the Mexican woman got out. She was alone. As she entered the house, Ronni sprinted for the truck. Crouching behind it, she heard a wail as

Ronni finished her beer. "Did you talk to Bob?"

"He wanted to jump on the first plane, but I told him to wait. I didn't know what shape you'd be in or if you might be stuck at the police station. I told him I'd have you call him as soon as you were able."

Ronni called, and Holly stepped out of the room to give her some privacy. A few minutes later Ronni stuck her head outside the door and beckoned her partner back into the hotel room.

"I told him I'm exhausted and that I'll call him tomorrow and fill him in on all the details," she said, a happy smile beaming through her weariness. "I'm going to bed."

"Here's something I want you to think about when you're dreaming," Holly said. "How does the guy with the accent know who killed Lorraine Blethen?"

"Be patient," Hawke advised Magnolia. "They may not have found the boat, yet. It will be in the news soon enough."

"What about the P.I.?"

"She escaped." Hawke said, like he was telling her the time of day.

"How did it happen?" The words were cold as ice.

"She killed the man that was watching her. Got away in his truck."

"I told you she'd be a problem," Magnolia snarled.

"I believe you may have me confused with the late Mr. Feldman," Hawke said. "You simply told me she was a P.I. You didn't mention that she was former special forces."

"She was a marine, military police."

"The technique she used was not part of any military police training."

"What are you going to do about it?" Magnolia snapped.

"Nothing."

Magnolia shrieked her disbelief. Hawke waited for the tongue-lashing to subside.

"There is no reason to do anything at the moment, and several good reasons not to," he said without emotion. "She never saw me. She saw no one involved in her abduction, except those who are no longer with us. She has nothing to connect the abduction to either you or me. And in my one conversation with her, I pointed her down a fork in the road that leads her away from both of us. As for the reasons not to take any action at this time, she and her partners will be uber vigilant, and she will be on the radar of every law enforcement department from here to Minnesota. So, no, I'm not going to do anything."

"I paid you to do a job, and you didn't do it!" Magnolia's anger had not subsided. "As far as I know, you didn't accomplish either of them. I want my money back!"

"Madam, as I said at the beginning of this conversation, *patience*. It is a virtue which you need to embrace more fully. You will see that what has transpired will all work out for the best." Hawke hung up.

Magnolia seethed. *That arrogant asshole is the next to go.*

OCTOBER 13, MONDAY

Ronni and Holly split up: Ronni heading to Boston Police Headquarters on Schroeder Plaza off Tremont Street to meet with Lieutenant Boyle, Holly to Cambridge to meet with Ham and Toni Blethen.

Holly was met at the front door by Toni and Barca, the latter more excited to see her than the former. Toni's greeting was cool, and the two didn't speak as they rose in the elevator to the third floor of the brownstone. Holly busied herself returning Barca's affection, emphasized by a steady tattoo beat on her leg and one wall of the elevator.

Hamilton was sitting in his wheelchair, looking tanned and fit, dressed in a white turtle neck and navy blue sweat pants.

"Ms. Bouquet," he acknowledged. "Toni says you have news."

"This is preliminary, but I had to be in Boston for another reason so I thought I'd pass it on," she said, not surprised by his abrupt demeanor. "We have a statement from a high school classmate that Magnolia Kanaranzi is your mother."

His mouth dropped open.

"Oh! Ham!" Toni blurted. She rushed and put her arms around him.

When she let go, Hamilton said, over Toni's shoulder, "You said preliminary. Why is it preliminary?"

Holly told the Blethens about how she and her partners had found Ken Olson and Olson had found Mary Blethen five or six years later in Las Vegas, going under the name Magnolia Kanaranzi,

"When you came here, I was going to excoriate you for continuing to investigate when we told you to stop." Hamilton said, "but now...."

"Wait," Holly cut him off. "There's more. We had someone research the name-change records in Las Vegas. We found Kanaranzi's name-change file, but the person who did the changing was named Mary Stumpf, not Mary Blethen."

"She must've gotten married after high school," Toni said.

"There's also some date discrepancies, but we're trying to track all that down," Holly said. "Ordinarily, I would have waited to tell you until we had those strings tied up, but since I was out here anyway......"

"I'm not sure what this means, but I'm glad you did," Ham interrupted.

"Me too," Toni added, with a sigh of relief. A little clarity for her husband—in their lives—was a good thing right now. "Can I get you something? I'd say mimosas to celebrate, but we're out of orange juice, and it *is* Monday morning."

"How about coffee," Holly suggested.

With Toni out of the room, Ham asked: "Here on pleasure or business?"

"Business of sorts," she said. She watched Ham closely, anticipating a reaction: "My partner, Ronni Brilliant—you met her—was kidnapped last Wednesday night. I'm out here to help with the investigation."

"Kidnapped!? Here?"

Holly nodded.

"My God," Ham said. "That's...that's...dreadful." Toni came back into the room with cups and a coffee pot. "Ronni Brilliant has been kidnapped," he exclaimed to Toni.

"What?"

"Kidnapped, here in Boston, last week," he said.

Under questioning by both Ham and Toni, Holly trickled out bits of information about the kidnapping. She held back telling them where the kidnapping took place, where Ronni had been beforehand, that Bob Decker had been with her, or that she had been held in a cabin in a forest in Maine. She kept waiting for the Blethens to slip-up, to say something that would divulge that they knew about the kidnapping, but they didn't. They seemed genuinely concerned for Ronni.

She connected with Ronni over lunch at Abe & Louie's.

"I'm pretty confident they didn't know about your kidnapping," she said. "They were genuinely surprised and, you should know, they were concerned about you."

"That's nice," Ronni replied. "Last time I saw them they were ready to toss me into Boston Harbor."

"Toni was more excited about the news that Kanaranzi might be his mother, than Hamilton was," Holly continued. "I'm not sure he knows how to handle actually knowing who his mother is."

"How much did you tell them?"

"Everything we know up to now. I told them I'd keep them posted as we dig into the Mary Stumpf issue. They're happy we're continuing to investigate."

"Did they offer to pay us?" Ronni asked.

"The subject never came up. I suppose I should've asked, but it just didn't seem like the right thing to do at the time."

Ronni nodded, understanding.

"How was your morning with Boston's finest?" Holly asked.

"FBI too," she answered. "They're taking over the investigation. Had the feeling I got caught in a jurisdictional battle. Feds will win, of course." She rambled on about the morning and her skepticism about whether anyone was going to find out who abducted her. "I can't give them anything to go on," she lamented. "I tried to describe the people at the shack, but I sounded like I was describing every Mexican stereotype. The only thing that stands out is that voice. I'll remember that if I hear it again."

Over ahi tuna burgers and sweet potato fries, they booked an evening flight back to Minneapolis-Saint Paul. "Did you call Bob?" Holly asked.

"He's working a twelve-hour shift. I'll call him tonight, after we get home."

It took several hours for the news to travel the eighty miles from East Dennis to Boston.

"East Dennis police have found signs of a struggle on a boat rented by former Magnolia Kanaranzi campaign worker, Aaron Feldman," the early evening news anchor intoned. "The boat was found abandoned Sunday morning in Cape Cod Bay. There was no sign of Feldman or the second person who was on board, whom local officials are still attempting to identify. A search...."

By the late evening news cycle, the next piece of the story had been put in place.

"It was learned earlier today that the boat rented by discredited former Kanaranzi campaign worker, Aaron Feldman, was rented from the same marina where U.S. Senator David Metzger keeps his boat. Feldman was accused of conducting a sex scandal campaign against Metzger. He was terminated from the Kanaranzi campaign staff last Thursday, immediately after his involvement in the campaign scandal came to light. Neither Feldman, nor the person who accompanied Feldman on the boat, who has yet to be identified, have been found. A search of Cape Cod Bay for the two men is still underway. Neither Senator Metzger, or anyone from his staff, could be reached for comment."

"I've got to get out of this fucking business," Bean growled, shaking his head in disbelief at the news. "Whatever happened to the days when two people just disagreed, ran campaigns on the issues, and whoever got the most votes won? This is insane."

He turned to Samantha. "Put together a press release: although he is no longer part of the campaign, praying for his safety, abhor violence, the usual stuff. Get it out so they'll have it for the early morning news. And call a staff meeting for tomorrow morning, ten o'clock.

Magnolia's new housekeeper, Pauline, was from a rural area south of Lyon, France. A farm girl of twenty-two, she checked all the boxes in Magnolia's required-traits list: she spoke no English, was a skilled cook and housekeeper, a hard worker, didn't complain, had no apparent agenda other than to get a start in America, didn't have a boyfriend and she was legal.

Pauline busied herself in the kitchen as Magnolia watched the large screen in the living room. The news of Feldman made her sad. She had to fire him from the campaign, but this was tragic. *Had Metzger actually done this?* She couldn't believe it.

"Pauline," she called. When the young housekeeper appeared from the kitchen, Magnolia asked, in French, "Would you please turn down my bed. I'm going to retire for the evening."

Magnolia switched to national news. The Feldman disappearance was on there as well. A marine expert of some sort was explaining how the natural currents in Cape Cod Bay would cause a body to drift around Wood End, past Race Point Lighthouse, over Stellwagen Bank and out to sea. "If the bodies aren't found in the first twenty-four hours, it's not likely they'll ever be found unless the tide washes them up on some beach days or weeks later."

She turned off the TV and swallowed the last sip of Absinthe. She handed the glass to Pauline. *"Bonne nuit,"* she said.

Magnolia crawled into bed, still in disbelief that Metzger would actually exact revenge in such a heinous manner.

OCTOBER 14, TUESDAY

The front door buzzer went off at two in the morning. Ronni pushed the button to let Decker in and waited for him to find his way upstairs to her condo. She opened the door at the slight knock and was immediately engulfed in his embrace. He was still in full uniform and she could feel his body armor and every tool in his belt on her skin, naked beneath her robe.

Twenty minutes later they lay side-by-side, sated, their legs intertwined, Ronni's head on Decker's outstretched arm. Her breathing had returned to normal, the transition from M to T to W complete.

So, this is what it's like. The dream-like thought passed through her head as her left hand wrapped around Decker's muscular back. She pulled herself close to him and found his lips. Her hand slid down his hip. *I think I'll call in. Take the day.*

Kanaranzi 49, Metzger 41, ten percent still undecided.

A new poll by the University of Massachusetts had the race holdings steady. That was comforting to Bean, but it gave Magnolia an anxiety attack.

"Our lead shrunk," she shrieked over the phone. "How could that happen?"

"Slow down, slow down," Bean replied. "Your lead didn't shrink. Remember, the poll last week had a plus-minus of three percent. This is well within that. We're doing just fine."

Magnolia was not to be mollified. "We need to do something."

"We'll keep doing what we've been doing that got you that lead. You've got a full calendar of events from now until the election. Our get-out-the-vote strategy is solid."

"We need to do another debate," she insisted. "Everyone said I won the last debate, and my lead increased. I want another debate."

"I don't think that's a good idea."

"I *do.*"

"This poll was taken before the Feldman disclosure, before he disappeared. Metzger issued a one-line denial this morning. Let's see what effect that has on the polls before we agree to another debate."

"I don't want to wait," Magnolia railed. "Schedule the damn debate!"

Bean exhaled loudly to show his displeasure. "All right."

He hung up, dialed his contact at New England Public Radio and informed her that he would agree to a second debate, conditioned upon Metzger's campaign agreeing to format and logistical issues. It was tentatively scheduled for October thirtieth.

There was a torrent of trepidation as he hung up. *There's nothing to be gained by this.*

"He won't be growing any hair, there," the surgeon said, pointing to the gash on Feldman's head that he had just finished stitching up.

Hawke looked through the plexiglass sheet that separated him from the anesthetized Feldman. "Did you do the implant?"

The surgeon grinned. "Two," he said. "I put one in his scalp under all those stitches, and I put a second one in his back, just in case he finds the first one. The one in his back is in a spot where he can't reach it. The incision was so tiny it didn't even need a stitch, but I put one in anyway, just to be sure. It will dissolve in about a week. When Feldman comes out of it, I'll tell him he can't wash his hair for a week because of the stitches in his head, and it would be best if he didn't shower, either, for precautionary reasons."

"Excellent," Hawke said, handing the surgeon a roll of hundred-dollar bills. "I will call you in the future should a need arise."

OCTOBER 15, WEDNESDAY

Ronni flowed into the office.

"You look pretty damn good for a woman who was kidnapped a week ago and spent five days in captivity," Holly said. Ronni's dark eyes broke into a tell-tale smile that soon consumed her whole face. "Must have been some reunion with Decker. You have flowers on your desk."

Ronni made a beeline for her office, followed by Holly and Carrie. A purple bag tied up with a purple bow sat atop her desk. She untied the bow and rolled down the bag, revealing a bouquet of daisies in a glass vase. Ronni took the card that was poking out of the flowers and opened it. Her smile melted into a shock.

"What?" both partners said simultaneously. She handed them the card. It read:

"Ronni. Happy you're safe. Maddy."

Ronni collapsed into a chair, her legs unable to support her. "How did she know?"

"I told her," Carrie said. "I thought you'd want her to know. Then I called her again when you got free."

Tears welled in her eyes as Ronni reached for the phone. She dialed and left a message. "Maddy. It's Ron...Ronni. I just got your flowers. I can't tell you how much these mean to me. Thank you," she sobbed. "I...I'll call...you later. Or call me back. I love you."

"Thank you," she choked out in the direction of Carrie. Memories of Maddy and her as kids flooded Ronni's thoughts. Good memories. Maddy had been the little sister, Ronni the big brother back when she presented as a male. They were inseparable. Maddy was the imp, always into mischief. Ronni's job was to look out for her, keep her safe and out of harm's way.

"Have you had a chance to check out the body shops?" Ronni asked, coming back to the present.

"No. Sorry. I haven't gotten to that yet," Carrie said.

"Could you do that for me?"

"Of course."

"And check Minneapolis and St. Paul to see if anyone reported a stolen white van around the time they ran Maddy off the road."

"Sure."

Eventually, conversation swung back to Ronni's reunion with Decker.

"I'll just say it was memorable," she said under the incessant teasing from her colleagues, anxious to change the subject. "Have you guys found out anything about Mary Stumpf?"

"No record of a Mary Stumpf in Goodhue County," Carrie said, "but I think I may have told you that already. I got ahold of the paralegal in Las Vegas, and he checked out the Clark County records.

No marriage certificate or name change for a Mary Stumpf between 1971 and 1980."

"Any chance he might be able to look at vehicle records to see if she had a driver's license or a car registered in her name?" Ronni asked.

"I'll get back to him and see."

"I didn't find anything in Massachusetts," Holly added. "I checked Suffolk, Norfolk and Middlesex Counties and there were no marriage records for Mary Blethen, Mary Stumpf or Magnolia Kanaranzi. I didn't have time to check court files for name changes. I'll do that today."

"That only leaves South Dakota," Ronni said. "I'll follow up on that."

"We've got to close this loop," Holly said. "The Blethens were pretty excited. We don't want to have this fall apart. I don't know that I'd have the courage to look them in the eye if it does."

Feldman sat in the dingy hotel room somewhere outside Boston, popping aspirin, drinking soda and watching television. The evening news said he was still missing, presumed drowned. The person who had accompanied him on the boat was still unidentified. The FBI was still investigating a kidnapping that occurred at the debate between Senator David Metzger and challenger Magnolia Kanaranzi a week ago. The name of the victim was still being withheld.

Feldman snorted. *Shit. I didn't even make it to the debate.*

He was watching the highlights of a Kansas City sweep of Baltimore in the American League championship series when there was a knock on the door. Feldman looked through the peep hole and opened the door. Hawke and Otto came in. Hawke took the lone chair in the room while Otto stood by the door. Feldman settled on the bed.

"How are you feeling today?" Hawke asked.

"Like shit." Feldman shot a sideways glance at Otto.

"This may make you feel better." Hawke took a flask from his inside pocket and poured two fingers into two plastic glasses that sat beside a beat-up ice bucket. "Armagnac." Hawke lifted his glass, Feldman reciprocated and the two downed the liquor in one gulp.

Feldman coughed, and tears rolled down his bulbous cheeks. "Good shit," he gasped.

"Indeed," Hawke replied coolly.

"I want you to rest here a few more days," Hawke went on. "Stay in your room. We don't want to take the chance of your being recognized. Is there anything I can get you?"

"Yeah. A hooker."

"That would be most unwise," Hawke responded. "You cannot have any human contact until we move you out of here; out of the northeast. This is a zero-tolerance situation. Do you understand?"

Hawke's eyes burrowed into Feldman. "So, I repeat, is there anything I can get you to make your life a bit more tolerable over the next few days?"

Feldman thought for a moment, almost scratching his head but stopping short when the anticipated pain reached his brain before his hand reached his wound. "Magazines. Boating and fishing ones. And girlie magazines. And have the newspaper delivered to my door daily. And a deck of cards. Yeah, a deck of cards."

"You will have all of those things tomorrow morning," Hawke said, looking at Otto. "I will see you in a few days with further instructions. Do not leave this room until I come back."

"And a bottle of whiskey," Feldman yelled as they left the room.

Hawke sat in the back of the black Escalade talking to Otto.

"Have Isabella gather up the things for Feldman--not the whiskey--and order a morning newspaper for a week." Otto nodded from the driver's seat.

"Without the woman P.I. we may have to change plans," Hawke said. "Unwise, I think, to have Feldman confess to the murder in Minnesota without the cooperation of the P.I. We could, of course, make her disappear, but she has partners. It would likely turn into a nation-wide manhunt. Dealing with the locals is one thing, but the FBI is something else altogether. Bad enough to have them snooping into the abduction. What do you think?"

Otto was silent for a moment, then: "Feldman is dead, right? Why don't we leave him that way?"

"You have such a way with words," Hawke chuckled.

OCTOBER 16, THURSDAY

Three Little Figs Coffee Shop is a neighborhood staple of the Somerville morning crowd. It's sumptuous breakfast menu and robust coffee concoctions bring a steady stream of patrons through its spartan seating area. In the busyness of the morning rush hour, it was easy to overlook a solitary woman sitting at a table-for-two along the wall.

A short, rotund man wearing a wide-brimmed fedora joined the line of customers.

"May I join you, Madam?" He inquired a few minutes later, holding his plate and demitasse in a pudgy hand. He pulled out a chair and sat without waiting, or expecting, a response.

"Do you know where she is?" The question was hissed at him at the same time his pants met the chair.

"Please, Madam, it is too early for questions. At least until I have my espresso." Hawke sipped the steaming black liquid. "This is usually the time I am returning to my home. I am not such a good morning person, except from midnight to six a.m."

Magnolia, wearing a hair kerchief, and sunglasses despite the dreary day, impatiently shifted in her chair. "Do you know where she is?" she repeated.

Hawke took another sip and sighed. "She is back in Minnesota. I am keeping an eye on her."

"Is she still investigating me?" Magnolia whispered.

"There have been no signs of that, but we will continue to monitor her actions."

"I want to know about it immediately if there's any indication."

"And you shall, Madam," Hawke replied.

"You're sure she doesn't have the recordings."

"One hundred percent."

Magnolia scowled behind her sunglasses. "Who, then?"

Hawke shrugged, the palms of his hands facing skyward.

"You are supposed to know these things," she hissed again.

"If any of your adversaries had the recordings, I would know it," he said.

There was a lull in the conversation as another cohort of the caffeine-starved cascaded through the front door of Three Little Figs. Magnolia watched to make sure there was no one she recognized.

"I will be returning to Barcelona tomorrow," Hawke said. "Anything that still needs to be done here can be done by my associates."

"There is the matter of money."

Hawke had expected this. "Consider it a deposit on my next project."

"What makes you think I'm going to want to use your services again, since you failed this time?"

"Ah, Madam, we are bound together, you and I. Like a married couple, 'til death do us part."

Sooner than you think, Magnolia thought.

On her way back to Pier 4, Magnolia got a call from Meredith Glenn.

"Next Monday the expert we hired to examine *The Reaper* will present his findings to the board. Can you come?"

"I'd love to," Magnolia replied, "unless I have a conflicting campaign event. What time is the presentation?"

"It starts at ten. We should be done by noon."

"I'll try to be there."

Carrie and Holly both struck out.

The paralegal wasn't able to access the Nevada Department of Motor Vehicle records without a court order, and there were no name-change files in any of the three counties that encompassed the Boston metropolitan area. Also, there was also no stolen vehicle report that involved a white cargo van. Carrie was still working on the body shop angle.

Ronni spent the morning digging around in websites for the city of Sturgis and Meade County and wondering why Decker hadn't called her.

The information provided by the web was either nation-wide, where she found an even one hundred Mary Stumpfs and eleven Mary Blethens, or state-wide where she found four hundred thirty-one marriage records, two hundred seventy-two birth records and four hundred sixty-five death records for Mary Stumpf, larger numbers for Mary Blethen and even a handful for Magnolia Kanaranzis. However, her attempt to narrow the search to Meade County or the city of Sturgis proved futile.

"I think I'm going to have to make another trip to Sturgis," she said. "Who knew that Stumpf and Blethen were such popular names."

"Do you really think that's a good idea." Holly said. It wasn't a question.

"If I left after lunch, I could be there tonight. That would give me all day tomorrow to look at records."

"I think you should check in with the FBI. Tell them you're going, or see if they advise against it," Holly persisted. "Maybe either Carrie or I should go with you."

"Do you think I should call him?" Ronni asked, ignoring Holly's suggestions.

Holly's shoulders sagged. "Are you listening to me? You've been the target of harassment. Then you get kidnapped, and the kidnapper threatens you if you don't stop investigating. You escape. Now you want to go back out in public and announce to everyone that you're still investigating. Do you think whoever is doing this is going to stop? You could be driving to Sturgis and a car could pull up next to you and blow you away!"

"Then it doesn't make much sense for you or Carrie to come along with me, does it?" was Ronni's snarky response. "I'm not going to live my life in a closet. I did that my first thirty years. Let them try to come and get me." Ronni patted the handgun she was now wearing on her hip. "I've got a bigger surprise for them waiting in the truck."

Holly sighed. "You're going, aren't you."

"Yup. I need to get out of here, feel the freedom of the road. A two-day trip to Sturgis is just what I need." Ronni paused. "Should I call him?"

"Yes. Maybe he can talk some sense into you."

Or maybe he'll come along with me. Ronni dialed Decker's number. *I've got to put him on speed dial,* she thought as she listened to the phone ring. She left a message.

Ronni eased out of St. Paul on 35E, a brand-new Remington 870 Police Marine Magnum 12-gauge short barrel lying on her lap with No. 4 buckshot in the chamber and four more rounds in the magazine. Her trusty Beretta lay in the passenger's seat within easy reach. With both driver's side windows open, blowing her short hair in multiple directions; the heater and her DVD player cranked up to high, and a YETI full of coffee, Ronni headed for Sturgis.

She watched her rearview mirror as she pointed the Dakota south, the cruise control at seventy-four and her head on a swivel. After the first twenty miles she was reasonably confident she was not being followed, but she exited at Faribault and again at Owatonna, anyway, to make doubly sure. By 3:30 she had turned right at Albert Lea and was headed west on I-90.

Somewhere between Albert Lea and Fairmont her phone rang and her heart jumped.

"Hello."

"Hi, Ron…Ronni. It's Maddy."

"Oh my God, it's good to hear your voice," Ronni said.

"Are you okay?"

"I'm fine. On the road right now, but I'm fine."

"Ron-n-n-i, I'm sorry I've been such an ass," Maddy stammered.

"I'm sorry I've screwed up your life. Do you think it's possible to forgive each other?"

"I'll try," Maddy said, her voice shaking.

"So will I."

There was a pause, until Maddy asked, "What happened? In Boston, I mean."

Ronni was in the middle of telling her sister the story when a car pulled alongside the Dakota. She jerked the wheel to the right and slammed on her breaks, realizing that she hadn't been paying attention. The shotgun, handgun and her phone all clattered to the floor as the truck careened down an embankment into a ditch. Ronni, fighting for control, managed to keep the truck upright. It came to a stop just short of a clump of trees bordering a field of corn stubble. Her head spun toward the interstate in search of the car. It was not there.

With her heart pounding, Ronni bent over into the passenger-side footwell to pick up the guns and her phone. When she looked up, the car was backing down the shoulder toward her.

Ronni crawled over the center console and slithered out the passenger-side door, taking the shotgun with her. She crouched and duck-walked to the rear of the truck, holding the shotgun in front of her. The car stopped, and someone got out.

It was a young man, college-age, dressed in khakis and a sweatshirt. As he got to the bottom of the bank, Ronni stepped from behind the Dakota, the shotgun held at waist-level aimed at his belly button.

"Stop right there," she barked. He stopped, his eyes grew wide and a stain appeared at his crotch, spreading quickly down his leg.

"Oh. What. Don't!" he stuttered, trying, alternatively, to hold up his hands and cover his crotch.

Ronni walked toward him. "Turn around," she ordered. Another car on the freeway slowed, and then sped away. She searched him with her eyes but there was no gun or knife attached to his belt and no bulges under his pants legs or around his ankles. There was a billfold in his back pocket.

"Take out your billfold and lay it on the ground," she said. "Turn back around. Now empty your pockets." Loose change and a pack of gum spilled to the ground as he turned his pockets inside out. He tried to cover himself, embarrassed by the wetness on the front of his pants.

"Man, I'm sorry," Ronni said, lowering the shotgun.

"What the hell?" the college kid said. "I was just trying to help, see if you were hurt."